GUILTY
by Association

To Gloria-

I hope you enjoy my first novel!

Sincerely,

[illegible signature]

GUILTY by Association

Rhonda Neville

Northwest Publishing, Inc.
Salt Lake City, Utah

Guilty by Association

For information address: Northwest Publishing, Inc.
6906 South 300 West, Salt Lake City, Utah 84047

JC 11.21.94

PRINTING HISTORY
First Printing 1995

ISBN: 1-56901-539-2

NPI books are published by Northwest Publishing, Incorporated,
6906 South 300 West, Salt Lake City, Utah 84047.
The name "NPI" and the "NPI" logo are trademarks belonging to
Northwest Publishing, Incorporated.

PRINTED IN THE UNITED STATES OF AMERICA.
10 9 8 7 6 5 4 3 2 1

To Terry—my husband, my best friend.
Thanks for making all my dreams come true.

Prologue

November, 1982

"It's happening, Doctor!"

"Are you sure?"

"Absolutely. She's even spoken."

"She's spoken? Where is she?" he asked, the telephone gripped tightly in his hand, his knuckles white.

"In her room, like always."

"Get back up there, don't leave her alone. And don't do anything to startle her, I'm on my way." He hung up the telephone with a calmness only years of training could have instilled in him.

A few moments later, Dr. Stuart emerged from his office, briefcase in hand.

"Connie, cancel the rest of my appointments, I'll let you know later if tomorrow's will have to be rescheduled."

Already reaching for the telephone, her appointment book open in front of her, Dr. Stuart's secretary began the task just given her. Although she'd only worked for the doctor a few months, she'd quickly learned that a psychologist's world consisted mainly of broken appointments and rescheduled meetings.

As he drove the short distance to his home, Dr. Stuart tried to keep his growing excitement in check. After years of waiting, could it finally be happening?

The rattle of the front door brought the nurse out of the bedroom where she'd been dutifully watching her charge. A little on the plump side, dressed in a neatly starched, brilliantly white uniform, tightly stretched over the her buxom chest, Nurse Katie, as she liked to be called, was the picture of restrained excitement.

Dr. Stuart quickly ascended the stairs and approached the patiently waiting nurse.

"Is she still with us, Katie?" he whispered.

"Yes, she's—"

"You said she spoke. Tell me exactly what she said."

"She told me she wasn't hungry," the nurse replied, matching his own quiet tone.

"That was it?"

"Yes," she murmured. "I'd just brought her lunch up, soup, like always. She looked me straight in the eyes and said she didn't want any."

"Eye contact?" he cocked his head, eyebrows raised.

"Very direct. I told you yesterday—"

"Yes, yes, I know, she seemed to be trying to focus on you. I didn't get a similar response. Anything else?"

Nurse Katie nodded her head. "She's in there now, sitting in front of the vanity mirror, brushing her hair, over and over again."

Dr. Stuart paused for a moment, then said, "A comforting reflex, no doubt. When she was younger, her mother used to brush it for hours," he replied, remembering. "Did you try speaking to her?"

She shook her head no. "After she refused the soup, I called you. When I went back upstairs, she was already at the dressing table. I thought it best not to say anything."

"Good. If she'd asked questions and you evaded answering them, she might've slipped back."

Dr. Stuart moved around the nurse and stepped into the bedroom. He hesitated for a moment, then softly approached the young girl still sitting where the nurse had left her, the hair brush moving slowly, rhythmically through her shiny, dark brown locks. She stopped the trancelike brushing only when Dr. Stuart's form appeared in the mirror alongside her own.

"Hello," he said calmly, closely observing the image reflected back at him.

She looked up; her dark brown eyes stared intently. "Hello," she murmured back.

"You've been back for some days now, haven't you?"

"Yes," she whispered.

"Do you know what your name is?" Dr. Stuart gently questioned.

"It's...it's Emma," she answered.

"Good," Dr. Stuart smiled, satisfied. Continuing, he said, "You've been away from us for quite some time, Emma. We're so happy to have you back." The doctor paused for a moment—the answer to his next question would set the tone for this young girl's entire rehabilitation, if rehabilitation was even possible—then plunged ahead with studied calm.

"Emma, do you recall anything about yourself besides your name?" He watched intently for her reactions to his question, trying to gauge the extent of her damaged mind.

Emma's face clouded over. "K...Katie calls me Emma, so I guess that's what my name is. But I...I don't remember *anything...*"

One

Eight years later…

"*Take five*," the cameraman yelled, then turned to the dapperly dressed man standing in front of him. "Come on, Teddy, some of us'd like to wrap this up before midnight, if you don't mind."

"All right, all right, it'll be word-perfect this time, I promise. Just get Emma out of my line of vision, will you? She keeps crossing her eyes and mouthing my lines for me." Ted glared over the director's shoulder in mock anger at his pretty co-host.

"I'm just prompting you, Teddy. You need all the help you can get," Emma teased.

With a chiding look at his two co-stars, the director said,

"Re-set the backdrop, and Ted, get back on your mark. Everybody ready? *Roll the tape!*"

"This is Ted Vinelli reminding you to be sure to tune in to tomorrow night's edition of *Evening Magazine,* where Emma and I will bring you up close and personal with..."

Emma found herself just half-listening to the closing remarks wrapping up yet another segment of their nightly magazine show; already her busy mind was leaping ahead to the next day's early shooting schedule.

"Emma!"

Emma turned and spotted a familiar figure striding rapidly toward her. She smiled and waved in acknowledgment.

"Niles, weren't you working late tonight?" Emma asked.

"I was supposed to. We came up with a counter-offer, the other side went for it, and here I am. I called the station and they told me where to find you. Thought I'd offer to take my favorite girl out to dinner. How does a quiet, romantic little place down near the waterfront sound to you?" he said, hooking his arm possessively through hers.

"Wonderful," she smiled up at him, "but we'll have to make it an early evening. Our shoot starts at the crack of dawn tomorrow, and I can't afford to have the discriminating eye of the camera pick up the fact that I was up too late the night before," she answered.

"All right," Niles sighed, "an early evening, I promise. But only if you promise to give me your undivided attention this weekend. No taking home notes, no going over new story lines, no ignoring me, got it?"

Emma laughed at his teasing—yet fairly accurate—description of her normal weekend routine.

"I promise," she said, crisscrossing her finger across her heart. "So what great plans do you have in mind that need my undivided attention?" she asked, only half-listening again, her mind whirling anew at what she'd need to wade through at the office in order to take a whole weekend off.

"There he is again, Frank!" Lenny said, nervously flipping

her auburn locks away from her face to get a closer look at the small screen in front of her. "See, it's not my imagination. I thought I recognized him last week."

"The shoot down at the coast?"

"Yeah, Haystack Rock," she replied. "Let's pull another tape out and see if we can spot him again." Lenny grabbed another tape off the growing pile in front of her.

When Lenny Wright, his assistant editor, had approached him with her oddball discovery, Frank Thompson was sure it was total fiction on her part, a little over-imagination gone wild. Now he wasn't so sure. Portland was just too big a city for this kind of coincidence.

Lenny scanned the screen in front of them, the film moving in slow motion. "There he is again!" she said, thumping his shoulder and pointing her finger at the offending figure.

"Where?" Frank moved in close, squinting at the screen just inches in front of his face.

"Right there," Lenny pointed, then pulled a felt-tipped pen out of the desk drawer and circled the shadowed figure of a man leaning half-in, half-out of the arched entryway to one of the many shops lining Pioneer Square in downtown Portland, Oregon.

"You can't tell that's him," Frank leaned back in his chair, unconvinced.

"But it is—"

"You can't even see his face," he argued.

"I don't have to see his face," Lenny said. "It's his hair I zero in on."

"Oh, yeah, I see what you mean now. Only about a third of the population of Oregon has blonde hair," Frank smirked, shaking his head. For a minute there, she'd actually gotten him to start believing there was something funny going on, but it was obvious she was overreacting.

"But don't you see, Frank?" Lenny went on, unfazed at his scoffing. "It's not blonde, not really. It's more of a silver-blonde. See how it almost shimmers, like a…a halo or something."

She leaned in close to the television monitor, her head just inches from her skeptical boss's as he moved in again for a better look.

"A halo. You see a halo there," he said, scrutinizing the small screen illuminated in front of him.

"Come on, Frank, you know more about camera angles and lighting than anybody I know. Look how, even though he's in shadow, the camera picks up that odd hair coloring. Not blonde, not silver...kind of luminescent." She tapped the pen against the screen for emphasis.

Frank pulled his glasses up on top of his head; looked again at the offending figure. Now that she'd drawn his attention to it, he had to admit she just might be on to something after all. In all the years he'd been in the business, he'd never seen a shading technique or camera angle that could generate this kind of effect on film. The hair did almost glow, halo-like.

"And that's not all," she said. She had his undivided attention again, and she wasn't about to squander it. "Take a look at his eyebrows. Here." She pulled out the tape and inserted another.

"They look black," Frank said, his eyes never leaving the monitor.

"They are black," she said, a trace of smugness in her voice. "Now how many times have you seen that combination? White-blonde hair and jet black eyebrows." She moved back to within inches of the screen again, closely studying the man frozen in place by the video film. "You'd think with such distinctive features, somebody in the film crew would've noticed him before now. I wonder what color his eyes are," she mused out loud.

Frank leaned back in his chair, crossed his arms and studied the back of his assistant's head. "Lenny, are we forgetting something here? If this guy is doing what you think he might be doing, we'd better concentrate on just what the hell he's up to, not what color his eyes are." The stranger seemed to be popping up in the background of segment after segment of their evening magazine program, and they needed to find out why. After that incident in Seattle, everyone seemed to be on edge. And now this. Could it be he had some unhealthy fixation on one of the crew—Emma being the most logical target? Frank wondered. Whatever this man's reasons for being there, it couldn't be ignored.

"You're right," Lenny agreed, reluctantly pulling her eyes away from the screen, ready to get back to business. "I say we start working our way backwards through all the old episodes, see if we can't get a fix on when he started showing up." She pulled another box of tapes off the shelf and started the tedious task of searching through volumes of past segments of *Evening Magazine*, frame by endless frame.

Two

Niles finished his telephone call and returned to the bedroom, where Emma was starting to undress. Coming up silently behind her, he wrapped her in his arms in what was meant to be a loving embrace. Instead, his quiet footfalls startled Emma, and, with a gasp, she threw his arms off her and broke away from him before she even realized what she was doing.

"Dammit, Niles!" she seethed through clenched teeth as she tried to quell her nerves. "How many times do I have to tell you, I hate it when someone sneaks up on me?" She turned her back on him so he couldn't see the momentary panic that had entered her eyes at his unexpected embrace.

"Emma, we're the only two people here, who else would be coming up behind you?" Niles said.

Reading the irritation in his voice, Emma whirled around on him. "I suppose you're going to try and tell me it's not natural to get upset when someone sneaks up behind you and startles you. Is that what you were going to say?" she asked, her arms crossed in sudden, angry defiance.

"No, I—"

"Because if it is," she continued, "I don't want to hear it. You might think it's strange, but all women react this way, not just me, so don't start with the lecture again." She knew it was much, much more than just being startled, but she'd never admit it to Niles. He already pestered her enough as it was when it came to her strange reaction to different things, and that was just what his keen observations picked up. Little did he know to what extent her aversions ran. And she certainly didn't need him to suggest, yet again, that her idiosyncrasies might be a direct result of her submerged past. How could he presume to know what effects her past had on her when even she didn't know?

"I wasn't going to lecture you, Emma. I was going to apologize. I know you don't like it, I just forgot, that's all," Niles answered, his voice contrite.

Emma sighed, relenting. "I know you're just trying to be affectionate, Niles, but there's a lot of crazy people out there, and with my job..."

Niles took her in his arms again, more carefully this time. "There's a crazy person right here, just waiting to ravage you." He swept her lithe form up in his arms, and, without relinquishing his hold on her, dropped heavily onto the large, four-poster bed.

He rolled until he was atop her, then sat up on his knees and began to unbutton her blouse, working slowly in the half light, knowing this was what she preferred. He removed the rest of her clothing, then his own.

Lying pliant beneath his nimble fingers, Emma was fighting down the urge to throw him off her and race out of the room; the light spattering of chest hairs coming in contact with her bare breasts sent a shiver of revulsion through her. Always it had been this way, and as much as she tried to relax during lovemaking, she couldn't seem to fight down the rising panic that seemed to grip her in her most intimate moments.

Fortunately, Niles was a patient, considerate lover, and he was careful not to rush her, knowing if he didn't take his time with her, she'd never be able to relax enough to really enjoy their lovemaking.

With great effort, Emma began to respond under Niles' knowing hands and rhythmic motions. As the budding excitement began to invade her limbs, she wrapped her arms around his neck, pulling him close. But once again, before she could experience the full measure of her desire lurking just around the corner, Niles reached his climax, and, spent, collapsed on top of her.

Long after Niles had gone to sleep, Emma was still awake. The unnamed anxiety she'd felt on more occasions than she cared to remember made it impossible to fall easily to sleep. And for some reason, she'd been especially restless and keyed up these past few weeks.

Had she really made the right decision when she'd accepted Niles' proposal? Sometimes she was so confused. After all, Niles Whitmann seemed to be everything she was looking for in the opposite sex. He was handsome, attentive, successful—she should feel lucky he'd chosen her to spend the rest of his life with. And she did. Sort of.

When he'd asked her to marry him several months ago, she'd been surprised, flattered, and scared to death. He'd had to do a lot of fast talking to convince her the time was right for both of them to make that final commitment to each other.

And she did love him, or at least she thought she did. And he was only one of a handful of people she'd trusted enough to reveal her deepest secret to. That he hadn't backed away from what she'd revealed had done much to convince her that perhaps it was time to start thinking about making their relationship a permanent one.

What really had her confused, however, was if everything about the two of them seemed so good, why didn't it *feel* good?

Three

"You've *lied* to me, Doctor. Now what am I supposed to think when a man with your reputation does something like that?"

"Hello, Andrew." There was no mistaking the owner of that low, whispery voice coming out of the past and through the receiver clutched in his hand.

"You remember me, how flattering," Andrew smirked.

"Believe it or not, I do think about you from time to time." And more often than he cared to.

"I bet you do, I bet it even keeps you up at night sometimes. Wondering, waiting for a phone call like this, hoping you'll never hear from me again, but never totally free of that nagging worry that maybe, just maybe, I'd stumble on the truth and be back in the picture again."

"What do you want, Andrew?"

"What I've always wanted, Doctor. Answers, *honest* ones this time."

"All right." There was no putting him off this time. "I take it you haven't approached her yet?" Dr. Stuart said, trying to keep his voice even.

"Not yet. I've seen her; I haven't talked to her."

Dr. Stuart breathed a silent sigh of relief. "Andrew, please. I'll answer all your questions if you promise you won't approach her."

"Promise you? I'm not inclined to promise anything right now, *Doctor.*"

"Just until we've had a chance to talk."

"So you can talk me out of speaking to her? Unh Unh, I don't think so."

"Andrew, please. Just a few minutes of your time."

"You want to see me. See me now, today."

"Today? You mean this afternoon?"

"No, now. I've already wasted seven years more than I needed to because of you. I'm not in the mood to wait any longer."

The doctor sighed. "All right," he said. "How soon can you get here?"

"I'll be right up. I'm in the lobby," Andrew answered, and hung up.

Although it had been nearly seven years since Ben Stuart had seen Andrew Brannigan, the younger man didn't look much different than he had back then, perhaps a little more muscular, more filled out, but otherwise it could have been yesterday that they'd last seen each other.

"Sit down, Andrew." The doctor directed him to a chair opposite his own. "You're looking fit."

"And you're looking old, worn out. It couldn't be the burden of a guilty conscience, could it?" Andrew taunted. Dr. Stuart's hair had gone from a grayish brown to a snow white in the years since they'd last set eyes on each other; the razor sharp part on his head made the deep pink of his scalp stand out in stark contrast to the wintry white hair.

"I had my reasons for doing what I did back then. Those reasons are still valid today." He was determined not to let Andrew ruffle him.

"Valid to whom? Not me. To Emma? That's a rich one."

"Look Andrew, if Emma saw..." his voice weakened.

"Just tell me about her, tell me the truth about what's happened to her," Andrew said. "And it had better be the truth! I'm warning you, this time I'll know if you're lying. Since finding her I've done a little digging of my own, so don't try to bullshit me like you did seven years ago."

"Where do you want me to—"

"With the day her father was murdered."

Dr. Stuart tried to contain his discomfort. "You...you want..."

"Yes, Doctor, the day her father was shot and killed. You look surprised. Do you find it odd I have no trouble talking about that day? Well don't. I've had ten long years to come to terms with what happened that day. My memories are still quite fresh, unlike poor Emma's. *Now say it!*" he hissed.

"On...on the day Emma's father was shot..."

"Murdered!" Andrew shouted.

"All right! For Christ's sake, murdered. What's the point of all this, Andrew? If you're trying to instill some fear—"

"In you? A trained psychologist? A professional whose job it is to get people to face their fears, not hide from them?"

"Then what do you want?"

"You?" Andrew continued. "A respected, no *revered,* criminologist who decided it was easier to lie and protect the status quo than tell the truth?" Andrew leaned back in his chair, a look of disgust on his face. "I'm not trying to scare you, I'm just trying to get the truth out of an old man who's afraid of losing control of a test subject he's been observing, manipulating and documenting for nearly ten years."

"That's not fair and you know it. She's like my own daughter. I even adopted her...," Dr. Stuart said.

"You adopted her to control her!"

"That's enough," Dr. Stuart stiffened. "You don't know

anything. It's pointless to try and convince you otherwise. But let's assume for argument's sake that you're right. Can you honestly say the course I've chosen for her is so wrong? You've seen her, Andrew. She's happy, successful...her life is full, even without a remembered past."

Andrew turned his head away and snorted. Dr. Stuart went right on.

"If you approach her now, confront her, you might undo everything I've accomplished—she's accomplished—over the last several years. Do you really want that for her? Do you really want her to remember the events of that awful night?"

"I don't know what I want," Andrew muttered. He brought his hands up to his face, gently massaging his throbbing temples.

"Leave her be, Andrew. All you can do is cause her harm now. It's time for you to forget, to bury the past like she's done."

Andrew's head snapped up at those words.

"No," he whispered. "That's the one difference between Emma and me. She's forgotten the past, but I remember every single, solitary moment of it. Every day of my life."

Four

Frank finished his umpteenth cup of coffee of the day, stretched his lean, whip-like body over the lip of his chair, tried working the kinks out of his back, then slumped back down and picked up the notebook in front of him. "So what do we know about this guy, Lenny?"

"Let's see." She shuffled through her notes, her normally vivid green eyes showing the strain of a long evening spent staring at the small, luminescent screen in front of her. "To the best of our knowledge, he started showing up in the background shoots about two weeks ago. He doesn't appear in every segment, and there doesn't seem to be any set pattern as to when he does or doesn't show up. For instance, he doesn't show up every Monday, or every Wednesday, or only on the local shoots."

"The Victoria, B. C. shoot?"

"Good example," Lenny nodded. "He was there."

"You got any theories on how he figures out where we're going to be every day?" Frank threw down his notebook, picked up his pencil and began nervously tapping it on the top of his desk, eyes locked on his assistant.

Lenny shrugged. "It's not common knowledge, that's for sure. My first instinct is to say he knows someone at the station—someone who's able to feed him our schedule."

"Or maybe he just follows the crew to each location," Frank threw out.

Lenny shrugged again, eyes wandering back to the scrawled notes in front of her. "That would entail a lot of sitting around—plus our shoot-times vary..."

"Maybe," Frank continued, "but say he enjoys our show so much he follows us around to see it."

"When he can just tune in at seven-thirty every night and watch it in the quiet comfort of his own home? I don't think so," Lenny shook her head, frowning, then said, "Maybe he's looking for a job."

"Nah," they answered in unison, shaking their heads.

"Camera hog?" Frank ventured.

"Don't think so. He seems to make a pretty good effort to stay in the background in the clips we've seen of him. He's there, but then he isn't—know what I mean?" she looked at Frank, saw the comprehension in his eyes. "Which brings up another possibility." Her voice had an ominous ring to it that made the hair stand up on Frank's arms.

"That he's been shadowing the film crew longer than we think?" he said, reluctant to face the possibility.

"And we just didn't get him on film," Lenny nodded, finishing his morose thought.

"Shit! It's Emma then, it's got to be," Frank said, giving voice to the fears they'd both been trying to avoid.

"Could be Teddy," Lenny offered.

"Yeah right, keep telling yourself that," Frank said, then regretted it. He could see she was beginning to get scared, really scared. For good reason. Not all that long ago, a newswoman up in Seattle had been brutally beaten by a man who'd followed her around for months before wheedling his way into her private life, only to turn obsessive and violent when she told him she no longer wanted to date him. He'd seemed normal enough, at the onset, but that was before she realized how he'd orchestrated all their 'coincidental' meetings. And she wasn't the only one this'd happened to. There were dozens of documented cases. Frank did *not* want Emma to become another statistic.

"Okay, say it's Emma," Lenny said, nervously twirling her empty coffee cup in her hands. "What do we do now? We'll have to tell her."

Frank shook his head. "No, not yet, not until we have something more concrete." He paused, then said, "Doesn't she keep a file of nutso letters she gets in the mail that have strange or sexual overtones?"

"Yesss. She even has a few pictures."

"You know where she keeps it?"

"In her desk."

"Can you get into it without her knowing?"

"Yes, but I don't like doing that." Lenny shifted uncomfortably in her seat, knew where the conversation was leading. "If we just ask..."

"Lenny, do you really want Emma all worked up over something that could turn out to be a figment of our imaginations?"

"Those films aren't a figment of our imagination, Frank, and you know it. If there's someone out there watching her, following her, she has a right to know about it. Remember what just happened—"

"I know, I know, and I agree," Frank nodded. "But if we approach her now with what little proof we've got, all we're going to do is spook her. *I'm* spooked, and I don't even know for sure if anything's really going on here."

"Then what do you suggest we do?" Lenny said, unconvinced.

Frank dropped the pencil in his hand and moved his chair closer to Lenny's. "How about we check her files, see if maybe she's got a photo of this guy in there. And we read her letters, see if someone mentions seeing her at more than one of our locations."

"And if nothing turns up in the file, then what?" Lenny persisted.

"Then you and I go along on tomorrow's shoot and see if we can spot him."

"And if one of us does spot him, what then?"

"I'll approach him, try to get a line on him. He may have a perfectly logical reason for being there. Whaddya say?" he cajoled. He could order her to do as he wanted, but he didn't want to take that approach, for two good reasons. First, asking instead of telling one of his subordinates to do something always garnered greater cooperation from them. More importantly, Lenny and Emma were best friends. He had no illusions about where Lenny's loyalties lay. If push came to shove, she'd go straight to Emma, no matter what he said to the contrary.

Lenny sighed, giving up. "All right, Frank, we'll try it your way first. But if we find this guy and you approach him, and he acts squirrelly in any way, we tell Emma, *and* we call the police."

"Agreed," Frank nodded. "Now go grab that file. I'll get us each another cup of coffee."

"Just one more thing, detective," Lenny pushed herself out of her seat and started toward the door.

Frank squinted at her through thick glasses. "What's that?"

"What explanation are we going to give the crew for tagging along with them tomorrow?"

"Um...good point." Frank rubbed his chin in thought. "I'll think on that one, come up with a good cover story for us both."

"Cover story? Oh brother," Lenny groaned as she opened the door. "What've I created?" she finished, wrangling a small smile out of her worried boss.

Five

"Hey, what're you two doing up so early? Don't tell me you're coming with us, I won't believe it," Emma said, eyebrows arched, a smile working at the corners of her mouth. She'd watched Lenny and Frank's approach and couldn't help but smile at the incongruous pair—Lenny with her vivacious auburn hair framing a startlingly pretty face, her petite frame matched up against Frank's long, lanky body and pale, washed out features. He was constantly getting teased that the lights from the editing machine were slowly bleaching out his skin.

"And what if we are?" Frank smiled back at her. "Did you and Teddy think you were going to get away with hogging all the festivities? It *is* Christmastime," Frank said, as if that covered every reason for their coming along.

Emma looked around to nobody in particular. "Did someone happen to mention in Frank's presence there was going to be free food today?"

"Hey, everybody knows the first day of the Treelighting Festival is always the best. Lenny and I have to work this weekend; this will be the only chance we'll get to attend." It wasn't the greatest excuse in the world for tagging along, but neither Lenny nor himself had been able to come up with a better one. Emma's file had turned up nothing—a big zero. This had been their best alternative. "Besides," he joked, "this is the only way to make sure Charlie gets all the background shots we need."

Emma cocked her head in Lenny's direction. "It was the free food, wasn't it?"

"As a matter of fact…"

"Okay, everybody, load up!" the director shouted, counting heads. "Hey, where's Teddy? Anybody seen Teddy yet this morning?"

"Right here," Teddy said, striding around the corner of the minibus.

"You're late!" Emma said, ready to start in on him, then noted the expression on her co-anchor's face. "What's wrong?" she asked.

Teddy shrugged, adjusting his tie. "Nothing, really."

"Oh come on, you can tell me," Emma persisted.

Teddy settled into the seat next to her, buttoned his coat up the front, pulling the cuffs free. "No big deal," he said. "Just got off to a rocky start this morning, that's all. I went to pick Nicholas up, give him a kiss good-bye before I left. He rewarded me with a gusher of steaming mother's milk all down the front of my shirt. I had to go back upstairs and grab a fresh shirt. What's so funny?"

Both Emma and Lenny were laughing. Teddy was known as the clothes horse around the office, never a hair out of place, his expensively tailored suits always neatly pressed, free of any wayward wrinkles.

"Oh Teddy," Emma replied through her laughter, "I'd

have given anything to see the look on your face." He was so finicky about his clothing, his morning just had to be ruined before it'd gotten a chance to really get started.

"Just wait, Emma, when you and Niles have some kids of your own," Teddy warned good-naturedly, aware of his reputation around the office. "You'll see how funny it is to have everything you own covered with sour milk stains. Ugh!" he pinched his nose, then spotted Lenny and Frank out of the corner of his eyes. "Hey, what're you two doing here?"

"Can you believe it," Emma remarked. "They're going on a field trip."

"Yeah, right. Frank found out there was free food today, didn't he?"

"Any sign of him?" Lenny asked Frank as they completed yet another meandering cycle through the crowded square. Although the downtown area was streaming with people, Lenny had felt certain they would have no trouble spotting their colorful mystery man if, in fact, he was there today.

"Nada. Think he took a day off?"

"Maybe," she replied noncommittally.

"It'd be just our luck," Frank said morosely. He missed his warm bed. "Shall we keep at it?"

"Why don't you stay close to where Emma's at, and I'll make another circle." She moved off to begin yet another winding trip through the busy square.

"*Goddammit!* How in the hell did we both miss him?" Frank raged. He stopped, backed up the film, and freeze framed the telltale figure staring eerily back at them both.

Teddy opened the door to the editing room, poked his head inside. "Hey, what's going on? I can hear you ranting and raving from forty feet away, even with the door closed."

"Huh? Oh, nothing," Frank replied, distracted. "I'm just irritated Charlie didn't get some close-up shots of the manger scene I asked him to get," Frank said.

Teddy rolled his eyes. "Editors...," he muttered under his

breath as he shut the door and returned to his desk.

"Maybe we should tell—"

"Not *yet,* Lenny!" Frank ground out harshly, frustrated. "And especially not to Teddy. He's the world's worst when it comes to keeping a secret." Frank turned his attention back to the film. "Look at this," he grumbled. "See the expression on his face? I tell you, this guy knew we were looking for him. See that grin?" Frank jabbed his bony finger at the offending figure on the monitor. "And he's looking straight into the camera! *Shit!"* Frank was beside himself with anger. "How did we miss him?" he repeated, shaking his head in disbelief.

"It was pretty crowded," Lenny offered lamely.

"Crowded! Crowded! Look at the *screen,* Lenny. He's right there in front of our eyes. How does he do that?"

"Keep your voice down," Lenny shushed.

As if he didn't even hear her, Frank continued his tirade. "He appears out of nowhere, then vanishes again. I'm telling you, this guy's spooky."

"That's what I've been trying to tell you. There's something not quite right here, Frank. I can *feel* it," Lenny said. She had described the stranger's hair as appearing almost halo-like, but now it seemed to appear much more sinister to Frank now, almost supernatural, and he had half a notion to blurt their findings to the whole office, alert everybody to be on the lookout for their mystery man, corral him before anything bad happened.

Instead, Frank backed the film up again. "Right there," he pointed again, "smiling right at us. Jesus...he must've known from the other shoots that we weren't part of the regular field staff. He probably saw us nosing around and put two and two together." Frank paused in his ranting, suddenly subdued as he let the implications of his statement sink in to both of them.

"Lenny," he said, worried. "Whoever this guy is, whatever he wants, he's one cool customer."

Lenny shifted uncomfortably in her seat as Frank continued on. "Instead of making himself scarce when he realized we were on to him," he said uneasily, "what does he do? He makes it a point to avoid the two of us, yet make himself known by blatantly showing up on our film again."

"He had to let us know he'd outsmarted us," Lenny said, shivering. "That's it, Frank. We can't keep this to ourselves any longer, not after today. Since he knows we're on to him, we might've just pushed him into taking some sort of action. I, for one, am unwilling to waste another minute speculating why he's hanging around our crew."

"After today," Frank agreed, "I don't think either one of us has any doubt his presence is more than just a little scary, or that it's pure coincidence." Frank turned in his chair, reached for the phone. "I'm calling Ray up right now, have him come down and take a look at what we've got."

Eyebrows raised, Lenny said, "Straight to the top?"

"I'm not about to take a chance of this getting buried before it reaches him," Frank answered, his voice firm. "It's too important." He remembered all too well how he'd almost dismissed Lenny's initial claims as being just too outrageous to give proper credence.

Frank hung up the phone. "Theresa says he's already headed this way, with a guest in tow." He shut off the editing machine, pulled himself up out of his chair and strode purposefully toward the door, intent on waylaying the news chief. There was no way he was going to sit on this disquieting discovery any longer, no matter who he had with him.

Frank opened the door and immediately spotted Ray making his way toward Emma and Teddy's desks. He took a step forward, then suddenly stopped in his tracks, mouth agape. Anticipating his continued movement, Lenny bumped into the back of the unmoving editor. She looked up, startled, her eyes wandering to where Frank's attention was so rigidly focused, then let out a gasp, shocked beyond words to find herself staring at the now familiar profile of the mysterious man who had been haunting their film sites for God knew how long.

Six

Immersed in her schedule for the next day's shoot, Emma was unaware of Ray Hollander's approach.

"Psst, Emma. Emma!" Teddy whispered out of the side of his mouth. His desk was just a few feet from hers, but with her attention riveted on the papers in front of her, it took a second or two for Teddy's voice to penetrate through her thoughts.

She looked up. "What are you whispering for?" At the look on her co-host's face, she said, "Is something wrong?"

"I don't know, you tell me. Look who's headed this way," he nodded discretely in Ray's direction.

Emma shifted around in her seat, a bit surprised to find Ray headed in their direction, his familiar, ramrod-straight body moving easily toward their desks.

This was odd, Emma thought. Normally, if Ray had something to say to them, he did it in the comfort of his own expansive office. Perhaps the fact that he wasn't alone had something to do with his unheralded appearance.

As Ray approached her desk, Emma turned her attention to the stranger accompanying the news chief, startled to find a pair of deep blue eyes boring directly into hers.

"Emma, Ted," Ray announced, "this is Andrew Brannigan." He turned back to the man accompanying him. He said, "As I'm sure you're aware, Mr. Brannigan, this is my *Evening Magazine* team."

"Ms. Stuart, Mr. Vinelli, it's a pleasure to meet you," the stranger answered, shaking their hands. His low, husky voice had a deep, almost rumbling resonance to it. Although it wasn't an unpleasant sound, and she had no trouble making out what he was saying, for some reason the timbre of it disturbed Emma.

"As I explained, Mr. Brannigan," Ray continued, Emma's sudden uneasiness unnoticed by either Ray or Teddy, "these two aren't just the co-hosts of our evening show. They're also directly involved in story development."

"You've got a story?" Teddy asked.

"That's for you to decide," Ray answered. "Mr. Brannigan approached me with an interesting idea for our show. I want him to pass it by you two, see if he's got a filmable story. I'll leave the final decision up to you."

As Ray talked on, Emma quietly studied the man standing so calmly in front of her desk, tried to put a finger on what so disturbed her about this stranger. It wasn't just his voice that had struck such an immediate, deep chord within her, but his overall appearance as well. And she realized with a start that, contrary to what seemed normal for her, she was not at all repelled by his dark, distinctive looks. Quite the opposite, in fact. She found herself inexplicably drawn to them, and this surprised her more than she could possibly have imagined.

"Mr. Brannigan," Ray shook his hand again, "I'm going to leave you in their capable hands. I wish you every success, with or without our help." With that, he left.

"Take a seat, Mr. Brannigan," Teddy offered. Emma still hadn't found her voice. She stared numbly as he took the seat directly across from her.

"Just Andy," he replied casually, taking the proffered seat.

"And it's just Emma and Ted," Teddy answered cordially. "Now that we're all on a first name basis, how about filling us in on your idea."

"In a nutshell," Andy said, "I'm working on a missing person case I thought would be interesting to chronicle on television."

Emma finally spoke. "Are you a private investigator?" she asked, clearing her throat as she tried to quell the odd sensations that kept rippling through her every time she made eye contact with the strange man sitting so calmly opposite her.

He shook his head no. "Not in the classic sense. I do investigative work for a non-profit organization," he replied, his piercing blue eyes locked on troubled brown.

"Like the National Center for Missing and Exploited Children?" she asked, mesmerized by the startling blue orbs that seemed to look straight through her.

"Close," he nodded. "We work in conjunction with them. In fact, most of our cases come straight from them, cases they haven't been able to resolve."

"But isn't that thousands of cases?" Teddy interjected.

Andy nodded again. "But what my organization does is pick a few we feel we might be able to have a positive impact on."

Emma had covered a missing person story just last summer, knew the success rate was terrible when it came to solving missing person cases, and she said as much.

"The statistics are depressing," Andy agreed. "But the Mizpah Foundation, that's the organization I represent, has a pretty good track record for bringing missing person cases to conclusion." His voice held a trace of pride in it as he told them he and his fellow investigators had worked long and hard for the reputation they now had, and he intended to extend that record with this current investigation.

"Mizpah," Emma repeated, mulling over the word. "That's biblical, isn't it?" she asked, surprised she'd made the connection. Now where did that little tidbit of knowledge come from?

Andy smiled at the look of confusion in her eyes. "Yes, he replied slowly, "Genesis 31:49. Our organization is loosely affiliated with the Catholic Church, thus the biblical name." He started to say something else, then abruptly stopped.

Emma looked up at him again, took in the odd expression on his face, and jotted the passage number on the notepad in front of her, then wondered why. Perhaps she'd find the time to look up the passage later, see what it actually meant.

"So who exactly are you looking for?" Teddy asked, seemingly unaware of the underlying tension around him.

"Two kids," Andy said, pulling his gaze away from Emma, shifting his attention to Teddy. "Brothers, five and seven years old."

"From around here?"

"No. They're from Philadelphia. The kids were kidnapped by their father."

"The parents divorced?"

Andy nodded. "The mother was the custodial parent, the father had alternating weekend visitation rights, along with a whole month in the summer. When his summer month rolled around, he took off with the kids."

"And you've traced them here?"

Andy nodded again. "He's somewhere here in Portland, or maybe one of the surrounding communities. It's taken me months to track the father and two boys this far, but I'm certain he's close by; maybe not in Portland itself—but close, very close."

"And you'd like our station to cover the story when you find him?"

"If you're interested. Or you could even cover some of the investigation leading up to his capture," Andy added.

"What if you don't find them?" Emma asked.

"You won't have a story," Andy answered simply. "But

I'll find them, don't worry about that. I've been on their trail for over three months, I'm not about to lose them now. Any investigator will tell you that finding people who don't want to be found takes a hell of a lot of time and a hell of a lot of energy. But most important of all is luck, pure and simple."

"Luck?" Emma replied, her eyes locked with his again.

Andy nodded, a smile played at the corners of his lips. "And I've got to tell you two, luck has definitely been on my side lately," he finished, the apparent irony of those words completely lost on Andrew Brannigan's two avid listeners.

"*Now* what do we do?" Lenny sat slumped in her chair, looking to Frank for some sort of direction.

They had stood at the open door just long enough to hear the introductions and Andrew Brannigan's reasons for being there before quickly backpedaling into the editing room again.

"I don't know, just let me think for a minute, will you?" Frank answered tersely. He should have been thankful their discovery had turned out to be nothing after all, but it just didn't sit well with him. He couldn't explain his feelings to Lenny—he wasn't even sure he should try. After all, none other than Ray Hollander *himself* had brought the mysterious stranger down to meet Emma and Teddy. What more proof did he need to have to believe the guy was legit?

"I'm just glad we didn't make fools of ourselves in front of Ray," Lenny sighed.

Frank looked up at her, only half-listening. "Yeah, I guess so," he mumbled.

"What's wrong?"

"Nothing."

"Come on, Frank," Lenny cajoled.

Frank shrugged his shoulders. "I dunno...it's just...just..."

"Just what?" Lenny prompted, trying to drag the words out of her reluctant boss.

"I don't know," Frank replied, squinting down at her. "I guess I'm bothered by the fact that this guy stayed in the background, haunting our shoots for how long we can't even pinpoint. Then, suddenly, he realizes we are on to him, and bang, next thing we know, he miraculously shows up on our front doorstep. Doesn't that bother you?"

"Frank," Lenny said with more firmness than she felt, "he was with Ray. Doesn't that tell you something?" a bit surprised at Frank's reaction, his unwillingness to let go of his suspicions.

"Yeah, it tells me something all right," he said, his head jerking up and down. "You heard the same things I did out there. Ray just met the guy today, so what does that tell you?" he asked pointedly.

"That Ray thought he was okay, and I for one am not going to question Ray's judgment. Are you?"

"No, I'm not going to question Ray, and you know it. But just because Ray thinks this Andrew Brannigan is on the level doesn't take away from the fact that he's been shadowing our crew, or have you forgotten that?"

"I haven't forgotten. But he's out in the open now, and he certainly doesn't seem so dangerous up close," she said, adding, "and if you're so worried about why he was at all those shoots, why don't you just ask him why he was there?"

"Don't worry," Frank replied, his face a determined mask, "I intend to. And while I'm at it, I'm going to ask him how in the hell he knew *exactly* where our crew was going to be every day."

Seven

Emma tried to tell herself she'd set up another meeting with Andy Brannigan only because she was interested in hearing more about his current investigation. She even tried to convince herself she was sorry Teddy wouldn't be able to devote much time to this particular story, what with his already overburdened schedule.

What she couldn't control, couldn't deny, however, was that she found herself inexplicably drawn to another man in a way she'd never experienced before, not even with Niles. And that thought both scared and thrilled her at the same time.

She scheduled their meeting to take place after the day's shoot, which thankfully had an early start time. This gave her time to do the wrap-up back at the office and still have plenty of time in the afternoon to meet with Andy. Freeing up an entire afternoon was no small feat for her, but luckily the shooting schedule had dovetailed nicely with her newly-laid plans.

She chose to meet Andy at a small restaurant several blocks away from the station instead of at the station itself in an effort to protect them from being interrupted unnecessarily. At least that's what she kept telling herself.

But she knew better.

She was more than a little aware of the budding excitement spreading through her at the prospect of their forthcoming meeting, and she wanted time alone with the man responsible for the odd sensations that had held her prisoner since she'd first laid eyes on him. These strange emotions had gripped her the moment she'd looked into his startling deep blue eyes, had kept her awake last night, defying easy explanation.

Emma maneuvered her white Camaro into an open slot in front of the restaurant, immediately caught sight of Andy through the window, his silver-blonde hair shining like a beacon, drawing her eyes to him. His fair hair seemed to corral the attention of the last meager rays of sunlight struggling through the cloudy, overcast winter day, creating an odd, shimmering reflection on the restaurant glass.

Again, that peculiar sensation rippled through her, leaving her with an odd feeling that if she reached out and tried to touch him, his image would fade from sight.

Andy watched Emma get out of the car and stride hurriedly toward the wood-framed entrance, again struck by how little she'd actually changed. It had been nearly ten years, almost half their lives, and yet he'd have recognized her anywhere. Her petite figure, the tilt of her head, the way the corners of her eyes crinkled when she smiled, all those special characteristics of the girl he'd known so well so long ago.

She slid into the seat across from him. "Sorry I'm a little late. A last minute telephone call took a bit longer than I expected." She had been halfway out of the building when the receptionist had signaled her. She'd motioned to the young girl that she was on her way out, but the girl had mouthed back that it was Niles on the line. Emma had felt compelled to run back to her desk and take the call. Unfortunately, Niles had been in a talkative mood, and she'd had to cut him short, but not before explaining her reasons why. Naturally, he'd then wanted to know all about the man she was meeting. Afraid her voice would give away some of the erratic emotions she'd been battling since she'd met Andy, she'd answered only a few of Niles' questions before begging off any further explanations on the excuse that she was already late for her meeting.

"No problem," Andy replied easily. "I've been watching the world go by from my strategic corner seat. Kind of an interesting neighborhood, isn't it?"

"Interesting?" Emma replied dryly. She looked out at the familiar street. "Quite the slice of life in this particular part of the city. This area is called 'Old Town.' I don't suppose any explanation is needed on the name," she smiled.

"But it looks like they're in the midst of refurbishing," Andy observed.

"The City of Portland has been working on it for the past decade, giving this portion of the city a badly needed face-lift. Unfortunately, we still have a long way to go. Our ongoing transient problem doesn't help. No matter what the city does, it can't seem to get them to relocate."

"I've noticed," Andy nodded as he watched a man in thin, ragged clothing, seemingly impervious to the cold winter chill, shuffle slowly down the sidewalk, stopping only long enough to rummage through the garbage cans on the street corners before continuing his disjointed meandering along the sidewalk.

"But every city has them, don't they? Mostly, they stay down near the waterfront area. But sometimes they wander further out, looking for new pickings."

Andy nodded in agreement. "Every large city in every town I've been in has had a homeless problem." Without realizing it, both he and Emma were sharing the same thoughts. What circumstances had driven these people to the streets in the first place? And why did they remain—away from their jobs, their families, their friends? Age old questions, never any concrete answers.

"You know," Emma fiddled with the buttons of her coat, "studies tell us that the majority of street people choose to live like they do, but when I see them living on the streets, in the cold, being rained on, yelled at, herded from corner to corner, I still can't help but feel sorry for them. Why is that?" she ruminated out loud, not really expecting an answer.

"Human nature," Andy replied softly. "And don't ever wonder why you feel sorry for them. When you can look at them and *not* feel something, whether it be pity, or sympathy, or maybe even disgust, regardless that it's their own making, that's when you should worry." Andy was remembering well how he could have so easily ended up in the streets as so many men with his sort of troubled past had. Luckily for him, there had been a few people still around who'd made sure he hadn't ended up like the transient slowly making his way down the street. He was eternally grateful for their intervention—but was he again about to embark down the same narrow path his friends had tried so hard to steer him away from? Only time—and Emma's reactions to him—would tell.

Before Emma could reply, the waitress came up to their table and asked them if they were ready to order.

"Are you hungry?" Emma asked.

"Not really," Andy replied, trying to shake off his suddenly pensive mood, return back to the present. "I'll just have a beer, whatever you've got on tap," he said to the waitress.

Emma wasn't hungry either. She ordered a white wine, then settled back in her seat and pulled her notepad and pen out of her scuffed, well-worn leather briefcase, ready to get down to the reason for their meeting.

The waitress quickly returned with their orders, placed the drinks in front of them, then hurried off to see to a new set of customers coming through the door.

"Tell me, with a little more detail, the events leading up to the abduction of the two boys, beginning with a background of the family," she started out, pen in hand.

Andy took a sip of his beer, then launched into his story, all the facts of the case tripping easily off his tongue. He'd spent so much time pouring over and over the details of this family he was searching for, he felt knew them intimately, perhaps even better than they knew themselves.

"David and Karen Carlson, a typical Middle America family," he told her. "The wife supported hubby while he went to school, chiropractic college, to be exact. When the boys came along, she stayed home and raised them while he built up his practice. Over the course of several years, discontent settled in on both parties, and they finally decided to divorce, but not before waging a bitter custody battle that the mother eventually won."

"So...even in today's liberated climate, more often than not, the mother usually gets custody of the children, is that right?" Emma asked.

Andy shook his head. "Not always," he said, then took another small sip of his beer. "In the past, yes. It usually didn't matter which parent was better suited to take care of the kids—categorically, the mother got custody. And to be brutally honest, most men preferred it that way. They didn't seem to want the day-to-day responsibility of their own children. They appeared to be content to give the mother custody and themselves take on the role of weekend father. Unfortunately, that feeling still prevails. Sure, the courts still see their share of custody battles, but they're more of a power play than anything else. The majority of men out there still give up custody of their kids without a fight."

"But not David Carlson," Emma said.

"Not David," Andy nodded, continuing his narration. "He wanted custody—fought hard and nasty for it—and lost. Actually, he was better equipped financially to care for the two children than Karen was, and that's the approach he took when they went to court. His business was thriving, Karen had no job to speak of, he felt he had a solid case for getting custody. But more important in the judge's eyes—and rightly so—was that the mother was better equipped emotionally to best meet their two son's needs."

"So he fought hard and lost...then what?" Emma asked, the drone of Andy's husky voice mesmerizing her.

"From what I've learned from Karen, David Carlson came away from the battle full of anger, full of threats. He tried to appeal, to no avail. But then, after a while, he seemed to accept the judgment. For several months, he followed the divorce decree to the letter. He was never late with his support payments, always brought the boys home on time from his weekend visitations. He was even, if not pleasant, at least civil to Karen."

"And her?"

"She never regretted getting the divorce, even though the custody battle drained her both emotionally and financially. But she'd found a decent job that paid enough for her and the kids to get by on, as long as the support checks kept coming in, so she was starting to get her life in order. Of course, we now know David hadn't accepted the situation at all, that he'd been biding his time, getting his affairs in order for a fast pull-out. Summertime rolled around, and Karen, lulled into false security by David's seeming acceptance of the situation, prepared her sons for their month-long visit with their dad. She packed up extra clothes, even sent along a few of their favorite toys and so on," Andy said, shaking his head.

"She never suspected anything?"

Andy shrugged. "She and David had been getting along so well lately, why should she? It never occurred to her that he was plotting a disappearing act." He shifted in his seat, steepled his hands around the half-empty beer glass. "Look at it from her point of view. Here's a professional with a lucrative practice, strong ties to the community, family and friends close by. How could she know?"

"So when did she find out they'd all disappeared?"

"They'd been gone about a week. She'd called them a couple of times, everything seemed normal. Then David called up and told her he was taking the boys camping for a couple of weeks, and that he'd have them call her when they got back in town. Little did Karen realize at the time that she'd just given him a minimum of two weeks head start on her when he pulled out."

"So at the end of the two weeks when he didn't return she started to get suspicious?" Emma said.

"And worried, as you can well imagine. The two weeks had dragged by slowly for her. After all, this was the longest she'd ever been separated from her sons, let alone just speaking to them on the telephone. And, although there was no reason for her to suspect otherwise, she told me that by the end of the first week, she'd begun to get a funny feeling about the whole thing. Maybe it was that maternal instinct kicking in, or maybe it was simply that she'd missed them more than she realized she would, who knows? For whatever reason, when the two weeks were finally up and she still couldn't get a hold of them, she wasted no time contacting his office to see if he'd checked back in at work. And that's when she received the shock of her life."

"He'd sold the business," Emma said.

A disgusted look moved across Andy's face. "She found out from his *secretary*. Can you believe it? He'd sold it over a month ago."

"And he'd been able to keep it a secret from her?" she asked, incredulous.

"Sure," he snorted. "How would she know what he did with his business? After the divorce, she no longer had a vested interest in his business, that'd all been settled in court. And she'd had no reason to call him up at his office in months. Like I said, everything had gone so smoothly, she was taken totally off guard, as he'd planned all along."

Andy drained the last of his beer, momentarily stopping his narration. Then he flagged the waitress over and ordered another, his last. Two was his limit. He had no intention of following in his mother's footsteps and dying of alcoholism. That alcoholism was hereditary was enough for him to always put a self-imposed two drink maximum on himself wherever he went. He'd made it through a lot of grief in his life; he wasn't about to let alcohol get a stranglehold on him, especially when everything seemed to finally be coming together for him.

"Anyway," Andy continued, "by this time Karen was beginning to get scared, really scared. So she decides to drive by the house David had moved into, and what does she find?"

"A *For Rent* sign?" Emma ventured eagerly, quickly caught up again in the narration.

"A *For Rent* sign," Andy repeated, his expression grim. "So now the panic really takes root. She drives home in a daze. She calls her ex-mother-in-law, who gives her no help at all, won't even speak to her as a matter of fact. So then she calls the police."

"She probably didn't get much help there," Emma ventured, shaking her head.

"No…she didn't." Andy was a little surprised at her cynical comment, then remembered Ray Hollander had mentioned Emma had done a story on a local missing person case a couple of years ago, so she was probably pretty familiar with police procedure.

"In my books, kidnapping is kidnapping," Andy remarked, his jaw set in an angry line. "But the police don't look at it with the same degree of seriousness as a total stranger taking a child."

"But that doesn't seem right—"

"It isn't right," Andy replied vehemently. "But the cold, harsh reality is, that's simply the way it is, period. And no amount of bellyaching about the system is going to change it one iota, not right now, anyway," he added, his tone dripping with disgust. "Believe me, I've tried." Christ, he wished he had a nickel for every irate telephone call he'd made to the police on some family's behalf in order to get some action going on a disappearance. Only occasionally had he been able to stir up some passion, shame some officer into digging a little deeper, but more often than not, he was butting his head up against a bureaucratic brick wall. And the worst of it was, he couldn't totally blame them for their seemingly unfeeling stance—the statistics on missing persons, especially children, were staggering. As much as he hated to admit it, he knew the police usually did what they could with the limited amount of funds and manpower available to them for that sort of crime. And crime it was, regardless of the fact that the perpetrator in this particular instance was the father.

"So then she called the MPAA, and they in turn got your organization involved."

"More or less," Andy nodded. "Like I explained yesterday, we look over a case file and if we see a glimmer of hope, we take it on. It sounds a little heartless, but it's important to know where to draw the line."

"And how do you draw the line?" she asked, curious.

Andy looked out the window for a minute, squinting out at the waning light, gathering his thoughts. He hadn't meant to get into this, but there was no stopping now. She'd asked him a question, seemingly interested in him, not just the investigation. And if meandering slightly off the topic at hand kept her there, near him, he was more than happy to share with her all he dared.

Shrugging, he shifted his gaze back to her. "For me, a lot of times it comes down to what my head tells me I should do and what my heart wants to accept." At her puzzled look, Andy tried to explain, "Some of the files I read are so gut-wrenching, they just cry out to me. My first instinct is to take the case on, regardless of whether it's got any real chance of being solved." He hunched over the table, his deep blue eyes intense, and suddenly troubled.

"You see, some families are just so desperate for information on their missing loved ones, all they really need is for someone out there to tell them they haven't forgotten about them, that they care enough about their plight to investigate a little further. The biggest problem I face with my job is that I want to help them all, and it's just not feasible, not with our own very limited resources," he shook his head, regret permeating his every word.

"So you take the ones that offer some hope. There's nothing wrong with that. At least you get results instead of wasting your time on something that has no real chance of being resolved."

Andy grimaced. "Except there's always that doubt, you know? The feeling that maybe, just maybe, you could have been the one to make a difference on a case." Andy's eyes focused on the glass twirling slowly between his two hands and thought back on some of the cases he'd wanted *so badly* to handle, yet had grudgingly, *painfully* put aside.

"Still, look at all the cases you've handled to fruition. There's no arguing your system for picking cases doesn't work," Emma said, trying to lift his spirits.

"True," Andy smiled, grateful for her effort. He leaned back in his seat and tried to dispel the helplessness that had suddenly come over him at the thought of the hundreds of cases he and the other investigators had had to turn down.

"And didn't you say yesterday that your organization had solved nearly every case you'd taken on? A pretty impressive record," she said, wrangling another smile out of Andy.

"That's because I've got a stubborn streak in me a mile wide," he said, the sadness falling away from him like a blanket. "I just hate giving up. As a matter of fact, I just solved a case I'd worked on several years ago." If she only knew how prominently she'd figured in on that particular case, he thought, harsh memories crowding in on him.

It was only after he'd recognized Emma on television that the idea to approach the station she worked at came to him. He'd been randomly flipping through the television channels in his motel room the first day he arrived in Portland when he'd stumbled on Emma's image staring back at him.

At first, he'd thought he was seeing things. It wasn't the first time this phenomenon had happened to him. Her image had come to him often, and at the oddest time, and he'd thought this was just another one of those instances.

After he'd finally caught his breath, he continued to watch the television screen, transfixed by what his eyes were telling him. And as he'd watched, he'd become more and more convinced it was her and not an illusion borne out of a desperate need to find her. Her dark brown hair was shorter, yes, but the large, expressive brown eyes, the voice, the mannerisms...they were all the same, just transported in a natural progression of time and age to the present.

And the more he'd watched, the more elated he became. And when her co-host had mentioned her by name, he'd been absolutely certain. Slowly, the idea to approach the station had formed, and his mind was made up. He had no idea if the program would be even remotely interested in his investigation, but for the first time in a very, very long time, his work didn't seem to matter all that much to him. Right then—that very minute—it was simply a tool to be used to get his foot in the door of Emma's place of business, to approach her legitimately.

And then the program had ended, and the two co-hosts had closed out the show for the day's edition.

And the camera had rolled, displaying Emma's full name, and Andy's elation had turned to anger.

He had been deliberately, cruelly lied to.

Suddenly, he had a second mission in mind.

Eyes narrowing, his thoughts had again turned to revenge on those individuals who had blatantly lied and misled him all those years ago, making him lose precious years in his pursuit of Emma's whereabouts.

"You've been investigating a case for years?" Emma broke into his morbid thoughts, surprise in her voice. "I know police departments keep certain cases, especially murder cases, open for years and years, but I thought I understood you to say your organization didn't take on an investigation of that magnitude."

"You're right. We don't...normally," Andy hedged, sorry he'd let those last words slip. "But this one was special. It was the very first investigation I was involved in, and I spent a lot of time on it without any substantial results. Bad timing and some misleading information threw me off the track for quite a while, and I just recently, and totally by accident, solved the case." It had started with one long year of searching, to be exact, only to be thrown off the track by her very own stepfather—one Benjamin Stuart—for another seven years. Twice, Ben Stuart had interfered with his unerring devotion in finding Emma. It would not happen again.

"Now that sounds like an interesting story for our show."

"Maybe another time," Andy said, effectively putting her off. Steering her back on a safer course, he said, "So what about this story? Are you going to recommend picking it up?"

Emma looked out the window, then back at Andy, trying to make up her mind. "You've tracked David and the two boys to Oregon, so you know you're close. But what if they slip away from you? I'm not so sure that's the kind of ending our viewers would particularly like," she stated honestly, giving voice to her fears.

Andy shrugged. "Unlike the movies, life doesn't always have a happy ending, but it's a risk your station would have to take. They'll be shelling out a few bucks on a story that may never have an ending. But that in itself is a story, too, isn't it? Either way, you'll have something to air. But believe me, it won't be wasted money, that I can guarantee. Think of the P.R. alone. Can't you just hear it?—*Evening Magazine* team helps in investigation of disappearance of two young boys..."

Emma leaned across the table, a twinkle in her eye. "You've thought of every angle, haven't you?"

Andy smiled as he thumped his empty beer glass down on the wooden table. "So it's a go?"

"It's a go," Emma answered as she brought her wineglass to her lips. She wasn't sure if her desire to continue seeing this enigmatic stranger was overshadowing her normally better than average intuitions on what did or did not constitute a good story line for her nightly magazine program, and, with a start, realized she really didn't care.

Eight

When she finally returned home, Emma was dismayed, then angry, at her own response at seeing Niles' black BMW in her driveway. She'd hoped to come home, stir up a warm, crackling fire, pour herself a glass of wine, and quietly digest all she and Andy had talked about during their time together. Spotting Niles' car had quickly put an end to her anticipated scenario. And instead of being happy at seeing her future husband, she was finding it difficult to quell the growing irritation at the disruption of her game plan for what remained of the evening. Reluctantly, she pulled her car into the garage and entered the house.

"Niles?" she called out, walking through the living room.

"In here," he replied, the sound of his voice emanating from the kitchen area.

She pulled her gloves off as she walked through the swinging doors separating the kitchen from the formal dining room, again dismayed to find Niles had already begun to make dinner for the two of them, silently berating herself for forgetting she'd promised to have dinner with him.

"Sorry I'm so late," she said, suddenly feeling horribly guilty over the fact that he hadn't entered her thoughts even once over the past several hours.

Niles glanced up from his preparations. "I take it the interview went well?"

"Ummm, pretty well," she answered noncommittally, leaning against the kitchen doorway, her eyes focused on his large, long-fingered hands, busily cutting up vegetables for a tossed salad. She didn't have the heart to tell him she'd already eaten dinner. The afternoon meeting with Andy had stretched into early evening, and they'd both decided to have a bite to eat. Emma had recommended the halibut and chips and they'd both eaten their fill, and then some. She was already hours later than she'd told Niles she'd be; the last thing he would want to hear was that she'd already eaten.

"I had a busy afternoon myself," Niles chatted conversationally, Emma's quiet mood going unnoticed so far by the observant attorney. "Didn't get here till about an hour ago myself. It was getting late and I figured you'd probably not want to go out for dinner, so I popped back out to the store and grabbed a couple of steaks. When I heard you pull up, I turned the broiler on." Checking his watch, he said, "Dinner should be ready in about ten minutes. Steak and salad, how does that sound?"

"Sounds great," she said with as much enthusiasm as she could muster. The thought of eating again after just finishing a big meal did nothing to improve her already souring mood. But Niles was being so sweet and thoughtful, she couldn't admit to him she'd already eaten, she just couldn't. She'd just have to try and force some of the food down her, if only a little bit.

They sat down to dinner, and Emma hoped Niles would be too involved in his eating and recital of his day's events to question her about this afternoon's meeting. Unfortunately, he hadn't forgotten her abrupt explanations earlier, and immediately brought the subject up again.

"So," Niles said between bites of his steak, "who did you say this interview was with?"

Emma slowly cut up her steak, took a small bite, prolonging her answer. "Andrew Brannigan," she managed to say between mouthfuls. "He approached us about a story." At his questioning gaze, she said, "Guess he'd seen our show, thought he might have something of interest for us."

"He approached you? Isn't that a bit unusual?" Niles asked, forking another bite into his mouth.

Her stomach rebelling, Emma tried pushing her food around to make it look as if she was eating more than she actually was. "He didn't propose the story to me personally, he went to Ray. And yes, it is a bit unusual for the station to be approached, but it has happened."

"And did you like his idea?"

Emma nodded. "I'm going to recommend to Ray we pursue it," she said, giving up on her steak and concentrating instead on her tossed salad.

"So what's it all about?" Niles said.

Emma could see that he wasn't all that interested, was only making conversation, so she filled him in on just the scantiest details, hoping he'd get bored and move on to a different topic. This one, and the enigmatic man at the center of it, coupled with her vacillating feelings, were still too close to the surface to be comfortable talking about, especially with someone as intuitive as Niles happened to be.

"But didn't you already do a story last year on something similar to this?" Niles said.

At first, Emma was surprised Niles had recalled that particular story, then corrected herself. Niles was blessed with a phenomenal memory, one of his greatest assets as an attorney.

"I think it'll be different enough for the viewers who happened to catch that particular episode—considering it's the father who kidnapped his children—that they won't remember and compare the two. Of course, the whole story hinges on whether Andy is able to pinpoint where the children are now living." Emma winced almost immediately, inwardly, aware of her mistake. Niles' eyes widened in sudden interest at the familiarity of her tone when she spoke of Andy Brannigan.

"So you'll be working on this story? Or did you just have to give it a thumbs up?" Niles asked evenly, his voice not betraying the wariness in his eyes.

Emma could tell by the tilt of Niles' head there was going to be no way of shaking him from questioning her about their meeting. The only good thing was that he didn't seem to notice she'd hardly touched her dinner.

"I'll be covering the bulk of the story. Teddy is also in on this, but in a more limited role. He's already committed up to his eyebrows in other segments. I'll probably be doing all the on-air narrative," she finished, then held her breath for his negative reaction. She didn't have long to wait.

"But you just told me a couple of days ago you were swamped with stories," Niles said, slowly putting down his fork, the food in front of him momentarily forgotten.

"We're *all* swamped down there. Ray gave this to us personally to handle." Although she'd always thought of Niles as a handsome man, it occurred to her that when he became angry, his voice took on a decidedly cruel edge, and his sculptured lips twisted into a thin, straight line, almost disappearing.

"So you'll be working pretty closely with this guy for the next several weeks," Niles said, trying, but not succeeding, to keep irritation out of his voice.

He'd tried to pose the question as innocently as he could, but Emma wasn't fooled by his simple inquiry. She knew how jealous he could get. His question might be cloaked in innocence, but she knew she had to be very careful how she answered him.

"Not exactly. He'll be doing the investigating, and I'll help out where I can. I still have my other duties at the station that can't be ignored in preference to this one." Now was not the time to tell Niles she'd more than likely be spending even less time with him. He was already resentful of her busy schedule, she knew he was not going to be happy at this new turn of events.

As if reading her mind, he said, "Helping out where you can…does that mean, like, after your regular work hours, or weekends…what?" he stared at her, eyes narrowing.

"I'm not sure yet. It could involve some extra work during the evening," she waffled, her eyes riveted on the salad in front of her, reluctant to continue.

"And weekends?" Niles persisted.

Emma's head jerked up and she met Niles' eyes squarely for the first time since arriving home, responding honestly, unable any longer to skirt the issue. "Yes, Niles, it'll probably spill over into weekends." She slammed her fork down. "And I know what you're going to say, but it can't be helped. You knew what my schedule was like before you ever became seriously involved with me. Just because we're engaged, doesn't mean I can ignore my responsibilities at the station, and I hate it when you try to make me feel guilty for doing my job," she finished, irate.

Niles picked up his glass of wine and angrily tossed down a gulp.

"It's not a question of you ignoring your responsibilities, Emma," Niles replied, his voice tight. "And if I make you feel guilty, well then I'm sorry. But you didn't have to take on this particular assignment. You can't tell me someone else couldn't have handled it," he finished harshly.

Emma responded slowly, trying to keep her mounting ire in check. "I suppose I could have given the story to someone else, but I didn't, for three good reasons. First, Ray personally asked us to work on this. Second, I find the story too interesting to pass along to someone else. But most importantly, if this pans out, it'll be given more air time than we've ever allowed for a single story, and consequently, *I'll* get more air time." Actually, the last reason hadn't even occurred to her until just moments ago, but it was the one reason Niles could identify with the most. She knew one of his greatest attractions to her was her celebrity, but that didn't bother her. What did bother her, however, was how he liked to brag about being engaged to the most popular television personality in Portland, all the while raging at her for the excessive amount of time she spent doing the very job that had attracted him to her in the first place.

Mollified, Niles sighed and reached across the table, grasping Emma's hand in his own, squeezing it.

"Emma, I know how important your career is to you, and if this story offers you an opportunity to gain a bit more exposure, than I'm all for it. But please, allow me to react a little selfishly when I'm told that I'll probably be seeing even less of you than I do now," he pleaded, the look in his hazel eyes sincere.

Emma lightly squeezed his hand in return. She knew he was waiting for some response, some reassurances that his fears were ungrounded, but she knew his assumptions were correct. And she wasn't about to lie to placate him.

Instead, she turned her attention back to her barely eaten dinner, unable to resist the unbidden comparisons that seemed to rise within her.

Niles, with his fair hair and complexion, had always appealed to Emma's rather mundane tastes. But suddenly, he seemed a pale comparison to the vibrant, blue-eyed, silver-haired man who'd so recently entered her life, disrupting it so completely in such a short time.

Later, as they were getting ready for bed, Emma knew Niles would want to make love to her. Always after a disagreement or a fight, he would approach her affectionately, in need of physical contact, as if the act of making love proved to her, and himself, that all was well between them.

Oh, how little men knew of women, she'd think at times like these.

As uninterested as she was at the thought of making love, she knew if she responded enthusiastically, it would, at least temporarily, allay any residual doubts that might be lingering in Niles' mind about her reasons behind wanting to work with Andy Brannigan and his investigation.

She sighed and closed her eyes as Niles hands began to softly caress her breasts, her thoughts a million miles away.

Nine

Emma glanced at her watch again. It was nearly eight o'clock—had he changed his mind? She did tell him eight, didn't she? Yes, she was sure she'd said eight.

She zipped up her jacket, shoved her mittened hands deep into its cavernous pockets to ward off the cold, and again wondered if spending the day with Andy was such a good idea. Teddy and the rest of the crew would be along too, so it wouldn't be like they were spending the day alone, with just each other, she rationalized, trying not to think about what Niles would say if he knew she'd invited Andy along.

"Emma, instead of freezing out here, why don't you get on the bus," Teddy remarked as he rushed past her and into the warm confines of the minibus.

Ignoring Teddy's advice, she glanced at her watch again. Eight o'clock on the nose. She turned to follow Teddy, trying to hide her disappointment. Maybe Andy's non-appearance was a blessing in disguise, she tried telling herself. But just as she started to step up into the bus, she saw Andy's rental car come whipping around the corner.

She hesitated for a moment, then waited for him as he quickly parked the car, then jogged over to her and the waiting bus.

"Am I late?" he said, smoothing back his windblown hair. "I got all caught up in an argument on the telephone with a stubborn bureaucrat and I kind of lost track of time," Andy said in explanation as they stepped onto the bus together.

Dressed in a faded pair of Levis and long-sleeved plaid shirt open at the throat, a dark blue jacket clutched in his hands, Emma was quick to notice how ruggedly handsome he looked, the slight flush on his face from the hurried sprint from his car gave him a healthy, outdoorsy look. He was shorter than Niles by a good four inches, but he had a heavier, more muscular build than her fiancé. It took Emma a full minute to realize she'd been unconsciously comparing the two men again, and she tried to cover her embarrassment by making small talk with the man who seemed to so easily confuse her without even trying.

"I'd just about given up on you," she said, taking the empty seat in front of Teddy.

Andy smiled and slid easily into the spot next to her, not waiting for an invitation, then he turned in his seat and stuck out his hand. "Good to see you again, Ted."

Teddy shook the proffered hand, startled at the other man's presence. He said, "Emma didn't tell us you were coming along today. Doing some sightseeing, or is this business?"

Andy glanced at Emma, surprised she hadn't mentioned his coming along. "As a matter of fact, Emma thought I might enjoy seeing a little of the Columbia Gorge. I also thought we'd get a chance to get you updated on what's been happening, maybe even get an opportunity to talk with the film crew, nail down a tentative shooting schedule."

Emma turned in her seat and tried to ignore the rush of pleasure Andy's close proximity caused in her. "And for your information, Teddy, I was going to tell you I'd invited Andy along, but you'd already left last night by the time I got back to the station. And you rushed by me so fast this morning, you didn't give me a chance to even say good morning, let alone anything else," she chided.

"Oooh, feisty this morning, aren't we? Looks like we better tow the line today, Andy, I've seen her like this before. It's not a pretty sight." Teddy pretended to move as far back in his seat as possible, his actions drawing a smile out of both Emma and Andy.

"He's right, you know," she said, her attention back on Andy. "But if you'd had to carry this deadbeat like I've had to for over two years..."

"Hey, who's carried who?" Teddy shot back, pretending hurt.

Emma leaned back and crossed her arms over her chest, looking over the heads of the other occupants of the bus. "I'm not going to embarrass you in front of our guest by pointing out all your shortcomings," she said. "Besides, he'll see for himself without me having to say a word."

Teddy rolled his eyes skyward. "See what I have to put up with day after day? And she wonders why I'm always the last one to get here in the morning. I'm just trying to put off the inevitable."

"You two sound like an old married couple," Andy said.

"That's what happens when you spend more time at work than you do at home," Teddy remarked, adding, "Hey, we're not starting to look alike, are we?" His brows wrinkled in feigned worry.

"Ugh, say it isn't so, Andy, say it isn't so," Emma grimaced, getting a laugh out of the two men. By no stretch of the imagination did Emma and Teddy look even remotely alike. Emma's dark brown hair and small, curvaceous figure contrasted sharply with Teddy's curly, sandy haired locks and rather stocky six-foot frame.

Andy's eyes rested on Emma. "I don't think either one of you have to worry about that," he said softly, his appreciation of her appearance came through loud and clear in his gently spoken words.

As the driver pulled away from the curb and the minibus began its journey eastward, Emma reluctantly broke away from Andy's penetrating gaze. She stared out the window, trying unsuccessfully to control the blush she felt working its way up her neck, painfully aware of Teddy's pointed stare.

Andy immediately recognized her discomfort and quickly turned his attention back to Teddy, thereby giving Emma a chance to regain her composure while he filled Teddy in on their progress thus far.

Emma was grateful to Andy for changing the subject, allowing her to collect herself. How was it that Niles, the man she was supposedly in love with, couldn't seem to generate the kind of response in her that just one fleeting, unwavering glance from this man sitting so close to her could? And to compound her problems, she found herself in the vulnerable position of letting others see how this man confused her. Teddy's knowing smirk had not been lost on her.

What was wrong with her? What had she been thinking when she'd invited Andy along today? Was she out of her *mind?* Niles was no fool, and if she was this way now, around just Teddy, she knew she was headed for big trouble with Niles if he and Andy ever happened to meet.

"One of the most popular sights in and around the Portland area, is Multnomah Falls. At six hundred and twenty feet high, it's the fourth highest falls in the United States," Emma said, directing her comments to the camera placed directly in front of her as she pointed to the historic falls off to the side of her, the camera following her lead. Andy watched, fascinated, as he'd done many times in the past few weeks, immersed in the sound of her voice, letting it roll over him, transporting him back to a time when he'd been the center of her attention, not a camera lens.

"Its origin stems from Multnomah Creek, a stream fed by snow melt and rain collected in a series of glacially carved basins. An unusually hard winter can reduce this turbulent flow behind me to a trickle, turning the falls into a masterpiece of twisted, sculptured ice. Quite a sight to see..." Teddy continued as the camera switched back and forth between him, Emma, and the swiftly cascading falls.

Andy followed the cast and crew as they sauntered along the main pathway, careful to keep Emma in his line of vision.

"You know, Ted," Emma continued, slowly making her way to the stone lodge perched at the bottom of the falls, "there's a legend surrounding Multnomah Falls."

On cue, Ted replied, "Of course. What would an impressive landmark be without some local folklore attached to it?"

Emma smiled into the camera. "And this one is about...what else? It's about love. It's said that many moons ago a terrible sickness overcame the Multnomah people. The medicine man of the tribe revealed to his people that the sickness would pass, but only if a maiden threw herself from a high cliff on the big river to the rocks below. When the chief's daughter saw the sickness on her lover's face, she went to the cliff and plunged to her death. And legend has it, when the winds blow across the falls, a silvery stream separates from the upper part of the falls, forming itself into the striking figure of the maiden who gave up her life for her people." Emma caught another glimpse of Andy out of the corner of her eyes. After just repeating that story of unrequited, tragic love, she found it comforting to find him within easy reach. Now why was that? she wondered silently.

Teddy turned once again toward the falls. "There...I think I see her. Is that her?" The camera loomed in for a close-up of the falls. "Well, maybe not. But next time, when the winds kick up through the gorge, come and see if you can spot the courageous maiden yourself. And even if you don't see her, there's plenty of other things to do along the gorge, including hiking up to the top of the falls. But a word of warning, be prepared, it's nearly a vertical climb, and by no means an easy one. Believe me, I know."

"You've climbed it?" Emma said, going by the scripted play by play. "So have I. And you're right, it's not a climb for the casual hiker." She smiled into the camera as it panned back to Teddy.

"And as I said before," he continued, the camera rolling, "Multnomah Falls is not the only sight to see along the Columbia Gorge. Not only are there several waterfalls along the scenic highway, there's also the Bridge of the Gods, which, of course, also has a legend surrounding it.

"Spanning the Columbia River between Oregon and Washington, the Bridge of the Gods' name comes from an old Indian legend about a natural land bridge that stretched across the Columbia River. The legend tells of the natural bridge's collapse during the eruption of two Warrior God volcanoes. Maybe you've heard of them—Mt. Adams and Mt. Hood, fighting over a third goddess, Mt. St. Helens."

Emma stood next to Teddy, cueing in on his dialogue, waiting for her turn, her mind wandering, drawn to the irony of the story she was helping narrate today, the similarity she seemed to be struggling with in her own life.

On the one hand, she had the rock-steady love of a man she'd known for some time and was planning to marry, while on the other, was a man who'd only just entered her life but seemed to have an inexplicable, almost volatile, pull on her.

She felt as though she was caught between the veritable immovable object and an irresistible force.

Without missing a beat, the turmoil inside her well hidden, Emma picked up right on cue as Teddy's voice faded.

"There always seems to be a woman involved in these legends, doesn't there?"

"Always," Teddy answered, smiling. Switching gears, he said, "And that's still not all the Columbia Gorge has to offer. Just minutes away from Multnomah Falls is another historical landmark with what has been described as one of the most spectacular, panoramic views in the world."

"When we come back," Emma interjected, nodding at her imaginary audience, "we'll show you that extraordinary sight." Cameras turned off, the crew packed up for a shift in location.

Back in the minibus, passing various waterfalls lining the lush, picturesque scenery rolling by them, the film crew kept busy panning the roadside for shots they'd incorporate into the evening's show. From past observations, Andy knew Teddy and Emma would do the backup dialogue when they returned to the station.

They progressed slowly up the steep, twisting, turning highway; the minibus finally cresting the top and coming to a stop at what Andy correctly assumed to be the historic landmark known as the Vista House at Crown Point.

Emma and Andy piled out of the minibus with the rest of the crew and wandered over to the rounded, domed structure as the crew busied themselves getting set up for the next shoot.

"This is Crown Point, the Gateway to the Columbia River," Emma said, waving her hand out as the two of them approached the stone railing circling the high cliff the Vista House had been built atop.

Andy leaned out across the railing, in awe of the wonderful spectacle laid out before him. High above the Columbia River, stretching out for miles and miles, he felt like he could see forever, or at least to the mouth of the mighty Columbia, a hundred miles away, pouring into the Pacific Ocean.

"This must be absolutely stunning at sunset," was all he managed to say.

Emma smiled, agreeing with him. "The film crew is coming back tonight to get a shot of it. We plan to close out the show with the sunset, so be sure to watch."

Teddy sauntered up to the couple drinking in nature's spectacular view. "They're about ready for us, Emma, and Starla wants to try and do something with your hair."

Windblown locks framing her pretty face, she shrugged her shoulders and reluctantly turned away from the panoramic scene laid out before her. To Andy, she said, "Duty calls. This portion of our shoot shouldn't take more than an hour to get the dialogue recorded and the backup shots on tape, so feel free to roam around. Inside the Vista House, the walls are crammed with tons of historical information about the Columbia Gorge and the early Oregon settlers. You might find it interesting."

"Thanks," Andy replied. "I'm sure I will. But I think I'll stay here for a while longer, enjoy the view. Don't worry, I'll keep myself occupied and out of everybody's way."

Teddy leaned against the stone railing next to Andy. "Quite a sight, isn't it?" he said conversationally.

"Ummm, yes," Andy answered. But he was no longer staring out across the colorful gorge. Instead, his eyes were busy following Emma's progress back to the minibus and the impatiently waiting hair stylist.

Andy strolled in and out of the old domed structure, able to catch fragments of Emma and Teddy's running commentary. He stopped for a few minutes to listen to Emma's description of the stone building, again marveling at her on-screen presence. Nobody watching her on television would ever be able to guess that this seemingly friendly, open woman held a secret locked within her that could destroy her career, perhaps even herself.

"Construction of the Vista House here at Crown Point began in 1916. Located seven hundred and thirty-three feet above the Columbia River, its scenic view, considered one of the best in the world, attracts tourists from all over the globe..." her voice hummed on as Andy glanced at his watch, then over at the *Evening Magazine* crew. He could see they were just about finished with the filming. Good. If they wrapped up soon, he'd still have time to place a few phone calls, spend some time working on what he was supposed to be in town working on instead of sidetracking to spend the day with Emma.

On the trip back, Andy and Emma spent most of their time with the film crew, tentatively setting up a timetable for filming some background on their story, thereby eliminating any chance of intimate talk between the two.

Instead, they agreed to meet the following day for what was to be Emma's first real contact with the investigative side of Andy's kidnapping case.

Ten

"So...who was that guy Ray brought around a couple of days ago?" Frank asked. He'd spotted Teddy as he entered the office, had nonchalantly approached the other man. Now, as he sat on the edge of Teddy's desk, pretending to make idle conversation, he was more than just a little interested in Teddy's impression of the silvery-haired, husky-voiced stranger.

"You mean Andy Brannigan?" Teddy said, thumbing through the messages on his desk. "He talked to Ray about a story idea for our show. Ray threw it in our laps."

"Oh yeah? What kind of story?"

"Two kids from Philly snatched from their mom by an unhappy ex. Andy Brannigan's looking for them on behalf of the mother. He trailed them here."

"He's a private investigator?" Frank asked, unable to hide his surprise.

"Nah, not exactly. I mean, he does do investigations, but he's not your standard P.I.—doesn't pack a gun or anything like that," Teddy said, dropping the messages and rummaging through his desk drawer, coming up with an open pack of lifesavers. "Want one?" he offered the editor before popping three of them in his mouth.

Frank waved away his offer, relieved to hear the little tidbit about the gun. "So...," he continued on, "you and Emma gonna take him up on his idea?"

Sucking loudly on the pieces rolling around in his mouth, Teddy said, "Yeah, I think so. Emma had a meeting with him the other day. From what she told me, she thinks it'd make for interesting viewing, *and* be great P.R. for the station—you know, helping a grieving mother get her kids back. The viewers'll lap it up," he smirked.

"So he knows where the kids are then," Frank said.

Teddy shook his head. "Not exactly. He's sure they're here in Portland somewhere, but he hasn't pinpointed 'em yet."

"So the story depends on if he finds the kids, right?"

"Well, yeah, it pretty much hinges on that. But he's tracked 'em this far, there's no reason to believe he won't find them. And Emma seems to think pretty highly of him," he said, a sly look coming over his face.

"After just a couple of days?" Frank said. He slid off the corner of the desk and took a seat across from Teddy. This didn't sound like the Emma he knew. She came across as a friendly, approachable person on television, but Frank knew full well that it took Emma a long while to warm up to people. And someone she'd just met?—never.

"Unh huh," Teddy answered, sucking the pieces of life-saver through his teeth, then rolling them around his tongue again. He leaned back in his chair and clasped his hands behind his head, cradling it. "In fact, she even invited him along on our shoot today—could hardly take her eyes off the guy."

"*Emma?* You're pulling my leg."

"No really." Teddy unclasped his hands and leaned across the desk on his elbows, all business now. "All the time we were talking, it was like I wasn't even there. And the other day, you should have seen her jump at the chance to work with this guy." He was embellishing his story a bit, but not to a great degree. He *had* noticed Emma's unusual interest in Andy Brannigan, and that was a fact. She hadn't exactly jumped at the chance to work on the story with him, but neither had she seemed overly disappointed when he'd said he wouldn't be able to devote much time helping her and Andy with it. And today, well, that had said it all. Those two had eyed each other all day long, too involved with each other to even realize they were doing it.

Eyebrows raised, Frank said, "Well, well, well, this could get pretty interesting. I'd love to be there when Niles meets this Brannigan fella. He's not the most tolerant guy in the world when it comes to men hanging around Emma, for whatever reason."

"Yeah, I was just thinking the same thing," Teddy smirked, a small smile flirting at the corners of his mouth.

It wasn't that he and Frank actually disliked Niles Whitmann, it was just that he was always so smug, so controlling, showing off Emma as if she was some sort of prize instead of a living, breathing human being with real feelings. And he didn't like the way Niles was always trying to monopolize Emma's time, making plans for them weeks in advance. She had a career, a highly visible career, that needed her total commitment. Teddy felt Niles too often pulled her in directions she didn't want to go, that his desires and demands came first. But he had to hand it to Emma—she was strong when she needed to be, and she managed to hold her own with Niles most of the time.

Still...he couldn't help but feel Niles didn't always have Emma's best interests at heart.

Frank's thoughts were paralleling Teddy's. If what Teddy said was true, and Niles saw Andy and Emma together, it wouldn't take him long to notice Emma's apparent interest in this mysterious stranger.

Yes, the next several days could prove to be very interesting indeed, Frank mused. And from what Teddy had said about Andy Brannigan, it sounded as if he was on the up and up, but he still had some questions he intended to get answers to, even if it meant waylaying the man and asking him point-blank.

Eleven

He was coming for her, and there was nothing she could do to stop it. She'd seen the look in his eyes before she'd fled to her room, and now she heard the sound of footfalls in the hallway outside her door. In terror, unable to hide, with nowhere to run, she watched in morbid fascination as the handle of the door slowly turned. Huddled in the corner of her bed, pressed up tightly against one wall, Emma's heart was beating so loudly, she was sure her unwelcome intruder could hear it. Slowly, ever so slowly, the door pushed inward, the dark, brooding figure outlined by the dim hallway light. She stifled a scream, clutched her bedsheets around her, gasping, "No...please...no..." to the figure now looming over her, reaching for her.

The sound of the ringing telephone shattered Emma's nightmare, startling her back to the present, away from the horrors that had plagued her on and off for as long as she could remember.

Drenched in sweat, it took her nearly a full minute to comprehend just what had pulled her out of her silent terror, away from the faceless, nameless intruder that seemed to spark fear and loathing to the very core of her being every time she experienced one of those hellish nightmares.

She turned on the bedside lamp, its luminescence bathing her bedroom in safe, brilliant light, chasing away the last remnants of her familiar nightmare. She glanced at the still-ringing telephone and grimaced, unsure if she was up to talking to anyone. But if it was Niles, and she didn't answer, he'd be worried about her. Sighing resignedly, she cleared her parched throat and scooped up the telephone.

"Hello?" she said, her voice raspy.

"God, it took you long enough! Were you in the shower or something?"

Emma breathed a sigh of relief. It was only Lenny—Lenny who knew her best. Lenny who knew of the nightmares.

"If the 'or something' means is Niles here, the answer is no. And I wasn't in the shower, I was sleeping, or trying to anyway. What time is it?" she asked, glancing at the clock on her nightstand.

"Eleven," Lenny answered as Emma's brain registered the fact that it was eleven-ten to be exact.

"Eleven!" Emma groaned, then shifted up on one elbow. "What's up?"

"Nothing. I just hadn't had a chance to talk to you much the last couple of days."

"So you're calling me now to chat—at eleven."

"Well...yeah. You've been so busy at the office."

"Len, you know how early I have to get up, and you know perfectly well that I'm always in bed during the week before eleven, so what was so important you needed to call me now for?" Actually, she was grateful for Lenny's intruding phone call. It had pulled her out of the scary netherworld she had no desire to be in, no control of. Just the sound of Lenny's cheerful voice was enough to chase away the last residues of fear the nightmare had spawned in her.

"All right," Lenny plunged right in, not mincing any words, "let's talk about Andy Brannigan."

Surprised, Emma said, "What about him? He's an investigator I'm working with on a story."

"I heard there's a little more to it than that," Lenny hinted. Neither she or Frank had shared with anyone else that they'd come in contact, albeit by film, with this mystery man already. They'd both agreed that, at least for the time being anyway, they'd keep that knowledge to themselves. But when Frank had shared with her what he'd learned from Teddy, it gave her the perfect opportunity to bring up the subject of Andrew Brannigan to Emma.

"What do you mean?" the beginnings of a flush already spreading up Emma's neck. She'd only known Andy a few days, and if Lenny was insinuating what Emma thought she was, she had to be more careful, reign her emotions in, or she'd find herself in the middle of a situation she was totally unprepared for.

"What's the matter?" Lenny cajoled. "Niles isn't there, you can come clean."

"Clean? About what?" Emma hedged.

"About the fact that you're attracted to this guy."

"And what makes you think I'm attracted to him?" Emma asked, unsure of whether she should reveal, even to Lenny, how much this Andy Brannigan's presence disturbed her. "Has Teddy been spinning yarns again?"

"Well..."

"Lenny, Lenny, Lenny," Emma admonished, still trying to decide how much she should admit to, even to her closest friend. "Of all the people in the world to listen to when it comes to idle gossip, you listen to Teddy. Haven't you learned *anything* in the last few years? Teddy is the *last* person you should listen to when it comes to rumors."

"So everything he said was just a figment of his overactive imagination?" Lenny persisted.

"I don't know, what'd he say?" Emma said, pushing herself up into a sitting position. This was not going to be a short conversation, she could see.

"That you seemed taken with him. And you're saying it's not true?"

"I didn't say that," Emma answered evasively.

"But you just said—"

"I said you shouldn't take much stock in what Teddy says *most* of the time because he's usually way off base."

"But not this time?"

Emma sighed. "I don't know...I mean...there's something about him that...that I can't quite pinpoint," she said, all the mixed emotions she'd been feeling the last few days popping easily to the surface again at the mention of Andy Brannigan's name.

Lenny smiled. "Could it be you're finally beginning to know the feelings of true and unabashed attraction toward another human being? Not just the comfortable, convenient relationship like the one you share with Niles, but *real passion?*"

"What do you mean by that?" a hint of irritation entered Emma's voice.

"You've got the hots for him," Lenny stated matter-of-factly.

Emma gasped. "Oh God, Lenny, what an awful expression."

"Then deny it," Lenny taunted.

"Deny what?" she countered, trying to back away from Lenny's pointed remarks.

"You know what. Does your heart go pitter-pat every time he comes near you? Do you have trouble getting thoughts of him out of your mind? Do you even *want* to get him out of your mind—"

"Enough!" Emma exclaimed. She didn't know whether to laugh or cry. "I'm already confused, now you've made it worse."

"Oh yeah, I can see that, I can see that. What with having

a fiancé and all, I can understand why you'd be a little confused."

Emma bit her lip. "Oh, Len, what am I going to do? Until I met Andy Brannigan, I was so sure what direction my life was heading. And now…" She let her words hang there. She wanted Lenny to step in, guide her, advise her, tell her she wasn't crazy, wasn't in danger of throwing away everything she'd built up with Niles over the last year on an undefined impulse. Lenny had described it as 'the hots,' but she knew instinctively that it was much more than that.

"Now I'm really surprised. What's happened to the cool, calm and collected woman I've gotten to know and love over the last few years? You sound frightened, so unsure of yourself," Lenny murmured, half to herself. A sudden thought, an eerie thought that brought goosebumps out on her flesh had just occurred to her. But should she even mention it to Emma? Maybe it's occurred to her too, but she's afraid to face the possibility.

"Emma," Lenny said hesitantly, "you said there was something about him you couldn't quite pinpoint. What exactly did you mean by that?"

"You said it was 'the hots,' remember?"

"No, really," she said, trying to be serious in the face of Emma's sarcasm.

At Lenny's suddenly somber tone, Emma too, became more thoughtful.

"I'm not sure I can explain it. It's like…like I've known him forever even though we just met. It feels so comfortable, but not comfortable—you know what I mean?"

"Maybe you have known him."

"What do you mean?"

"I mean maybe you knew him before." At Emma's continued silence, she said, "You know, from when you were growing up."

It hadn't even occurred to Emma that the strange, vacillating feelings permeating her senses since the moment she'd laid eyes on Andy Brannigan might have something to do with her lost years, her childhood and early teen years. And yet it seemed so obvious.

Or was it?

After all, if Andy was someone out of her past, wouldn't he have mentioned it? Or would he—considering the circumstances surrounding her memory loss? Even she didn't know the whole story, remembered or otherwise. She only knew that it was traumatic and that it had precipitated in the death of her father. She hadn't *wanted* to know any more, was instinctively afraid of knowing anything more.

"So you think this attraction could be the result of a long forgotten connection to him?" Emma asked, her voice subdued as she rolled the idea around in her mind.

"What do *you* think?"

"I'm not sure. I...I guess it could be a possibility. But why wouldn't he say something if he recognized me?"

"I don't know. Maybe he wasn't sure. I mean, your last name is different, and since you didn't say anything to him either...Maybe you should mention his name to Dr. Stuart. He knew you as a child, maybe he'd remember him."

"Oh sure," Emma replied dryly. "How many of your friends' names do you think your own mother remembers?"

"It was just a suggestion," Lenny said, piqued.

"And not a bad one, really," Emma conceded. "If Ben and Niles didn't get along so well I just might consider it. But I can't imagine what Ben would think of me if I told him I was strangely attracted to someone I'd just met. And it really wouldn't surprise me if he *did* know some of my friends' names. And if he is someone out of my past, that might explain..."

"Explain what?"

"Have you seen him, Lenny?" she asked slowly, reluctantly.

"Frank and I saw him when Raymond brought him down to meet you," she answered cautiously. "Why?" Not a lie. Not exactly the whole truth either.

"Did you notice anything in particular about him?"

"He's a good-looking guy, Emma. I'm not surprised you're attracted to him."

"But didn't you notice anything else?" she probed.

What was she trying to get out of her? He was a very attractive man—she'd already said that. What else? Lenny racked her brain, but she could think of nothing other than his strange coloring. That was it! "Got it!" she answered triumphantly. That's what was bothering Emma. Or to be exact, *not* bothering her. "He's got that gorgeous mane of silvery-blond hair, but then he's got those dark, brooding jet black eyebrows."

"And...," Emma said.

"The nightmare...you're usually *repelled* by those type of looks because of it," she answered, connecting all the pieces to what Emma was trying to tell her. "The only thing you remember in that awful nightmare are the eyes, the eyes, the heavy brows, the dark features. But Emma, Andy's eyes are blue, maybe that's why it doesn't bother you."

"But in the dream, I can't make out the color of the man's eyes, I only know they're dark. They could be dark blue for all I know."

"Then maybe it's the combination of his hair in contrast to the rest of him that keeps you from being repulsed by him."

"Mmmm, maybe," Emma said, still mulling over the possibility that Andy was someone she knew from before.

"There's no chance he could be the guy in the dream, could it?"

"Oh God, no," Emma blurted out with more conviction than she felt. He did cause a stir in her. But fear?—it didn't *appear* to be fear. She said, "The man in the dream scares me to death. Andy's presence seems to do just the opposite. He's so calm, so easy going, I'm comfortable around him. Not even Niles makes me feel so comfortable."

"Which reminds me...what about Niles?"

Emma frowned. "I don't know. I don't know what to do. He's already angry at the time I'm going to be spending with Andy, I can't imagine what he's going to do if...if..."

"If he finds out you've got the hots for this guy," Lenny said.

Emma groaned and laid back up against the pillows, covering her eyes. "Oh, Lenny," she cried, "what am I going to do?"

Twelve

Emma sat at the oblong table in Conference Room B, surrounded by the paperwork Andy's investigation in the disappearance of David Carlson and his two young sons had generated. With his hand on her chair, Andy leaned over her shoulder, explaining the many steps it had taken him to get to the point of cornering David Carlson in Oregon.

When the National Center for Missing and Exploited Children had approached Andy and his organization, and Andy had reviewed the file, he knew immediately that he had a good chance of finding David Carlson. David was a chiropractor, a professional, and experience told him that David would continue in that field rather than start something new. According to Karen, his wife, he loved his work, and she'd felt as he did, that David wouldn't stay away from it for long. And, like doctors, lawyers, teachers and many other professionals, Andy knew David would have to be certified to practice his trade in whatever state he settled in. Andy's approach to this particular investigation was to canvas various certification boards in different states and try to trace David that way.

It had taken months and months in front of his computer, keeping a list of all the agencies he contacted, hours and hours on the telephone talking to those different agencies in the hundreds of different cities.

His diligence had paid off, finally.

Just weeks ago, he'd called Salem, Oregon, been put on hold for what seemed like an eternity, and been rewarded for his patience and perseverance with a certification number on David Carlson.

"This is a copy of the form he filled out." He leaned across her shoulder again, barely touching her, and pulled a buff colored piece of paper out of the stack in front of her.

Emma tried to ignore the shock of pleasure that ran through her at his fleeting touch, concentrated instead on what he was showing her. "Just his name and certification number? No address?"

Andy shook his head. "He doesn't have to give an address, just that he's going to practice somewhere in Oregon."

"So what makes you think he's around here and not somewhere else in the state?"

"Because Portland meets his current needs, or at least I think it does. While I was searching for his certification number, Karen and I also worked up a profile on David—you know, his likes and dislikes, hobbies, so on. Here." He pulled another piece of paper out of the stack.

She skimmed down the list, impressed by the thoroughness, the professionalism of the report. It had everything on it from his favorite colors to what kind of climate he preferred.

"I knew he would head west, try to put as much distance as possible between himself and his ex. When I was calling around to see if he'd applied for certification, I concentrated on the western portion of the United States. If I hadn't been able to eliminate so many states, I'd probably still be trying to zero in on him."

"And this profile narrowed it down even further."

He nodded again. "As you can see," he pointed to the report, "he doesn't like a real hot climate, so that alone ruled out the southwestern states. He likes to snow ski, likes to watch professional sports."

"But all we've got is basketball."

"But Seattle is what...three hours away? And they've got it all."

"So why didn't he relocate there, instead of here?"

Andy shrugged. "I'm not sure, to be honest with you. In fact, I concentrated heavily on the Seattle area for a while. After reviewing his profile, Seattle was my first choice. But maybe he's smarter than even I gave him credit for, maybe he realized Seattle would be too obvious. Anyway, he's somewhere here in Oregon, that we know for sure. He applied for certification less than a month ago, so I think he's still around."

"So what's next?"

Andy sat down in the seat next to her, starting Emma's heart triphammering anew. "There's a couple of things we can do to zero in on his home address. First, his older son, the seven year old, Tyler, is probably enrolled in school by now. And the five year old, Jacob, might even be in kindergarten. I'm going to concentrate my efforts now on the grade schools, looking for Tyler's registration."

"But what if he's registered in a different name?" she asked, pleased at his close proximity. He had full, sensuous lips, and she had to fight back the impulse to reach out and trace them with her finger.

"Do you know how difficult it is to try and teach a seven year old *not* to say his real name after you've been drilling it into him for as long as he's been alive?"

Emma laughed at the look on Andy's expressive face.

"Couldn't you just picture what would happen?" Andy continued ruefully. "This poor little confused kid, in a new town surrounded by strangers, blurts out to his first grade teacher that his real name isn't Bobby, or whatever name his dad has convinced him to use, but really Tyler, Tyler Carlson and that he hasn't seen his mommy for a long time."

"And the teacher would ask him what happened to his mommy."

"And he'd probably repeat what his dad had told him—that she was sick and couldn't take care of them, that she didn't want them anymore, that she was unhappy and left, that she died—any one of these scenarios. I can only guess at what David told his boys, but I bet it was one of the four things I just mentioned."

"And the teacher would get suspicious."

"If she was on the ball she would. And hopefully, if she's thorough, she'd do something about it."

"Like call the police?"

He shook his head. "Maybe not initially. She'd probably start with the school counselor, have him talk to the boy, see what his impression is. Then go to the police if necessary."

"Okay, so Tyler's probably registered in his own name, if he's registered at all."

"There again, it'd be too conspicuous not to have his sons, at least Tyler anyway, in school—after all, it's the law. David Carlson isn't going to do anything to call unwanted attention to himself, you can bet on that."

"So...you've zeroed in on David, now you concentrate on the boys."

"Right. Unless something better occurs to me. For now, unless David opened up his own practice and called it the David Carlson Chiropractic Clinic, or something to that effect, I think it'd be easier to trace the kids. That's not to say I still won't be working on David's location either. Yesterday when I got back from our excursion through the Columbia Gorge, I tried calling information around the state, just on the off chance he'd registered for a phone in his own name. Pretty much a wasted effort, but what the hell, I've gotten lucky before," he grinned. "My guess is, he probably won't open up his own clinic, but go into partnership with an already established one—he's got money from selling his practice to buy into another one easily enough."

"Thereby obscuring his trail even more."

Andy smiled and touched her arm. "There you go. You're already getting the hang of this."

And that's the picture Niles Whitmann was greeted with as he walked into the conference room unannounced. His fiancée, smiling and laughing with a man whose hand was resting possessively on her arm, his head just inches from her own, talking intimately.

Emma and Andy glanced up in unison, surprised at the sudden intrusion.

"Niles!" was all Emma could think of to say. It was obvious from the look on his face that he was angry, yet struggling to control it.

"It's almost lunchtime, I thought you might like to have a bite to eat," Niles said woodenly as he turned his attention to the man seated next to his fiancée.

Emma noted the direction of his pointed interest and hastily introduced the two men. Andy slowly took his hand off Emma's arm, stood up, shook the other man's hand.

"Emma tells me you're in town on a missing person investigation. I imagine being a private investigator must be interesting work," Niles said, all thoughts of going to lunch with Emma totally pushed out of his mind.

"Actually, I'm not a private investigator. I work for an organization that helps find missing persons. I'm an investigator within the framework of that particular association."

"Is there really a difference? You still carry on an investigation, don't you?"

Andy smiled, aware of Emma's fiancé's keen interest. "There's a lot of differences," he said. "For one thing, I don't carry a gun like some investigators do, and I don't need a license to do what I do either." He didn't add that, because of his juvenile record, he *couldn't* carry a gun. Adding a touch of humor, he said, "And I don't drive a hot-looking car and get beat up as often as the stereotypical television private eye does either."

"You've been beaten up before?" Emma asked, trying, but not succeeding, to quell the nervousness the two men together in the same room was causing her.

Andy shrugged his shoulders, disliking the topic. "Nah, not really. Roughed up a few times maybe, when I stuck my nose someplace where someone didn't particularly like it," he said, downplaying the violence he'd encountered more than once during the course of his investigations.

"Is that why you prefer to work for this organization instead of branching out on your own—to avoid any potential violence?" Niles remarked, annoyed at the obvious concern in Emma's voice, and aggravated with this line of discussion. The last thing he wanted was for this Brannigan fellow to come across as having a glamorous, yet dangerous job.

The point behind Niles' innocuous query was not lost on Andy. The battle for position had begun, and he was ready for it. Andy tried not to let it show that Niles had struck a painful chord with that last remark. What Andy would have preferred was a moot point in his life; his dreams of one day following in his father's footsteps were just that. There was no reversing the past, and no point in dwelling on what might have been, what he might have been able to accomplish if not for a devastating turn of events.

Instead, Andy said, "I think only a foolish man courts violence, don't you? Besides, I felt the Mizpah Foundation—that's the organization I work for—was in dire need of competent investigators. Not to mention the fact that I fell into the manipulative hands of a very persuasive recruiter. I've been doing this for several years now, and I've never regretted the decision to work for this particular organization," he said. Gathering up his papers, he said, "What about you? What keeps you busy here in Portland?"

Niles answered curtly, "I'm an attorney."

"Oh?" Andy said, eyebrows raised, and left it at that, the workings of a smile played at the corners of his mouth, telling both Emma and Niles exactly what he thought of Niles' chosen profession without uttering another word.

Emma could see that Niles was struggling mightily to control the angry flush beginning to spread across his face. "I represent some of the largest corporations in the state of Oregon, including the Nike Corporation," he added stiffly, then wondered why, all of a sudden, it was important to try and impress this man standing so calmly opposite him.

"Ummm, a corporate attorney," Andy murmured. "That's where the big money is, I suppose. And I imagine criminal law, on the other hand, can get pretty down and dirty…violent even…sometimes." Andy let his statement hang, the obvious parallel he'd drawn between what Niles had tried to trap him on and what he'd just neatly turned to his advantage not going unnoticed by the two other occupants in the room.

Emma watched Niles' face turn a dangerous hue at these last words. She wasn't sure what she should do. On the one hand, she was fascinated by the underlying animosity that had quickly sprung up between the two men. Niles was one of the premier corporate attorneys in the state of Oregon, but he was getting pummeled verbally by the upstart investigator. And she was finding it difficult to come to Niles' rescue when it was he who had initiated this thinly veiled war of words and ideals with Andy. For the first time, she found herself almost embarrassed at Niles' profession. The comparison between the two men's work was so great, she couldn't help but feel almost guilty at being engaged to someone such as Niles. It was patently clear to her that the two men were worlds apart when it came to what mattered in their lives. Niles' focus had always been success and money. Being a corporate attorney had allowed him to be both successful and affluent. Andy, on the other hand, seemed to care less about money, or power. His focal point was people, and he spent his time trying to help resolve other people's problems.

Yes, the gap between the two men was great, and she found herself almost physically pulling away from Niles and his seemingly narrow minded ideals.

Above all else, Niles was an attorney, and a very good one at that. He'd lost his composure for a moment or two, but Emma could see that years of training his emotions, allowing the jury or a witness to see only what he wanted them to see, enabled him to recover quickly, could almost *hear* him grudgingly reassessing Andy.

Niles turned his attention back to his fiancée, unwilling, it seemed, to continue his battle of words. "Are you ready for a break yet? How about that lunch?"

The last thing Emma wanted at this point was to have lunch with Niles, but she could find no other way of diffusing the present adversarial situation. It was obvious Niles had no intention of extending the lunch invitation to include Andy, so that meant only one thing. He was going to want to discuss what had just transpired during that time, and there was no way to avoid it.

Resigned to her fate, she nodded yes, then turned back to Andy and asked him if he'd like to join them. Even if Niles wouldn't extend the invitation, she couldn't be so pointedly rude.

Andy shook his head. "Thanks, but I'm going to talk Ted into letting me use your fax machine to get the boys' pictures out to some police stations. Maybe we'll get lucky and a patrol cop'll spot one of the boys playing in a schoolyard or park. I like to play a hunch now and then. Sometimes it works, sometimes it doesn't."

Trying to get in one last parting shot, Niles said, "Too bad their mother's hunches didn't play out as well as you say yours sometimes do. Maybe she could have seen this coming and done something to prevent it. If she had, I suspect you probably would never have made your way to our fair city." And suddenly wreaked havoc on what had heretofore been a perfectly satisfactory relationship, he longed to add.

"Oh, I don't know," Andy replied evenly. "Fate has had a way of intervening at the strangest times for me. Somehow, I can't help but believe that I would have made my way here to Portland anyway, for one reason or another," he finished, his unwavering gaze never leaving Emma's face.

Thirteen

From the moment they'd sat down in the restaurant and been afforded some semblance of privacy, Niles and Emma had been arguing.

"Thanks for your great support back there," Niles snipped at her.

"Since when do *you* need any support, counselor?"

"You completely ignored me."

"I ignored you because you were being an ass," Emma replied hotly, then glanced at the other tables to see if anyone was listening.

"An ass!" he seethed. "What do you mean by that? I was just being polite."

"You were grilling him like a hostile witness, and then you

became angry when he bested you at your own game."

"Bested me? Where were you? He comes off like a sanctimonious prick, and you eat it up!"

"Where was I? Where were you? You acted like a spoiled rich boy that had nothing better to do with his time than represent a sneaker company, while Andy, on the other hand, spends his time and energy locating missing children for distraught families!" she hissed back at him.

"Oh, so now all of a sudden I'm a slimy attorney. Is that what you're implying?" Niles replied, his voice taking on an angry, clipped tone.

Eyebrows arched, Emma countered, "Why, is that how you feel?"

For a long moment, Niles just stared at her, then his anger seemed to wane. He said, "It's how you're making me feel, and that's not fair. Emma," he said, shifting forward in his seat, a hurtful look in his eyes, "I've worked hard to get where I am, and before today, I thought you were pretty proud of what I did for a living. Now all of a sudden my career isn't good enough anymore. Suddenly, I'm the bad guy, and I don't like it."

"Niles, if you're feeling like you're the bad guy, then you've only got yourself to blame," Emma countered, not fooled by this switch in tactics. "Admit it, you were trying to bait Andy, for some godforsaken reason. And when you couldn't corner him, you started sulking like a little child. What's worse, you've put me in a very difficult position. I have to work with that man. How am I supposed to explain your behavior back there?"

"Neither one of us owes him an explanation," Niles said, his jaw set in a stubborn line again.

"You still don't think you did anything wrong, do you?" she said, incredulous.

"No," he answered, his eyebrows drawn together in a frown. "What did I do? I was only trying to find out a little bit about the guy. You seemed so taken with him, I wanted to see what was so special about him."

Emma gasped, at a loss as to how she should answer this last remark. As hard as she'd tried to hide her vacillating feelings, he'd obviously noticed more than she'd given him credit for. She knew how astute he was, she'd only hoped that, if he was going to accuse her of undue interest in Andy Brannigan, he'd done it somewhere not so centered in the public eye. Emma glanced around her, then back at Niles.

"I think for both our sakes, we should put off any further discussion of Andy Brannigan and my supposed interest in him until we're alone," she replied stiffly, trying to regain her composure.

"Then let's go," Niles said, pushing back in his chair, ready to rise.

"Niles, our food will be here in a minute," Emma hissed, sitting firm.

"I'll just pay the check. Let's go," Niles stood up, motioned toward the front of the restaurant.

Emma continued to sit unmoving in her chair, arms crossed defiantly in front of her. "Niles," she said through clenched teeth, "When I leave here, I'm going back to the office. I have too much work to do. We'll discuss this later."

At the look in Emma's eyes, Niles slowly sat back down. "All right, Emma," he said, pulling his chair back in close to the table, seemingly resigned to Emma's edict. "I promised you lunch, and lunch it'll be. No more arguing for now, okay?" He was relenting, but only temporarily, they both knew.

Emma breathed a silent sigh of relief anyway, and rewarded Niles with a small, tight smile. If he'd insisted, she'd been prepared to sit firm and let him leave without her. It would have been a bit awkward when the waitress arrived with two lunches and only one person left sitting at the table, but Emma suspected it wouldn't have surprised her overmuch, considering they'd been arguing from the moment they'd sat down. The waitress would have had to have been deaf not to have overheard at least part of their heated conversation.

The rest of their lunch was eaten in strained silence.

Fourteen

Lenny spotted Andy at the fax machine feeding paper into the slender opening and decided to approach him. At the sound of her footfalls, he looked up and smiled, taking in the cautious look in her luminous green eyes.

Andy nodded in acknowledgment as she sidled up next to him, half-turning as he punched in a number and fed another copy into the hungry fax machine.

Lenny was surprised to find that Andy Brannigan was even better looking than she'd previously thought him to be. Although she'd seen him on film, and briefly at the station, she hadn't been close enough to him to get the full impact of his deep blue, penetrating gaze. Definitely a plus, those eyes were—as if he needed anything else to compliment his already better than average good looks. Finding her voice, she stuck out her hand and said, "Lenny Wright, assistant editor."

"Andy Brannigan, resident investigator," he answered, taking her slender hand in his.

"We've met before, haven't we?" she said, already on the attack, ready to test him. Handsome or not, she had some questions she wanted answered.

Andy grinned broadly. "If you mean vicariously by film, I guess we have."

His forthright admission caught Lenny by surprise. She caught his infectious smile and grinned back, infinitely more comfortable now that it appeared he wasn't going to deny his odd presence at their shooting sites. "It *was* you."

"Guilty," he said disarmingly.

"And now you're working on a story with Emma."

"Guilty again."

"So why were you hanging around our sets?" Short, sweet...straight to the point—Frank would be proud of her.

"Why do you think I was hanging around?" he countered, his smile still in place, accentuating the deep dimple on his left cheek.

"Well I...I wasn't sure why you were there," she said, his open, friendly face was taking the edge off her desire to interrogate him on Emma's—and Frank's—behalf. "At first I thought that maybe you were a...a fan of the show or something...," she stumbled over her words, embarrassed all of a sudden at the multitude of suspicions that had crossed hers and Frank's minds.

"And then?" Andy urged her to continue.

She shrugged, looked away for a moment, then back at him. "And then...then Frank and I—Frank is my supervisor—Frank and I thought that maybe you were hanging around because of Emma...that maybe you were fixated on her or something."

"Frank..." Andy murmured, brows wrinkled, "was he the guy with you down at Pioneer Square when you were trying to find me?"

Lenny gasped. "So you did guess what we were doing!"

Andy nodded, a devilish grin on his face. "You were pretty obvious. Did you know I was standing right behind you at one point?"

"You're kidding! I don't believe it. Right behind me?" she grimaced.

"Within inches," he laughed, holding up thumb and forefinger to illustrate how close they'd been to each other. "I couldn't resist the opportunity."

"God, how embarrassing. So much for the super-sleuths. Pretty impressive, huh?" She covered her face, blushing a pretty pink, and shook her head in disbelief, a mental picture conjured up in her mind of her and Frank slinking through the crowd like the amateurs they were, while Andy, pinkpantherishly, followed behind them, mimicking their every move.

Andy shrugged away her embarrassment, slipped another sheet of paper into the fax. "Actually, it was kind of funny. At the same time, it was really quite sweet. It didn't take any great deducting on my part to realize you two might've thought I was shadowing your shoots for some nefarious reason. I was glad, actually, to see that someone in your organization was on the ball, had finally spotted me. It was you, wasn't it, who first noticed me in the background shots," Andy said, the tone of his voice held admiration, not accusations.

Lenny nodded, confessing, "And I'm the idiot who convinced Frank you had some ulterior motive for being there."

"And you were right, you know," his husky voice took on a conspiratorial note. "I did have an ulterior motive." His words caused her emerald eyes to light up in lively interest, along with just the slightest touch of fear. Their eyes locked, and Lenny felt herself being pulled into the deep blue orbs, more afraid to break their deadlock than to continue it. Was that cruelty she glimpsed in the depths of his eyes—or pain? Suddenly, he looked away, as if *he* was the one touched by fear.

"What," he began, looking over her shoulder, " what if I told you that you and Frank were right in the first place?"

"What do you mean?" She wasn't sure she really wanted to hear this.

Andy seemed to sense her growing discomfort; but instead of backing off, he leaned in close to her, still not meeting her studied gaze. "What if I told you I *was* watching Emma, following her. What if I told you I spotted her on television and decided then and there that I had to know more about her...what would you say to that?"

Lenny shifted uncomfortably from foot to foot, but willed herself to turn, force him to look at her. "I'd think it was pretty spooky," she answered candidly, concerned now that she might have read the situation correctly the first time around, the tone of her voice serious as she looked unwaveringly into his deep blue eyes. "*Is* that why you were there?"

Eyes locked on hers, Andy again broke contact and shrugged, seemingly losing interest in what he'd just stirred up. "I'm here investigating the disappearance of a couple of kids, remember? And your station is now an integral part of that investigation, right?" He nudged her gently with his shoulder and smiled that brilliant smile, then moved away from her and fed another copy into the insatiable fax machine.

Lenny studied him for a moment, automatically returning his dazzling smile. She watched him work, satisfied, for the moment, with his explanations.

It didn't occur to her until much later that he hadn't actually answered her question.

Fifteen

With great effort, Niles had refrained from lashing out at Emma during the remainder of their lunch. And now, back in his office, he was finding it difficult to concentrate on the brief his secretary had just laid out in front of him. Instead, his mind kept wandering back to Emma and this Andy Brannigan.

Somehow, in a very short period of time, Andy Brannigan had made a very disturbing impression on his fiancée, yet it had taken him months to get her to take him seriously. Somehow this…this *interloper* had done it in just days, Niles ground out furiously, remembering well how he'd relentlessly pursued Emma.

And when he'd finally gained her interest, her trust, her love, Emma had shared with him her deepest secret. Although he'd been shocked beyond words, he had been understanding, and quite concerned at the trauma she must have suffered through at some point in her life—a trauma that had caused her mind and memories to retreat in protective reflex of a young soul struggling to survive a circumstance she was obviously unable to cope with. And knowing that she'd shared something so private, so painful to her, he had been careful in his inquiries of what she was able to remember. And so far, he had been able to successfully hide his shock at finding out that she had absolutely no cohesive memory of *anything* before the age of seventeen, just snippets of a lost past.

But what had surprised him the most about this strange phenomenon, was that she seemed to have no desire whatsoever in trying to reconstruct her past, no curiosity of what had transpired so many years ago causing her mind to rebel, her memories to retreat—no recollections of a family she must have loved, and loved her. He only knew that the man who eventually became her adopted father had tenderly nurtured her during her illness.

Although Niles had been, and still was, respectful of her wishes to keep her unknown past just that, he found it difficult to understand why she had no curiosity *at all* about it. His view of her stance had been the only sour note, until now, in their otherwise almost idyllic relationship.

He'd even gone so far as to speak privately with her stepfather, only to find that Ben was even more adamant than she was about not dredging up the past. Niles had been surprised at the man's position, considering he was a psychologist, a man with years and years of professional training on how to deal with just this sort of problem.

But therein lay the root of the problem, as Niles saw it. Emma categorically denied she had any adverse side effects from a life that didn't actually start—in her memory anyway—until she was seventeen. As far as she was concerned, she not only looked up to Ben Stuart, her adopted father and mentor, she relied heavily on his judgment that it was best to go forward with her life, not dwell on a past that could only bring her pain.

Besides, she'd said to him, she knew the salient facts. Ben had shared some of her family history with her many years ago, and they both felt she knew all she needed to. Of course, Niles didn't have to be a psychologist to understand that Ben, and even Emma if the truth be known, was afraid that by facing her past head on, her mind might again seek refuge in oblivion rather than face the truth of what had pushed her over the brink in the first place. Neither one of them were willing to run the risk of plunging her back into a situation that could cause her to retreat again, perhaps permanently, this time. Ben was content to play a waiting game with Emma. He felt that if or when her mind became strong enough, the memories would come flowing back on their own. In his mind, as in hers, there was no need to force the issue.

As he'd talked to the distinguished psychologist, Niles had had a feeling the older man knew much, much more than he was willing to share, but no amount of coercing on Niles' part would get him to indulge any more information than what he felt was necessary. As highly as Ben Stuart regarded him, the very strong message coming across from the older man was simply to let things be.

And he'd tried. *God knows* he'd tried. But he didn't know if it was that characteristic in him that made him a successful attorney, the urge to dig and dig until a satisfactory answer surfaced, that kept him from taking the doctor's advice, from dropping the whole matter, or simple curiosity. All he knew was there were times when he was with Emma when he would see her react to a situation in a totally different way than most people normally would, and he would again quietly probe her about her past. Unfortunately, these times did little to spark an interest in her of her forgotten youth; rather, he could feel her almost physically withdrawing from him. She would become uncharacteristically brooding and silent toward him, as if she resented his studied observations of her.

And he also knew that, although they were engaged to be married, it was times like these that he could read in her eyes she was having second thoughts about their future together.

So, rather than drive her away from him with his probing questions, he tried to keep his observations to himself. He loved her, and the last thing he wanted to do was drive her away from him.

Besides, if he was to be absolutely honest with himself, he wasn't so sure it wasn't that very quality in Emma, the air of mystery and hidden vulnerability, that had initially attracted him, and had ultimately been the catalyst to his asking her to marry him.

He hated to think he loved her more for the challenge she represented than for herself alone, but he was honest enough to admit that this was at least part of his unflagging interest in her.

He'd been initially attracted to her because she was a beautiful, successful woman with a reputation of being very discriminating when it came to dating the opposite sex, a challenge he hadn't been able to pass up. Her large, dark brown, almost black eyes, easily her most prominent and attractive feature, went well with her dark brown, shoulder length hair, and her shorter than average height was often remarked upon by watchers of her evening program when they spotted her in person for the first time. Her full, soft lips, ever-curved in a knowing half-smile and her unforced, natural, girl-next-door image made her one of the most popular local television personalities in the city of Portland, and he enjoyed the sensation of attending high profile events with her on his arm. He had been smitten by her from day one, had relentlessly pursued her thereafter.

And now he sensed their future together was in jeopardy, caused by a silver-haired stranger who had no business interfering with them. Instead of Emma, Andy Brannigan had now become the focal point of Niles' undivided attention. Within a few days, he expected to know everything there was to know about Andy Brannigan. And with that knowledge, he hoped to find the key to unlocking the mystery surrounding Emma's apparent fixation on the man.

Niles flipped through his rolodex and found the number he was looking for, picked the telephone up and dialed.

"Karl? Niles. Got a pencil? I want you to find out everything you can about an organization called the 'Mizpah Foundation.' And while you're at it, I want you to find out if there's a sheet on a guy by the name of Andrew Brannigan..."

Sixteen

For some reason, it irritated Emma when she walked over to the fax machine only to find her best friend laughing and smiling up at Andy. She'd never experienced the painful surge of jealousy before, so it took her a minute to recognize exactly what was bothering her. Lenny was flirting outrageously with Andy Brannigan and she didn't like it one bit. Unsettled, she approached the laughing pair.

"Since when does it take two people to work a fax machine?" she said, her voice even, belying her discomfort.

"Emma! How was lunch?" Lenny asked, unaware of her friend's uneasiness.

"Fine." She couldn't even remember what she'd just eaten.

"I'm glad you're back, Emma," Andy said. She looked

none the worse for wear, maybe a little harried. "I thought if you'd like, we could visit some grade schools, give 'em my pitch, hand out some flyers—if you don't have anything special scheduled for this afternoon."

"Sounds great. Let me just delegate a few things off my desk. I'll be right back. Lenny?"

Delegate? Since when did Emma delegate *any* of her work? Lenny wondered silently. "On my way," she said, turning back to Andy one last time. "It was nice talking to you. Good luck on your investigation. I'm sure we'll be running into each other again."

"But probably not on film anymore. At least, not until the story is taped."

Lenny laughed. "No, I suppose not." She turned and followed Emma, sensing as only a woman can that Andy's eyes weren't following her retreat, but Emma's. Teddy had been right, for once. Whatever emotions were raging through Emma, Andy Brannigan was not unaware of them, of that she was certain.

"Have you asked him yet?" Lenny asked without preamble.

"Asked him what?" Emma said, shuffling through the papers on her desk.

"What we talked about last night, you ninny! Does he *know* you."

"I'm working up to it." She nervously rearranged the papers, her hands busy. She hadn't really had any work to farm out, she'd just wanted a minute or two alone with Lenny. "So what were you two talking about?" she asked nonchalantly.

Lenny wasn't fooled. She knew Emma too well, knew she was too well organized, almost fanatically so, to be shuffling through her papers so randomly, for no apparent reason. Arms crossed, a smile playing at the corners of her mouth, she answered, "You."

"What did he say?" Emma asked, a note of urgency in her voice, the papers on her desk forgotten.

"Nothing really. That he'd seen you on a couple of your shoots, how impressed he was by your professionalism."

"Anything else?" she persisted.

Lenny didn't deem it necessary at this point in time to tell her they were discussing his presence at several of their shoots. What was the point?

"No, not really. When I saw him over by the fax machine, I went over and introduced myself. We'd just started talking when you came in. He's a nice guy, Emma."

"But did you…"

"Any strange sensations, an odd pull, déjà vu?" Lenny teased. "Unh, unh, that's all yours honey."

"Nothing?"

"Hey, he's a good-looking man. I'm not saying I didn't feel *anything*."

Reassured, Emma said, "So you really think I should ask him if he knows me?"

"It couldn't hurt." Or could it?

"But wouldn't he think it was, like, the oldest line in the world, with a strange twist to it? Hi there, don't you know me from somewhere?" she sing-songed.

Lenny giggled. She had to admit it did sound funny. And it would put Emma in a position of having to explain herself, something Lenny knew she wouldn't do, not to a stranger, even if that stranger happened to be Andy Brannigan. Very few people knew Emma's story, and that's the way she preferred it.

"And what if he thinks I'm coming on to him?" Emma added.

"Honey," Lenny said, waving away her friends protestations, "the way he looks at you, I wouldn't worry about who's coming on to who," she grinned broadly.

"Andy Brannigan?"

Andy turned around to find Lenny's supervisor and fellow sleuthing partner, Frank, waiting for a response. The fax machine seemed to be a hotbed for meeting people.

"Yes?"

"Frank Thompson. I'll be editing your story." They shook hands.

"From the looks of your programs, I'll be in good hands," Andy said, feeding another sheet into the machine.

Frank smiled at the compliment. Up close and personal, Andrew Brannigan didn't appear to be the least bit dangerous.

"I saw you and Lenny talking, so I thought I'd come over and introduce myself."

"If you're going to chew me out about getting you two all worked up at my showing up in your background shoots, you're too late. Lenny already beat you to it."

Frank laughed, glad everything was out in the open, glad he wasn't going to have to pretend it didn't happen. He just had one last question he needed cleared up, then he'd divorce himself from the whole silly matter.

"So how did you know where we were going to shoot every day?" he asked casually, as if the answer held no real meaning to him.

"How do you know where they're going to be?" Andy countered.

"We keep the show's itinerary on our computer. I just punch up the schedule..." At Andy's broadening smile, Frank said, "Hey...did you get into our computer? How did you manage that?" Now he *was* impressed. Out of all the strange and stupid ideas he and Lenny had come up with on how Andy might have come by their schedule, this one had never occurred to either of them.

Before Andy could answer, Emma interrupted the two men.

"Hey, is this old home week or something?" she said, nudging the lanky editor.

"You didn't tell me the fax machine was such a happening place to be," Andy replied, gathering up his remaining papers. "If I stay here much longer, I'll know everyone in the building. It was nice meeting you, Frank."

Frank nodded, then watched them walk off together, wishing he'd had a chance to get an answer out of the other man before Emma had shown up. He hadn't wanted to pursue the subject, not with Emma there. He had to admit, though, as his eyes followed them out the door, that they made a striking couple—her dark hair and petite frame played well against his mixed features of dark and light, his muscular, stocky build. At least he now knew how Andy came to be at their shoots.

He just didn't know *why*.

He shrugged his shoulders and returned to the editing room.

Seventeen

"Why don't we hit some of the Portland Public schools first." At her nod of agreement, he pulled away from the curb and quickly merged the dark brown Taurus, a rental, into traffic.

Emma was just glad to be away from the office, away from prying eyes and ears. She didn't mind that Lenny was aware of what she was going through, but it bothered her to know that Teddy, and now Frank, seemed to be scrutinizing her every move. As good of friends as they all were, she still felt uncomfortable at their studied appraisal of her. And for once, she didn't feel compelled to be at the office, not wanting to leave until every last little project on her desk was finished for the day.

Again, she found it odd that Niles couldn't pry her away from her desk with a crowbar, yet Andy did it almost effortlessly.

Granted, she was working on a story with him, but he didn't really need her today, and they both knew it. He wanted her company, and she'd responded.

Now, as she sat next to him, watching him out of the corner of her eyes, taking in the firm grip of his hands on the steering wheel of the car, in control, always centered on the problems at hand, she felt a deep contentment she'd never felt before—or at least that she could remember—come over her.

Andy was aware of her quiet perusal. There was something different about her today that he couldn't quite pinpoint, different than how she'd been with him the other times over the last few days.

He'd first sensed it when he'd arrived at the station, as if she was looking at him in a new light. He wondered if she was beginning to remember. Was it possible? She had blanked out for so long what had happened to her, could it be possible it was coming slowly back to her?

Dr. Stuart had warned him she'd have no recollection of him, but he'd been wrong. Something had been tugging at Emma from the moment she laid eyes on him, he could almost physically feel it. He wanted desperately to confront her, but he dared not. Not yet.

More importantly, if she was beginning to remember, was there any way for him to control, for both their sakes, exactly what she remembered?

Neither one of them had mentioned the incident between himself and her fiancé, and since Emma hadn't said anything about Niles or remarked on their lunch, Andy wasn't about to bring the subject up.

For now, he felt his best approach was to say nothing, act as if Niles was invisible, nonexistent, unimportant.

Emma was still struggling with whether she should ask Andy outright about herself. But she was afraid, afraid if they had no shared memories, she'd look foolish to him, and it was very important to her that she not look silly in his eyes.

It occurred to her as she sat quietly next to him, that perhaps if she learned a little bit more of his background, where he was from, where he grew up, she could garner, without outright asking, if he and she could possibly have known each other long ago. She knew enough about her own past, where she lived, where she went to school, to be able to ascertain if Andy could have been in the area when she was growing up. Maybe that would be the best approach, she thought, thereby reducing the odds that she'd sound like a screwball to him.

Deciding on this line of approach, Emma broke the comfortable silence. "You mentioned Karen Carlson was from Philadelphia. Are you from that area?"

Andy shook his head. "I was born in the Midwest—Winona, Minnesota to be exact," he answered, his eyes on the road.

There went one point against Lenny's theory, Emma thought. She had been born and raised in Boston, the daughter of a prominent circuit judge.

"I haven't lived there in years, though." he added. "I've got a small apartment in Washington, which I'm never at. But it's close to the Mizpah Foundation's official headquarters, if you call a small office with no secretary a headquarters."

Strike two, she thought, although at least he was on the right coast.

"Your work keeps you on the road a lot, I imagine."

"Constantly, but at least I've gotten a pretty good feel of this country of ours."

"And your parents? Are they still back in Winona?" she continued, not giving up hope.

Andy took his time answering. This was the first question she'd asked that could truly connect him to the time before her blanked-out years, something concrete she just might remember about him.

"My father was killed when I was nine," he answered slowly. "He was a cop—a big, dark featured Irishman with a tough reputation—popular with his police buddies, well respected. When he was shot down, his funeral was the biggest attended event for a cop, ever."

It wasn't difficult to read the pride with which Andy talked about his father, the love he must have felt for the man who'd never gotten the chance to see his son grow into manhood.

"And your mother?"

"My mom," Andy said, "never got over my father's death," he said quietly, the words coming easily to him. He'd had a long time to come to terms with his parents' death. "She was a pretty, blonde, petite little thing that always relied on my dad for everything. When he died, she couldn't cope, just gave up, didn't care anymore."

"But what about you? She had you."

"But I wasn't enough," he laughed softly, belying the pain, the loneliness he'd felt as a child. "She found peace in a bottle," he continued. "One-hundred proof peace—there's nothing quite like it in the whole world," Andy said, no trace of resentment in his voice. There had been nothing he could do for her back then, a small, scared boy of nine, but stay quiet and out of the way, let her find her own peace.

"And that explains my strange looks," he said, trying to lighten the mood a bit. "The Black Irish features, the Scandinavian coloring."

"I wouldn't exactly describe them as strange." Emma pretended to size him up, thankful he didn't seem depressed about his childhood memories. "More like, distinctive—striking even."

"So you don't mind them?" he said, a twinkle in his eye.

"Not at all," she replied, then blushed at her quick response.

As they pulled up and parked at the first school on his list, Andy pretended not to notice the pretty flush on her face.

"She died when I was seventeen. People say she drank herself to death, but the truth is, she died the moment she opened the front door and found my dad's partner standing there with tears streaming down his face. They'd been partners, and the best of friends, for sixteen years, longer than my dad and mom had even known each other. He took my dad's death just as hard as my ma. But he pulled out of it. My mom couldn't, didn't really want to, I guess." He switched off the engine but made no move to exit the car.

"Did...did your dad's partner keep in contact with you and your mom?" The lump in her throat made it difficult to get the question out.

"Oh, yeah," Andy grinned. He paused for a moment, then said, "His name's Jack O'Malley, another big, brooding, hard-drinking Irishman." He stopped for a moment, saw no recollection in Emma's eyes, so he continued on. "He fell into the bottle for a few months after my dad's death too, but he finally pulled himself out of it. When he started coming around again, it didn't take him long to realize my mom was on the skids. He tried to help her—for months he hounded her, tried to get her to stop. Then it finally dawned on him that she wasn't going to stop, didn't want to, and nothing he could do or say could change that."

"But what about you?"

"He even laid that guilt trip on her, but all she'd do was start crying louder, drink harder. When he realized there was nothing he could do for her, he kind of took me under his wing, made sure I stayed out of trouble, went to school, that sort of thing. I learned to keep out of her way, talk quietly, tread softly, keep a low profile at home. Jack and I are still real close. I think of him as the dad I never had the chance to finish up with."

Talk quietly, tread softly. Years of trying to suppress his boyish enthusiasm in an effort to stay out of his mother's way had left its indelible mark on him. To this day, he found it difficult to raise his voice beyond the low, husky tones that were now such an integral part of him.

"And the Mizpah Foundation?"

"Jack was instrumental in getting me involved with that, too. See, much as he tried to keep me on the straight and narrow, I got into a little trouble and ended up in reform school."

"Reform school?" Emma said, eyebrows raised. "Now I am surprised. For some reason, you don't remind me of a reform school type of guy," she teased. Both his parents were dead, and so were hers. Was that the strange tie that bound them?—tragedies that seemed to parallel each other? She'd have to mull that over later. For now, she was more interested in what had landed him in reform school in the first place.

"Oh, you'd be surprised. Sometimes us innocent-looking, baby-faced boys'll fool you. Even now, I keep Jack on his toes trying to keep me out of trouble."

"Really?" She wasn't sure if he was kidding her or not.

"Let's just say that there's been a time or two when I stretched the boundaries of the law—and his patience—to get what I wanted."

"Really? I'd think with your organization being affiliated with the church and all, you'd have to be pretty careful."

"That's what Jack keeps telling me every time he pulls me out of another scrape," Andy admitted.

"It sounds like you keep him pretty busy."

"Sometimes," he agreed, a lopsided grin on his face, remembering all too well the times he'd stretched his surrogate father's patience to the limit, and then some.

"It doesn't sound to me like you resent his interference," she said, noting his expression.

"Resent it? No, I don't resent it," he answered, shaking his head. "Like I said, Jack was the one who recruited me for this job in the first place—a little fact I remind him of every now and then when he starts lecturing me about some of the more questionable tactics I've used in the course of a few of my investigations. I tend to get a little overzealous at times, especially if I'm on the trail of something really pivotal to my case."

Emma shifted in her seat and smiled, in no hurry to leave the comfortable confines of Andy's rental car. She was content to sit back and learn all she could about the fascinating man sitting next to her. She felt relaxed—chatty almost—and felt no great pressure to leave the warmth of the car and get on with their business. Instead, she kept up with her soft interrogation.

"So what were some of these 'questionable tactics' Jack took exception to?"

Andy rubbed his chin. "Let's see...there's so many things to choose from, where should I start?"

"How about with the one that made him the maddest?"

The maddest? No, he couldn't start with that one, not with her being the central figure in it. Jack had been hot, hotter than he'd ever seen the man, ready to flay him down to the bare bones. The best he'd been able to do for Andy that time was a two year stretch in reform school, and four years probation. He tried to push away from thoughts of that black time.

Instead, he said, "He was pretty rattled at me the time I dressed up as a parish priest so I could get into a maximum security prison."

"A parish priest?" she echoed, surprise on her face.

Andy nodded, a sheepish grin on his face. "I'd been told one of the inmates there had some information he was willing to share with me but he was in lockup for thirty days, which meant no visitors, period." Andy cocked his head and shrugged. "I couldn't afford to wait thirty days to talk to him."

"But they'd let a priest in."

"That's what I was hoping. And they did, and I got the information I was looking for."

"And Jack was angry over that?"

"You've got to remember, we're talking about an Irishman here. There ain't nothing more sacred to these old Irish cops steeped in tradition than their faith," Andy said, exaggerating in an Irish brogue. "It's what keeps them going on the job, especially when they get older, seen all that garbage on the street. It's the only solid concept they have to cling to—that and their family—in their often crazy, often uncaring, brutal world."

"So he felt you were making a mockery of the faith?"

"More or less. And the fact that I kyped his brother's robes—his brother the priest—to get in in the first place."

Emma laughed at Andy's expression. "So he found out from his brother?" she asked, fascinated at his story.

"Nah, he wouldn't tell, he's a great guy."

"So how did he find out?"

Andy shook his head, smiling back at her. "That's just it. I have nobody to blame but myself. Somehow, I always end up telling on myself. Maybe subconsciously I like to get him all riled up. It's like, during my briefings with him, the story just pops out, then all hell breaks loose. He rants and raves for a few hours, tells me how the means don't justify the ends and all that jazz, and then it passes. All's well...until the next time it happens."

"So what else have you done?" she asked, her mission to find out whether he knew her or not totally forgotten in the wake of his interesting revelations.

"Um...," he said, scrunching up his face in thought. "There was the time I was thrown in jail for a few days for tapping into the Internet Research Computer Network. That's a big no-no, by the way," he smirked, merriment twinkling in his eyes. "The U. S. Government didn't take too kindly to me over that one," he said, remembering full well the verbal threats thrown back and forth over that escapade. "Jack pulled some major strings to get me out of that particular jam, but not before he let me stew in prison for a few days, just to let me get the feel of the place."

"What on earth did you need to break into the Government's computer for?" Emma asked, amazed at the multi-faceted man sitting so calmly next to her.

"I needed to look at the service record of a guy I suspected of abducting a teenage girl I happened to be looking for. The Internet Network Computer includes those at the Air Force and Aeronautics and Space Administration facilities. I'd found out this guy had been dishonorably discharged out of the Air Force, and I wanted to know why."

"And they wouldn't tell you." Privileged information, she knew.

"Hey," he shrugged, "I tried all the lawful means possible.

When that tactic didn't work, I improvised, and got the information I needed. I bypassed the computer's security system, and, using my suspect's social security number, accessed his service record." No small feat, and one he wasn't particularly proud of, but necessary at the time.

"And you found what you were looking for?"

"Exactly what I expected to find," he replied, his voice suddenly grim. "He had been stationed over in West Germany, that I knew. What I didn't know, was that while he was over there, he was accused, and found guilty of, kidnapping and raping—and nearly killing—a fourteen year old girl on one of his weekend passes. Our glorious government, always so worried about its sterling image, hushed up the incident, threw him in the brig for a couple of months, gave him a dishonorable discharge, then sent him on his way. All I needed was some proof that he was capable of what I suspected him of, then I zeroed in on him."

"Figuring it was only a matter of time before he tried it again?"

Andy nodded. "They always do," he added, the disgust standing out in his husky voice. "I caught him in the act of trying to force a young girl into his pickup truck. The police arrested him, and he ended up confessing to a number of murders." And Andy spent the next two months flat on his back in a hospital, recovering from a nasty knife wound that'd nearly killed him. The man had wielded around on Andy as the two of them struggled over the girl, and the suspect had knifed him before Andy'd had a chance to react. Andy had been just angry enough, and coherent enough, to slam the other man's head into the door of the truck, knocking him unconscious before he, too, had slipped under.

"Including the girl you were looking for?"

"Yeah," was all he said, his voice subdued. He glanced out the window, fogged over from the heat generated by their bodies and breath in the small confines of the car. He remembered well that day, the day the young victim's parents had learned their only child, their beautiful little girl, had been raped, murdered, and buried in a shallow grave in the middle of the Mojave Desert.

"At least you kept him from killing again, which he surely would have done. You have that consolation." He glanced back in her direction, the pain evident in his eyes.

"That doesn't help much when you have to go to those people that have…have looked to you for support and hope, only to tell them the horrible truth. It's awful, and I'm a coward when it comes to facing people with that kind of news. I usually take Jack's brother with me when an investigation turns out that way. He's a master at consoling people."

"Jack's brother. And Jack. They've been good friends to you over the years, haven't they?"

"I don't know what I'd have done without them. Even when I was in reform school, Jack was always coming out, talking to the counselors, getting me involved in different projects going on. I could've easily fallen into the reform school trap—you know—drugs, violence, gangs. Hell, I escaped without so much as a tattoo," he said, his mood lightening. "He just kept at me, at me, at me—made me believe I could come out of that school a better person than I went in—not worse, as so many of them do. He taught me I could leave my past behind, really do something with my life."

"And you did," she said matter-of-factly. Leave his past behind…at least he'd had a choice.

"I like to believe I did."

"Don't you believe you did?" she said, surprised at the dubious tone of his voice.

"Most of the time, I guess," he answered truthfully. "But sometimes, when I've been working on an especially frustrating case, or the kid I've been looking for winds up dead, I start questioning. Insecurities set in. Self-doubt starts gnawing at me."

"But those feelings pass," she prompted.

"Yeah, they pass," he nodded. "And I start to believe again, believe I can make a difference. And when it comes right down to it, I guess I do."

Both of them sat silently for a few minutes, digesting what had just been said, revealed. Emma felt mesmerized by Andy's reminiscing, and again felt that now-familiar pull, that sensation, that inkling of curiosity about her buried past. What *was* it about this man who sat so quietly, so self-assured, next to her that brought out all those untapped feelings? Without even trying, without even realizing he'd done it, he had her wondering about the complete Emma, not the cardboard Emma people saw on television five days a week, the Emma from *before,* not just after.

"Tell you what," Andy said, breaking the silence. "We'd better get inside the school now, while we have the chance, 'cause in about ten minutes, what looks like a million kids are going to be spilling out of those two small doors and streaming down upon us."

That night, alone in bed, Emma went back over their long afternoon conversation and wondered again what Andy had done to land himself in reform school in the first place. Somehow, they'd never gotten back to the subject.

And thinking back, she found it odd that, although she knew beyond a shadow of a doubt that Andy was attracted to her, he hadn't asked her even one question about herself.

Eighteen

Emma knew the time had come to make a decision. There was no sense in trying to postpone it, or think that the situation would change, go back to what it was before. It wasn't fair to either her or Niles to continue in this way. More importantly, she didn't *want* to continue, and the sooner she got it over with, the better.

She now knew it wasn't going to work with Niles. Perhaps she'd always known it, and meeting Andy Brannigan had just brought all her fears and doubts to the surface. The fact that she was so confused about her feelings toward the two men was enough to prove she was not yet ready for marriage, not to Niles anyway. That Andy had been the catalyst to all those untapped feelings just added to her resolve to tell Niles she couldn't, wouldn't, marry him. Even if nothing more than a strong mutual attraction came out of her meeting Andy, she knew it was over between herself and Niles.

And why?—because she couldn't possibly love Niles if another man was able to affect her so—and Niles deserved better than that. He deserved someone who would love him completely, not out of obligation, as she'd sometimes felt. It was clear to her now that she'd been fooling herself all along with him—why she'd been so unsettled on so many occasions, why she'd put off setting a wedding date, why she'd put her work before her fiancé so many times. If she really loved him, wouldn't she have wanted to spend all her free time with him, instead of grasping at other things to work on?

But how was she going to tell him? She knew instinctively Niles would put up a horrible fight over her decision, surely as intense as the arguments he'd used to convince her to marry him in the first place.

For a moment she thought of taking the coward's way out and simply tell him over the phone that she was breaking off their engagement. Then she realized that, if nothing else, he deserved to hear her decision face to face.

With a determination that surprised even her, Emma picked up the phone and dialed the familiar number.

"It's Andy Brannigan, isn't it?" Niles raged, disgust pouring out of his heated words.

"No," Emma vehemently shook her head, "it's me. I just don't love you Niles, not the way a future wife should." This was the most difficult thing she'd ever remembered doing; she could see the hurt her words were causing, but she needed to stand firm. For a moment or two she'd wanted to waver, unsure if she could withstand the pain she was causing. But then a new rush of resolve had washed over her at the mention of Andy's name.

Niles sneered, unable to control his raging jealousy, his temper. "Are you going to stand there and tell me it's just coincidence that you meet this guy and less than a week later you're breaking our engagement? Just what the hell were you two *doing* at those so-called meetings?" he snarled.

If Emma had been feeling guilty, Niles' nasty words put a halt to those thoughts. "What you're thinking is disgusting, and you're better than that, Niles! *Nothing happened.*" Niles shook his head in disbelief.

"Niles," she said, her voice taking on a pleading, yet resolute tone, "take a look back at our relationship...a good, hard look. Can't you see something was just not...quite...right? Be honest with yourself," she beseeched, hoping, somehow, he'd agree with her.

Niles only half-listened to her heated explanations, unwilling to drop his earlier accusation. "Emma, no relationship is perfect," he started out. "Can't you see how he's influenced you? Since he entered the picture, it's like...like you don't care about anything anymore—not me, not your work. It's just not like you!" He tried to pull her close, make her understand, listen to reason.

Emma slapped his arms away. "How do you know who I am, Niles?" she angrily shot back at him. "How do you know this isn't the real me—the me even *I* can't remember?" Tears of frustration flowed freely now. "If Andy is guilty of anything, it's allowing me to be just me—no questions, no expectations, no recriminations."

"So it *is* him—"

"No, dammit!" she stomped her foot in frustration. "Aren't you *listening* to me, Nileås?" she cried. "It's *me! I've* changed. Or maybe I've been this way all along and didn't really realize it until now. I...just...don't...love you," she finished, turning away from him.

"How do you know that?" he said, stunned, following her, forcing her to turn around and face him. "How can you love me one day, and not the next?" he demanded, refusing to believe what she was saying to him, his face screwed up in anguish.

"That's just it, Niles," she cried softly, her large brown eyes brimming with sorrow. She didn't want to hurt him any further, but she could no longer avoid the truth just to spare his feelings. "I don't think I ever really loved you."

Nineteen

"Good, you're back. I've been trying for hours to get a hold of you," Jack said.

"Why didn't you just leave a message, I'd have called you back," Andy answered, pleased to hear his gruff voice.

"Sure you woulda, whenever you felt like getting around to it."

"If I avoid your phone calls, Jack, its only 'cause its usually bad news."

"Then I won't be disappointing you. What've you stirred up out there anyway?"

"Why?" Jack's tone of voice didn't bode well for him.

"Someone's trying to get a copy of your record, that's all."

Niles. It had to be. Who else would be interested?—

Emma? She wouldn't have the clout to get it even if she *were* interested. And why would she want it, anyway? No—it had to be Niles.

"You can withhold it, can't you?"

"The juvenile portion, probably, if they don't come back asking for it. The request came straight from the D. A.'s office in Portland."

"But how—"

"I know, I know, the *law* says juvenile offenses are supposed to be written off within two or three years after the offenders are freed of court supervision, when you reach twenty-one. And you kept your nose relatively clean—we were supposed to expunge your records. But the D.A., he has the authority to see that old stuff." Jack hated wholeheartedly the idea that, poof! arson, killings, drive-by shootings, armed robberies, all those things could simply vanish off a juvenile's record. Since 1989, the only crimes that supposedly couldn't be written off were sex crimes committed against children. Those stupid juvenile laws that permitted records to disappear were written over twenty years ago, when shoplifting was considered a heavy crime. It was a different animal out there now, running the streets. Young teens out there with no conscience, no remorse at all, would just as soon cut your heart out as look at you.

But Andy didn't fit in that category. All bringing his records to light would do was muddy the waters even more, cause old injustices back to the surface. Jack didn't want that, but his hands were tied.

"I can't believe—"

"Look Andy, we're doing what we can for you, you know that. There's more…"

"What else?" Andy whispered, almost afraid to ask.

"They want a profile on the Foundation."

"Is that so?" Andy said, recovering a bit. So, Niles was going for a complete profile. Perhaps he had underestimated his competition. "Give it to 'em, the Foundation records can't really hurt me."

"So you gonna tell me what's going on?" Jack persisted.

Andy ignored his question. "You say you can suppress my juvvie records for a while. What kind of time frame are we looking at here before you might have to cough them up?" Niles would ask, he was sure of it. His current record he wasn't too afraid of, and foundation inquiries, well, he could handle those too. It was his sheet prior to turning eighteen he didn't want Niles, or anybody else for that matter, to see.

"I'm stalling sending what I've got already. If they come back and ask for a complete…maybe a day or two."

"Can you make it a week?" He needed all the time he could get. He had no illusions at what Niles would do with the information on his juvenile sheet if he got his hands on it.

"Not if you don't give me a good reason why I should."

Andy hesitated, unsure if now was the time to reveal what, or more specifically, whom, he'd discovered living in Portland.

"'Come on Andy boy, don't make me ask again or I'm on the next flight out there," Jack threatened.

Andy sighed. There was no putting off Jack this time, not when he needed his help. "She's here, Jack," he said, his voice barely above a whisper.

"What?"

"Emma. She's here. After searching everywhere for her, after….after almost giving up, I've found her," he said, unable to keep the wonder out of his voice.

Shit! Just when the boy'd seemed to have gotten the girl out of his system, he'd stumbled on her whereabouts, Jack muttered to himself. He didn't know how, or why, not that it really mattered. What mattered, was that Andy was messing with something he shouldn't be messing with, and Jack knew there was no way he'd be able to talk him out of this one. Anything else, anything else in the *world,* but not Emma.

Instead, he said, "Is the doc still in the picture?"

Andy snorted in disgust. "Yeah, he's still around, still trying to be the master of his own little universe." He didn't find it necessary to tell Jack the permanency of the doctor's relationship to Emma. Why worry him further?

"Andy—Andy listen to me," Jack said sternly. "He's gonna stir up trouble for you. He's already requested your files."

"Why would he want them? He already knows what's in them." Andy paused, knowing how Jack was going to react to his next bit of news. "It's not him. I'm pretty sure it's an attorney by the name of Niles Whitmann who's trying to get at them."

"He a D.A.?" Jack didn't like the sound of this, not at all.

"Nah. But I'm sure he's got enough clout to ask the D.A. to get the records for him. He's a local hot-shot corporate attorney who just happens to be engaged to Emma."

"Ah shit, Andy," Jack groused into the telephone, "this just keeps getting worser and worser."

"Jack…Jack, listen to me. You've got to trust me on this one. I know what I'm doing."

"Buddy, you better know what you're doing, 'cause I'm getting too old to keep dragging your ass outta the fire," he said, afraid for Andy, *really afraid* for him for the first time in ten years.

"Don't worry," Andy said with more conviction than he felt, "nobody's gonna lock me up this time."

Andy was going to have to move a little faster now that Niles was on his tail. As soon as he got a copy of his record, it'd be bye-bye Emma if he didn't convince her in the meantime she was meant to be with him, regardless of what happened in their shared past.

Taken at face value, his record would crucify him in her eyes. He needed to convince her right now, before word got out, that what was, was, and there was no going back, no need to go back. As much as he would have liked her to remember him, remember the wonderful times they'd had before the bad times, he was content to settle for the here and now—it was much safer that way, for her as well as himself.

Niles asking for his record threatened all his well-laid

plans, so it was important for him to be the one, not Niles, to tell her about their past, or at least select portions of it. Perhaps coming from him, it would lessen the blow a little.

And maybe, just maybe, she'd remember...remember and forgive.

He'd had it in his mind to call her anyway, after glancing through today's newspaper. An idea had hit him right square in the face and now it afforded him the perfect excuse for calling her at home.

He picked up the telephone and dialed her number.

Emma was determined not to answer the telephone. She'd said all she was going to say. To rehash their argument, their breakup, was pointless. After hours of arguing, Niles had angrily stormed out of her house, vowing not to give up on them. As soon as he'd left, she'd turned on her recorder, intent on screening her calls for a while, but at the sound of Andy's deep voice, she quickly rushed to the phone.

"Hello?" she said, out of breath.

"Oh good, you're there. Did I catch you at a bad time?"

A bad time? Just the understatement of the year, she thought as she tried to push the unpleasantness of a few hours ago out of her mind.

"Uh...no. I was just about ready to go to bed."

"Oh...well, I won't keep you long. A great idea occurred to me and I thought I'd run it by you."

"Oh?" she said, curious.

"You know the profile on David Carlson I was showing you this morning? If you remember, one of his favorite pastimes is snow skiing."

"Yes," she said, "I do remember. Downhill, wasn't it?"

"Yeah. Anyway, I was thumbing through today's paper, and when I came to the Arts & Entertainment section, you know, the one that comes out once a week telling you all the good events going on over the weekend, I noticed there's a big bash going on up at Mount Hood."

"The annual Starlight Skifest at Timberline Lodge," she

finished, knowing exactly what he was talking about. *Evening Magazine* had covered the popular event just last year.

"That's the one," he said. "Anyway, I was thinking maybe David, being the ski hound he is, might be up there tomorrow, what with it being a once a year type deal and all, and with him being a stranger in a strange land, so to speak, he might be attracted to the event. And I thought I'd go up there, kind of wander around, see if I get lucky and spot him. And I thought, since you probably know your way around up there, you might be interested in being my tour guide—if you didn't have any plans for the weekend." Andy held his breath, waited for her answer.

His invitation was delivered innocently enough, but they both knew this was a turning point in their heretofore overpowering, yet not openly acknowledged, mutual attraction. If she accepted, Andy would know he'd succeeded in pulling Emma, at least temporarily, away from a rival who was even now trying to gather information that could destroy them both.

Emma knew if she went up to the mountain with Andy tomorrow, there'd be absolutely no turning back for her. Somehow, some way, she'd find the courage to ask Andy about herself—if he knew her long ago—if the compelling alliance she felt, and was certain he did too, was simple desire, or much more.

"I'd love to," she answered breathlessly, her heart racing.

Twenty

The first thing Andy noticed when Emma slid into the seat next to him, was that she wasn't wearing her engagement ring. As much as he wanted to remark upon its absence, he kept quiet. He knew instinctively that when the time came, she would tell him the reason for its absence.

Instead, he smiled and greeted her warmly, commented on how stylish she looked in her black ski pants and colorful Edelweiss sweater. He'd rushed out the evening before and bought a pair of ski pants, black, like hers, to better blend in with the crowd assembling on the mountain. The last thing he could afford in this juncture of his investigation, when he was so close to finishing it up, was to tip David Carlson off to his presence. And although he and Emma both skied, they'd decided last night not to bother with taking up equipment. Andy's plan, if they spotted David, wouldn't involve any skiing on their part.

"You look pretty stylish yourself," she said, smiling back. The blue in his ski-sweater perfectly matched the deep blue of his eyes; the snug, stretchy material of his ski pants revealed well-muscled legs. She started to blush when she realized where her eyes had wandered. "I...I brought some coffee along." She fumbled for the thermos in her bag, trying to cover her embarrassment.

"Great, I'll take some." He steered the car away from the curb, unaware of her discomfort, and the reason behind it.

She handed him a mug of steaming coffee, more composed now. She couldn't help but notice how right everything felt this morning; the cheerful mood she'd greeted the day with continued to linger.

Up before the crack of dawn, knowing Andy would soon be there, she'd been pleased to find the weatherman had predicted a clear, windless day on the mountain. A dusting of about six inches of new snow overnight guaranteed perfect skiing conditions up there, meshing perfectly with their plans. They hoped David Carlson wouldn't be able to resist the temptation to join in on this once a year bash, the lure of new powder the greatest incentive of all.

And best of all, last night, she'd slept clear through until morning, an unusual feat for her. Normally, her nights were filled with restless tossing and turning, reoccurring nightmares, insomnia. And on the occasions when Niles stayed over, her unease intensified, instead of lessening, which always surprised her. She'd have thought his presence would make her feel safer, more secure, but for some reason it had always worked just the opposite.

Emma kept them both well supplied with coffee during the two hour trip up to Timberline. They spent part of their time going over how they planned to approach David Carlson if luck happened to smile on them and they spotted him in the throngs of people expected to attend the day's events. If things played out as they hoped they would, they needed to have their act down pat.

The two hours it took to reach the summit passed quickly with Andy regaling Emma with highlights of some of his more interesting cases. Emma, in turn, shared a few anecdotes on the pitfalls of working on television. Theirs was an easy conversation, and when they fell silent from time to time, it was a companionable silence, not one strained by the need to say something just to fill in the void.

And if they didn't touch on the subject that was uppermost in both their minds, they both knew the day was young and they had several hours ahead of them to explore the strange and fascinating ties that seemed to bind them inexorably to each other.

Niles tried for four hours to get in touch with Emma. She had her recorder on, and the first three times he'd called he left messages. Now he just slammed the receiver down in frustration each time the hated recording came on.

Where was she? Was she at home, avoiding his calls? He'd called the station an hour ago, but the receptionist had said Emma wasn't expected in. He grabbed his car keys and stormed out of his house. If she wouldn't answer her telephone, fine—but let her see how difficult it was to ignore someone beating on her front door.

The twenty minute drive from his house to hers gave him time to calm down again. It had taken him all night to get a grip on his jealousy and frustration, only to have it rekindled in the morning when he couldn't reach her.

He pulled into her driveway and got out of the car. Striding over to the garage, he peeked in, barely able to make out the outline of her white Camaro. He quickly checked his appearance in the reflection of the garage door windows, then walked briskly up to the front door and knocked.

No answer.

He knocked again, leaned sideways, and tried to peak through the heavy curtains of the bay window. No movement.

He knocked again.

No answer.

He angrily jerked his key ring out of his pocket, flipping quickly through the half-dozen keys for the one he wanted, then inserted the key Emma had given him and entered her house.

"Emma?" he said loudly, his voice echoing through the house.

No answer.

As he walked through the empty rooms, Niles began to get worried. Her car was in the garage, where could she be? Just as he was about to call Ben, see if she was hiding out there, he noticed a slip of paper near the telephone. He scooped it up off the table, quickly read through it; the few unemotional words on the paper fueling his anger once again.

It was a note addressed to him, asking him to please leave her key when he left, and for him not to worry over her not being home. She'd said all she needed to say last night, and she'd gone out of town for the day with a friend, just to get away.

Niles crushed the note into a small, angry ball, white-hot stabs of jealousy roiling through him. His stomach in knots, he stormed around the small living room, unable to control his rage.

"Friend," he seethed. "Friend! *Goddammit!* When I get through with him he won't have a friend in the world!" he vowed, slamming out of the empty house.

Twenty-One

Although they'd left Portland early in the hopes of getting up to the mountain and settling in before the surge of skiers arrived, Emma and Andy were surprised to find the huge Timberline Lodge parking lot nearly full by the time they'd arrived. Before long, the Lodge shuttle buses would be commissioned into action, picking up skiers from the other lots located further below the popular resort area.

Andy was impressed by his first view of the historic Timberline Lodge, and said as much. The huge stone and wood structure sprawled against the south flank of Oregon's highest peak, Mt. Hood, blending well with the rugged landscape surrounding it. The Wy'East Day Lodge that had been built a few years back to handle the ever-increasing influx of skiers was just far enough away from the main lodge that it didn't detract from the natural beauty of the distinctive stone structure.

They pulled their gear out of the car and walked the short distance to the main lodge. As they passed through the lobby, Andy was quick to notice the homey, rough-hewn atmosphere of the place—four writing nooks tucked naturally in the corners of the main lobby—complete with wrought iron lamps and hand-carved writing desks and walls on three sides—gave complete privacy, if it was what one desired; the main stairway enhanced with hand-carved shapes of animals and birds from cedar utility posts, polished to a high gleam. Heavy timbers and floor-to-ceiling windows gave a spectacular view of Mt. Hood's snowy summit, the free-form glaciers held at bay outside helped in creating an atmosphere of deep rustic warmth. The magnificent lodge played well against the majestic, jagged, razor-sharp peak of Mount Hood. Emma told him four hundred men and women, part of a WPA project, had built the lodge during the Great Depression.

"This way," Emma directed as she steered him toward the Ram's Head Bar, already more than half full, the waitresses already busy serving up hot drinks with trendy names attached, spiced with just about every liquor available for the early morning skiers. The chairlifts didn't open until nine, which gave the skiers a chance to buy their lift tickets, eat a hearty breakfast at either one of the two lodges, or just gather in the bar for relaxing conversation before hitting the slopes.

They threw their gear on a table nestled in one corner of the bar, giving them clear view of the entrance to the lodge. Once settled, they pretended to casually scan the crowd already assembled in the bar, their eyes peeled for any sign of their quarry. No David Carlson—not yet anyway. Andy hadn't really expected it to be so easy; it rarely was. But he had a positive feeling about today—always a good sign. He wasn't sure, however, if it was simply because Emma had accompanied him, or he was about to break the case wide open.

David was close, he could *feel* it. But would today be the

day? After months and months of often tedious investigation, would it end as so many of his investigations had?—with a whimper and not a bang, closing in for the kill with a simple visit to the local police station, giving them his spiel, laying out the facts, perhaps even accompanying them on the arrest.

Not much fanfare usually, but maybe that's the way it should be after all the pain and suffering the family had gone through.

"What're you thinking about?" Emma asked, watching the play of emotions cross his face.

"Ummm?" he said, breaking out of his reverie.

"You had the strangest look on your face just now."

"I did?"

She nodded and smiled. "Kind of, unfocused, dreamy."

Andy smiled back at her. She was beginning to know him again, without even recognizing it, without even realizing they'd known each other better than they'd ever known anyone else in their lives.

Instinctively, he clasped her hand resting lightly on the rough-hewn, hand carved table. "This is the day, Emma, I can *feel* it." His soft, gentle voice sent shivers down her spine.

Did he mean this was the day they found David, or the day they confronted the overwhelming attraction they felt for each other? she wondered, enjoying the feel of her hand in his.

When the cocktail waitress came around, she made a fuss over Emma, immediately recognizing her from her nightly program. It was the one thing Andy found a little unnerving, her celebrity. In his line of work, it was important to blend into the background, keep his quarry unaware of his scrutiny. But, now, everywhere they went, people came up to them and chatted with Emma as if they knew her personally. That she was a popular local celebrity was easy to see, and Andy was banking on her credibility to sucker David in on their story if they happened to run into him, playing on the fact that he wouldn't be suspicious of Andy if he was with her, her status assured and quite visible in this west coast area.

They each ordered a 'Mogul Masher,' the waitress's

recommendation, which was simply hot chocolate with a splash of butterscotch schnapps in it, topped with a generous dollop of whipped cream. Side by side with their feet up on the empty chairs in front of them, they looked like everyone else in the bar who'd stopped in for one last warmer-upper before getting out onto the well-groomed slopes. Only the sharp once-over they gave every newcomer to the lodge separated them from the other occupants of the quickly filling bar.

"Do you think we'd have a better chance of spotting him if we were near the ticket office? He'll have to buy a lift ticket to ski, won't he?" Andy asked, trying to cover every angle.

"I thought about that, but you can buy tickets all over town, at just about anyplace that sells ski equipment, and usually for a few dollars less than you'd pay up here," Emma replied.

"So you think he probably bought one in town?"

"I'm saying the odds are he did, if he correctly guessed how crowded it might be up here. The lines can get pretty long, and since he's new to Oregon, I think he'll be attracted to here, the main lodge, instead of the Wy'East Day Lodge, at least initially. Much more the touristy thing to do. This place is going to be a madhouse in a couple of hours. You're new here, what would you do?"

"I think I'd buy my ticket in town and, with the time I saved doing that, come in here and have a quick one before going out."

Emma smiled. It'd been her idea that they come in the bar and wait and Andy had just given her his stamp of approval of her plan. And even if he didn't end up coming into the bar, it had still been a good idea.

"If he doesn't show up in here within, say, the next few hours, we should probably move over to the day lodge. You can watch people come in off the slopes from the bar over there, too, plus the whole place is a lot bigger than over here. It'll be easier for him to find a place to eat if he comes in for lunch," Emma said, her knowledge of the area coming in handy. Andy agreed.

"Or we could split up, one of us stay here," she threw out.

Andy pretended to give the suggestion serious thought. He said, "We'd increase our odds of spotting him, but I think we'd be too conspicuous. One person, sitting around in one place, staring, or wandering around, giving everybody the once over might be noticed by someone aware he's being looked for."

His argument was a good one, but it wasn't the real one. He didn't want to split up, it was as simple as that. He wanted every minute he could get with her, every second. After years and years spent apart, he wasn't going to waste away any opportunity to be with her. His investigation was important—especially since his personal goal was to get the two boys home to their mother by Christmas, and time was running out. He had no intention of endangering the outcome of his investigation, but having Emma near him, instead of off on her own would not compromise the outcome, of that he was certain. If David was up there, they'd find him, without having to split up.

"So we'll just sit here talking, like we're old friends, with our eyes peeled on the doorway. Very normal, nothing unusual to the casual observer," he added with just a trace of sadness.

Talking, like old friends. Why did his statement bring on such a sudden bout of nostalgia in her? As if...as if she'd done this very thing with Andy before.

They sat quietly for a while, watched the people milling around them, jockeying for a spot in the popular lounge, until Emma could resist the strange pull of Andy's presence, his words, no longer.

"Old friends," she murmured, breaking the silence, dark brown eyes staring directly into deep blue. "We are, aren't we, Andy?"

Andy's eyes widened at her simply stated, yet wondrous words. He only wished the setting of her query, these important revelations, could have been different, more private, perhaps more romantic, but there was nothing to be done about it now, not without out and out lying to her, and he wouldn't do that.

With just a moment's hesitation, he said, "Yes," his penetrating gaze never left her own searching eyes.

Emma tried to blink back the tears welling up in her eyes. "You...you and I knew each other from...from before?"

Nodding, Andy gently held her hands in his own, his eyes growing soft. "We grew up together, back in Boston." At the look of confusion in her eyes, he said, "I was born in Minnesota, but when I was about six years old, my family moved to Boston, right next door to you."

"But didn't you recognize me? Or were you waiting for me to say something?"

"Emma," he began slowly, feeling his way. He'd dreamed for years of this moment, he needed to be very careful now what he revealed. "I'd have recognized you anywhere, no matter how many years had passed. But I had a pretty good idea you wouldn't recognize me. I...know what happened, what you went through. Running into you at the station was no accident. I've been searching for you for years. When I found you here, I didn't want to upset you, scare you away from me with knowledge of your past. I was afraid that...that if I blurted out I knew you from before, you might not believe me, or that it might trigger some adverse reaction. It was enough that I could feel you knew me. And I hoped that, given time, you'd remember me, or at least surmise you knew me. And you did."

"But Andy, I still don't remember anything!" she cried, tears of frustration spilling out onto her cheeks. She must have known, deep down, unconsciously, from the moment she'd been introduced to him, that Andy had played an important part in her life, a part she'd suppressed in the deep recesses of her damaged mind. Those were the feelings that had been tugging at her so furiously since the moment they'd met.

"I didn't recognize your name, your face; I don't know how well we knew each other or if we'd even done anything together, but I knew you Andy, I knew," she shook her head, still reeling in surprise at her own subconscious feelings.

"Sssh," he said, trying to stem the flow of tears. He moved

closer to her, put his arm around her, tried to calm her. "Don't you see? Your *feelings* are all that's important, not that you couldn't remember my name. Those same feelings we've felt for each other so many years ago have stood the test of time, of those awful circumstances beyond our control that pulled us apart in the first place. And whatever questions you have, I can answer them—I was there—if it's what you want, if you feel strong enough to handle the burden of the past now. And you'll know the truth of what I say, you'll *feel* the truth, Emma, like you have since the first day at the station when Ray Hollander brought me down and introduced us. And if you don't want to talk about the past, that's fine too." In fact, it was better for them both if she didn't press him too much for details.

He pulled one hand free and drew a handkerchief out of his pocket, gently brushing away her tears.

"Us," she murmured, her voice hoarse, "I want to know about us."

Andy smiled at her, squeezed her tightly held hand. That she had zeroed in on their relationship, and not her father's death was the direction he had hoped she would take.

"Not long after my family moved in next door to you," he told her, "we took a shine to each other. You were kind of a tomboy, even at five years old, and you used to follow me everywhere. I pretended I didn't like it at first, but you were never fooled. From almost the first day I moved in, we've been friends, good friends, inseparable. And, as the years passed our friendship grew to something even more permanent, more meaningful."

"More permanent?" she sniffed, drying her eyes. She found the story mesmerizing, not only because she was such an integral part of it, but because it was almost as if she was re-experiencing it as he related it. Was it snippets of her memory finally coming back?—or simply the comfort of memories shared, surrounding her like an old woolen blanket, making her feel warm inside, cared about, loved...missed even.

"Our friendship evolved into something much deeper, for

both of us. I couldn't even tell you when exactly it happened, but suddenly, or maybe it wasn't even suddenly, I don't know, but suddenly we weren't just good friends anymore. By the time we were in high school, we both knew we wanted to be together, always. Maybe it was because we'd grown up together and knew each other so well that we were able to identify what we felt for each other as the real thing, even at such a young age, I don't know. All I know is what we had back then was *real,* Emma." He brought her tightly held hands up to his face, keeping them there, pressed warm against his cheek. "We loved each other, and after all these years, searching for you, nearly giving up hope that I'd ever find you again, you've come back to me. I'm still in love with you, Emma. I've never stopped loving you through all these years. And I never will."

Oblivious of the crowded tables surrounding them, their corner table giving them at least some semblance of privacy, the tears began to flow freely again, for both of them, as they realized the truth of his simply stated words. That they'd found each other after nearly ten years was remarkable; that they still loved each other with the same intensity of their shattered youth was nothing short of a miracle. For Andy it was the culmination of years and years of frustrating search, of heartbreaking disappointments, this love of his life sitting next to him. With Emma, it was like coming home to her feelings, feelings she never remembered having, never realized she was capable of, until now, until Andy's words brought back those same feelings she'd missed all these years but never been able to quite identify in the recesses of her damaged memory.

"Oh, Andy," she cried, "You've been looking for me all this time?"

"I wouldn't have ever stopped looking for you Emma, not ever. Sometimes it was the only thing that kept me going, the hope that I'd find you again one day."

Slowly, with infinite care, he pulled her close, his lips descending softly upon hers, the remembrance of hundreds of just such kisses flowing through him, thrilling him. A gentle kiss, a kiss full of promise and longing, lasting forever and just moments, never long enough, yet enough to convey the deep and abiding love they'd felt for each other. If nothing else ever came back to her of her buried past, the texture, the softness, the *taste* of Andy's kiss was enough.

And she reveled in the fact that she *did* remember. Everything he'd said about them had a ring of truth to it and his searing kiss confirmed it. Maybe this was why she'd never been able to truly give herself to Niles—or any other man, for that matter. Perhaps she knew, even if it was only subconsciously, Andy would come for her, find her again someday.

"Andy..." she hesitated, trying to catch her breath at these new, yet wonderfully familiar sensations. "I...don't believe in love at first sight...and...I didn't remember you that first day, and yet...I just knew there was something about you, something special."

"I'm not sure I believe in love at first sight, either. Lust maybe," he answered honestly, "but not love. But I do believe in destiny," he smiled, looking deep into her eyes. "I know it sounds kind of corny, but how else can you explain how we've been able to find each other after so long, never finding anybody else, never marrying. Even with you and Niles—"

"I broke off our engagement last night," Emma blurted out. It was important Andy know she was through with Niles.

"I thought something like that must have happened." At her look of surprise, he pulled her left hand up to his lips and kissed the spot where her engagement ring had been. "I noticed it missing the minute you got in the car this morning."

"I've never been really comfortable with the thought of marrying him," she sighed. "I don't think I would have gone through with it, even if you hadn't shown up and gotten me all confused."

"And do you know why?"

"Why?" she asked, her eyes never leaving his.

"For the same reason I never found anyone to take your place. You were always there, whether you knew it or not. Just like I was here with you. The way we feel for each other has stood the test of time—don't you see? It's why you never fell in love with anyone else, not really. We both might have tried to fool ourselves, consciously or otherwise, that we were over each other, or that we'd find someone else we'd want to spend the rest of our lives with. But it wouldn't have ever worked out." He pulled her close, his eyes caressing her face. "We were lucky back then, and now too. We'd found each other, chosen each other, and we never, ever let go."

Twenty-Two

Andy spent the next few hours sharing with Emma stories of their growing up years. Mindful of the reason for being there in the first place, they managed to keep up their vigil of any newcomers to the bar, although their mission was decidedly overshadowed by their desire to get to know one another again, catch up on each others' lives. And anybody who happened to glance in their direction would have seen a very affectionate couple seemingly engrossed in themselves, content to shut out the rest of the world.

Around them, the Ram's Head Bar filled up to overflowing during the height of the morning rush, then slowly the crowd receded a bit as the skiers took to the slopes. And although they'd meant to move over to the Wy'East Day

Lodge around lunchtime in the hopes of spotting David over there, before they knew it, the lodge was filling up again with skiers with wind-reddened cheeks and healthy appetites clomp clomping through the bar in their heavy boots looking for a place to put their feet up, grab something hot to eat, something refreshing to drink, thaw out.

At the realization it was already lunchtime, they decided to stay put. There was no way they'd find a table in the other lodge now, better to keep the strategic spot they had and hope David would somehow—if he was even there—make his way to them.

They had deliberately strung their stuff out on a table for four, a luxury during the busy part of the day, and they had precariously hung on to it all morning in the hopes it would draw David Carlson to them. The chairs had been especially hard to hang on to during the rush hours—they'd turned away a half dozen or so requests for the chairs with the excuse they were expecting another couple. They had no idea whether David, if he was up on the mountain, would be alone or with someone, so they needed both chairs, just in case, to reel him in.

It was Emma who first realized that the bearded man weaving through the packed bar was David Carlson, and even then she almost missed seeing his meandering search for a place to sit, she'd been so engrossed in Andy's reminiscing. They'd both passed over his entrance; his heavy, snow-encrusted beard had thrown them both off, and they had just enough time to inconspicuously clear the gear off the table before David's eyes turned their way. Before they had a chance to exchange another word, he was standing in front of the empty chairs, asking if they minded if he sat down for a spell.

Barely able to hide the triumph in his eyes, Andy swung his feet off the chair in front of him, sat up slowly and invited the other man to take a seat. The first part of their plan seemed to be working to perfection; hopefully the rest of their strategy would.

Andy stuck out his hand and said, "Bob Anderson," as David took a seat. He'd decided earlier not to use his own name on the off chance David had found out from relatives or friends he was dogging his trail. "And this is—"

"Emma Stuart," the other man finished, taking her hand in his. "I've seen your show on TV. I'm Jim Carlson. Thanks for letting me join you." He sat down opposite them.

"No problem." *David James Carlson!* It was him, no doubt about it. Andy could tell by the pleased look on Emma's face that she, too, had easily made the connection. David probably thought her smile was in response to being recognized. Andy gingerly sat back down in his chair, grimacing slightly.

"Take a bad spill?" David inquired as he signaled the passing cocktail waitress.

Shifting in his seat as if trying to get comfortable, Andy nodded. "I think I must have pulled a muscle or something. No big deal."

"I told him he should go in and get it checked out," Emma said, shrugging, "but he doesn't listen to me."

Seeming to ignore her, Andy said, "You up here for the festivities?"

David nodded. "I was up here a couple of weeks ago, and I heard a lot of people talking about it then, saying how fun it usually is. Thought I'd give it a try if the weather cooperated. You can't ask for better conditions than they've got up here today."

"I know," Andy shook his head, regret in his voice. "We came up yesterday for a little night skiing. We've had reservations for this weekend for six months. But the snow was a little icy last night and I took a spill. I woke up this morning to several inches of new snow and my back hurting like hell. Good timing, huh?" he grimaced, playing his role to perfection.

David nodded in sympathy and accepted a beer from the harried cocktail waitress. "Your girlfriend's right. You might want to go in and get it checked."

"I've already gone down to the First Aid room here. They said I might have jammed a vertebra or something, nothing real serious," Andy shrugged.

"You still might need to see somebody about it, just in

case," David said, pulling a brown paper bag out of his backpack.

Emma was silent, listening closely as Andy orchestrated the conversation exactly to his liking.

"Oh? You have back problems?"

"I certainly hope not," he smiled, then added, "I'm a chiropractor. You may have just kinked your back up a bit. If that's the case, a chiropractor could fix it in a snap," he said, busily unwrapping his sandwich.

"See, I told you, honey," Emma said. Turning to David, she said, "I told him this morning we could run into town and see if we couldn't get him in to see a doctor, or maybe even a chiropractor, but he wanted to stay up here," she shook her head in mock dismay.

"We've had these reservations for *six months,*" Andy protested. "Besides, it doesn't hurt all that much."

They argued good-naturedly between themselves as David Carlson quietly sipped at his beer, observing the two of them.

"Tell you what," he said, setting aside his half-eaten lunch. "If it's still bothering you when you get back to Portland, come see me." He fished around again in his backpack and pulled out his wallet. "Here's my card, give me a call," he said. This was the first opportunity he'd had to use his newly-printed cards.

Andy accepted the card. "Thanks," he said, pleased with himself. He didn't dare look at Emma, he'd never be able to control the joy threatening to spill out of him at the slightest provocation. He glanced down at the card before tucking it away in his pocket, just to make sure it was real. East Portland Chiropractic Clinic, it said, with a Gresham, Oregon address. Andy knew from studying the city map that Gresham was on the outskirts of Portland. In fact, if he remembered his map correctly, they'd passed near David Carlson's office on the way to Multnomah Falls the other day.

As they watched David continue on with his lunch, it occurred to both Emma and Andy that they hadn't eaten anything all morning. Two Mogul Mashers hardly constituted a meal—they'd had other, more important things on their minds.

But now, with their mission pretty much accomplished, their appetites came flooding back to them. Emma pulled out the lunch she'd quickly prepared for them while waiting for Andy to pick her up that morning, and the three of them ate companionably together.

Emma found David Carlson to be quite pleasant and easy to talk to, which surprised her. For all intents and purposes, this man was considered a kidnapper—a felon—but she didn't find it difficult to pretend otherwise. He seemed perfectly normal. Nobody would believe by looking at him that he was leading a dangerous double life. At least his apparent normalcy gave her hope that the two boys were doing all right.

Andy, too, was not finding it hard to stay in character. However, unlike Emma, he was not at all surprised at the other man's demeanor—he'd dealt with too many of his kind to be fooled. In fact, to him, these were the most dangerous kind—the most unpredictable—*because* they seemed so average, so normal. Fitting in well within a structured environment, they were the hardest to spot. He'd learned long ago, the hard way, how deceiving appearances could be.

Before he took his leave of them, David said he planned to do a few more hours of skiing before calling it quits, and perhaps, he'd offered, if they were still around, they could all get together again for a last drink before he headed back down the mountain. Emma and Andy had nodded in agreement, although they had no intention of taking him up on his offer.

As soon as David left the bar, Emma squealed in delight, holding Andy close. After congratulating themselves on a job well done, he pulled the card back out of his pocket and gently touched the raised letters with the tips of his fingers.

"Amazing, isn't it, how a simple little piece of paper could mean so much." He sat staring at the address, memorizing it, just in case, then tucked it carefully away in his wallet.

"Andy...what if he does come back in and tries looking us up?" Emma asked.

Gathering up their belongings, Andy said, "We just won't be here when he comes back, that's all. I think we've hogged this table long enough, don't you?" He didn't want to risk another meeting where an accidental slip of the tongue on either one of their parts could ruin everything.

"But we told him we were staying here tonight. What if he checks the register, tries to look us up that way? Won't he get suspicious if we're not registered?" she persisted.

She had a good point, Andy conceded. After he'd made such a fuss about not wanting to give up their reservation, it might appear a little odd to someone perhaps already paranoid, looking over his shoulder at every strange occurrence, scrutinizing everything. Of course, he might assume Andy's back had finally driven them off the mountain, but did they really want to take the chance?

Andy put their gear back down on the table, slumped back into the chair again and motioned Emma to sit back down.

"You're right," he said, a frown creasing his face. "Any suggestions?"

Emma shrugged, looked away from him. "We...could stay the night," she said hesitantly.

Andy stared intently at Emma, surprised at her suggestion. They both knew she was talking about getting a room, one room, a room they'd share.

Emma looked back at him, meeting his pointed stare unwaveringly. "This place is packed. Chances are, they'll laugh at us when we ask about a room. But lets try anyway."

Andy pulled her close. "Are you sure, Emma?" he said, searching her face.

She took his face between her hands, kissing him gently, her heart beating wildly at her bold suggestion. "We've got ten years to make up for, Andy. Don't you think we've wasted enough time?"

He smiled broadly and held her to him, could feel her tremble in his loving embrace. "Ten years...it felt like a lifetime. *Ten minutes* is too long for us to be apart any longer," he whispered softly in her ear.

Twenty-Three

It took no small amount of wheedling to get them a room for the night, and then only after Emma promised to bring the *Evening Magazine* crew up in the spring for another story on the famous lodge. There had already been a long waiting list of people wanting to stay the night if, by chance, there happened to be a last minute cancellation, and Emma's promise of a story finagled them to the top of that list. Luckily, not long after negotiating themselves to the number one spot, there had been a cancellation.

The room they were given was certainly not luxurious, but then none of Timberline Lodge's rooms were. In fact, compared to other resort hotels, they were quite stark, part of the international appeal and charm of the popular lodge. The walls made of knotty pine planking, hardwood floors covered with thin throw rugs in Indian patterns, an old-fashioned telephone on the wooden, crate-style bedside stand, and the trundle-like bed, combined to give the small room a rustic, outdoorsy feel.

But the furnishings mattered little to Emma and Andy. They were so wrapped up in each other, the spare surroundings could have been the most luxurious in the world and they wouldn't have noticed. All they were aware of was each other, and what this long awaited moment meant to them both.

They no longer cared about David Carlson. And if, by chance, he did come looking for them, they were safely registered. But he would not be able to contact them—Do Not Disturb firmly in place on the door to their room, and the telephone safely off the hook virtually guaranteed no interruption.

Entering their room, they dumped their gear on the floor just inside the door, and Andy led Emma to the bed, where he left her briefly while he shut the curtained windows, dimming the room just enough to bathe it in a soft light, illuminating her face, a face he had held so dearly in his memory, had cherished, had longed for.

There was a small fireplace in their room, and Andy quickly stoked up the glowing embers as Emma lay across the bed, fully clothed, quietly watching him, a look of apprehension mixed with subtle desire on her face.

Even though there was still waning daylight outside, the heavy snow pack surrounding the lodge had illuminated their room, but with the curtains closed their small room seemed sheltered, the rest of the world far away, a world they were both determined would not intrude on this day they had waited so many years for.

Andy returned to the bed. He smiled down at Emma, then stretched out beside her and pulled her close. He kissed her gently, slowly, savoring the taste of her soft, full lips. As his kisses increased in intensity, her tongue moved within his mouth, hot, searing, begging him for more. His hands moved to caress her breasts, and he could feel her erect nipples, even through the thickness of her ski sweater. He slipped his hand under the soft folds and captured a hot, swollen peak. Emma moaned at the electrifying contact of his warm, sensitive fingertips, wanting more, much more.

She broke free of his embrace just long enough to pull her sweater and bra off, then took his head in her hands, guiding him to her throbbing breasts, the first contact of his searching lips pulling a cry of pleasure from her. He bent over her and licked her swollen nipples, taking first one, then the other in his mouth, sucking gently.

"Andy..." she moaned, her husky whisper thrilling him to the innermost reaches of his being as her body arched up against his. She'd never felt such pleasure, such outright *lust* for a man, as she was experiencing under Andy's exploring hands. She could feel him long and hard against her thin ski pants, and suddenly, she *had* to see him, *had* to feel him inside her.

For the first time in her life, she became the aggressor as she pulled away Andy's thick sweater, thrilling at his bare, heavily muscled chest. She ran her hands across the smooth broad expanse, reveling in the feel of the taunt, sculptured muscles, her silken touch sending shivers through him as he lay pliant beneath her. She stopped briefly in her explorations when she came to the raised scar on his lower abdomen, running her fingertips across it, then following it with her lips, making Andy shiver in delight.

Moving lower, she unbuckled his pants and helped him pull free of them. Her hand touched him, moving gently up and down, caressing him, and Andy felt as if he'd go mad with pleasure and desire. Pulling her on top of him, he kissed her slender throat, her throbbing pulse beating hard against his lips. Then she sank down upon him, impaling herself as the heat of her womanhood and the quickening tempo of her hips sent a fire raging through his loins.

Never before had Emma felt such intense pleasure, a pleasure bordering on pain, driving every thought from her mind. From far away she could hear Andy calling her name, whispering words of love. The pace of their lovemaking quickened, every nerve in her body was at the peak of sensitivity, every kiss, every stroke of Andy's hands filled her with pleasure until she thought she would pass out from the intensity of it.

When he felt Emma near her climax, Andy gripped her tightly to him, arching against her, stroking, stroking, trying to prolong the pleasure for her. As she cried out his name, climaxing with him, her breath came hot and quick against his neck; her eyes shut tight, trembling with astonishment at the intensity of her first orgasm.

"Andy," she whispered hoarsely as she struggled to right her reeling world. "I never knew..." she gasped, eyes widening as she felt him harden inside her, ready for her again.

With infinite care, Andy maneuvered himself so he was atop her, never once losing contact with her smooth, silky flesh. Slowly, he began the sinuous rhythm again, watching the wondrous expression on her face, driving him on and on and on, wanting to satisfy her like he'd never satisfied anyone before, knowing instinctively that she was new to this pleasurable world of sex and sensuality.

Emma was certain she'd never be able to experience what she'd just gone through with the same urgency, same intensity again, but she was wrong. Andy's skillful lovemaking moved her closer and closer to her climax once again, and she felt the expanding, erotic heat grip her, sending rippling flames of desire through her. And when it was over, they both trembled at the magnitude of their desire and love for each other.

They lay quietly for a time, neither speaking, holding each other close, afraid to break the idyllic mood. Spotting the dying fire, Andy moved away from Emma's warmth, reluctant to leave her side even for a moment as he quickly stoked the dying embers back to life, then returned to Emma's waiting arms. They dozed for a time, a deep, contented slumber. And when they awoke, they made long, languorous love again, both seemingly insatiable, as if they wanted, *needed* to make up for the years they'd lost in just a few short hours.

Emma reveled in Andy's sensuality, amazed at the depth of passion she felt for the man lying next to her. Unbidden, tears of love welled up in her eyes at the thought of those lost years. With simple understanding, Andy kissed away her tears, his heart filled with a joy and contentment he'd almost forgotten he had the capacity to feel.

They slept some more, then woke up ravenous. As neither one of them seemed to have the energy it would take to get dressed for a meal in the main dining area, they decided to stay sequestered a bit longer and just order something to eat from room service. Feeding each other from the plates strewn out on the bed in their temporary haven, they exchanged kisses, laughing, immersing themselves in the simple pleasure of each other's company.

Morning came sooner than either of them wanted or expected, and they lolled around in the bed, exploring each other's bodies, making love passionately, then slowly, learning each other's likes and dislikes, probing, sharing, memorizing every inch, as if they couldn't get enough of each other.

It amazed Emma how she was able to give herself to Andy with such total abandon, never once feeling the familiar tug of revulsion she'd so often felt with the few lovers of her past. Could it be because she was truly in love for the first time?—or was it because she had been the aggressor with Andy, the one to initiate the lovemaking?

Or could it be because Andy was the best she'd ever been with? She smiled and held him close, never wanting to let him go.

"Andy?" she murmured, her face nestled in the comfortable crook of his shoulder.

"Ummm," he said, his eyes closed, enjoying the feel of her next to him.

"Did we...when we were younger..."

"Fool around?" he said, a languid smile on his face, his eyes still shut.

"Unh huh." She pulled her face up next to his, kissing him. If they'd been intimate in their youth, perhaps it would explain why she seemed to be so comfortable, so sensually abandoned with him.

Andy grinned widely. "Emma, we'd been going together for years, what do you think?" he said mischievously, a twinkle in his deep blue eyes.

"So did we?" she said, wrapping her arms around him, pulling him close again. Surely she should have remembered *this!*

"You really want to know?"

"Yes."

"We fooled around a little."

"What do you mean by a little?" she persisted.

"Let's just say I was on familiar ground here," he turned in her arms, caressing her soft breasts. "Although I have to admit, they've filled out some since then," he leered at her.

Emma, embarrassed all of a sudden, blushed and buried her head in his neck.

Andy gently pulled her away, looked deep in her eyes, serious all of a sudden.

"You were a good girl, Emma. Your mother brought you up right. We never did anything but a little heavy petting. I never really pressed you beyond that. We both knew we were going to marry each other, we thought we had all the time in the world, so the pressure to have sex was never a major issue with either of us." Smirking, he added, "Of course, if I knew back then what I know now, I probably wouldn't have been so patient." He pulled her to him again, desire welling up inside of him.

Emma could feel his passion flaming again, was pleased she could arouse him so easily. But at the mention of her mother, she was suddenly curious to know more about the woman who had died so abruptly when she was just a young girl of fourteen.

"What was she like, Andy?" she asked hesitantly.

Andy paused in his caressing, and wondered if now was the time to tell Emma the truth about her family. He had to tell her, at least part of it, before Niles did, or she would never understand his actions on the awful day her father was killed.

Andy smiled into her eyes, his voice gentle, belying the sudden turmoil inside him. "I knew your mother well. I was always underfoot at your house, especially after my dad died, but your mom didn't seem to mind. You're a mirror image of her, Emma. And you've even inherited her drive for perfection." He smiled at her, a small, sad smile full of memories. "When she died," he said, "I think I took it just about as hard as you did." She'd died suddenly, and without warning, when a blood vessel had burst in her head. A brain aneurysm, he remembered them calling it.

"And my father...he grieved terribly," Emma said.

"Yes," Andy said, surprised. "You remember?" Emma's mother had been only thirty-six years old when she'd died, and her death had cast a pall on Emma's father's life—he never recovered from it.

"No, I...I'm not sure. It's kind of like when I met you. Somehow, I just sense he suffered terribly."

"Emma," Andy said, his voice serious. "I think it's starting to come back to you, your memory. Slowly...little bits and pieces of it." Perhaps he wouldn't have to tell her the whole story after all. Perhaps she'd remember it all by herself.

"It's so frustrating. It's like...like it's just sitting there in the back of my head, waiting for me to call it forward. But every time I try, nothing seems to happen."

"It'll come, just don't fight it. Maybe it's like when you're trying to remember the name of something you know you should know the name of—like a book title, or who starred in what movie, but it just won't come to you. Have you ever noticed, if you turn your thoughts to other things, the name or title you were kicking yourself to remember all of a sudden just pops up in your brain? I know I'm simplifying what might be happening to you, Emma, but something definitely seems to be going on in there," he said, kissing her forehead.

Emma moved out of Andy's embrace, sat up on one elbow, scrutinizing him.

"Or maybe it's you, Andy. Maybe...maybe seeing you again has sparked something in my memory. To be honest with you, I wasn't all that interested in trying to recover my past—or maybe I was afraid to, until you appeared. Do you think it's possible that, subconsciously, I never thought I was strong enough to face my past unless you were there to help me?"

Andy rolled onto his back, his arms clasped behind his neck. He stared at the ceiling, contemplating Emma's latest theory. She'd already told him she remembered nothing about her past—what little she did know of her family had been provided by Ben Stuart. When he'd mentioned to her that he, too, knew the doctor, she'd seemed pleased, and he hadn't shared with her his true opinion of the man. The fact that Dr. Stuart had given her such a limited, sanitized version of her family life after the death of her mother made Andy's job all the more difficult. He wasn't certain just what truths Emma was strong enough to handle—or even what he should reveal—if she continued to press him on details of her buried past. That he might be the catalyst to her memory returning bit by little bit was hard to determine. The timing did seem to indicate he was, at least partially, responsible for portions of it flooding back to her, and her newfound desire to know more about herself seemed to be directly tied to him. Perhaps this was exactly what Ben Stuart had been afraid of…

"Is it really…that bad?" she said, worried at his hesitation, still unsure if she really wanted to know. If the reality of what happened so long ago was devastating, perhaps the truth of it, coming from Andy, wouldn't be so horrible, so hard to face.

Andy kept his gaze on the ceiling, afraid to meet her eyes, afraid she would be able to read the evasiveness of his answers.

"Emma," he said slowly, choosing his words carefully, "after your mother died, things were…were never the same for…for you or your father again. Especially for your father. You see, we still had each other, and just like when my own father was killed, you and I found comfort in each other. But your dad, he had nobody to share his grief with." He remembered well how, if it hadn't been for Emma, he probably would have collapsed when his father had been mercilessly shot down, just as his own mother gave up. When things had become especially rough for him at home, he'd always sought out Emma, knowing she would be there to soothe over his hurt and humiliation. And later, when Emma's mother had died, they had drawn even closer to one another, each suffering, each with their own personal demons. Only the two of them knew the full extent of their shared anguish, and what caused it. Only the two of them knew the truth. And now, at least for a while longer, only he knew. And that thought both saddened and relieved him. He was thankful in many ways that Emma had blocked out the horrible events that had taken place so many years before; he just hoped that if, or when, her memory did return, she would remember what they had together before the bad times, before the accusations, before the long separation—and especially what they had now. But would it be enough?

"He had me..."

Andy grimaced, not wanting to hurt Emma, but knowing there was no way around it.

"Yes, but...Emma you were the spitting image of your mother, and when your father looked at you, it always brought the pain and longing of his loss back to the surface where he couldn't control it."

"You mean he wouldn't have anything to do with me?"

If only it had been that simple, he thought sadly, how different their lives would have been today. Instead, he said, "No, not at all. He was still attentive to you, it's just that...that he never really *accepted* your mother's death, never really believed she was lost to him forever." His and Emma's lives had paralleled each other in many ways—the death of a parent at an early age, the tragic loss of the other as a direct result of the first one's untimely death.

"Ben told me he continued to sit on the bench after my mother's death, that he seemed to recover—"

Andy tried to keep his voice calm, tried to keep from shouting out to Emma that Ben Stuart was a liar, and worse than that, he was gutless and manipulating.

Ignoring his dark thoughts, he said, "Your mother had always been the driving force behind your dad, Emma. She was the one who talked him into vying for a judgeship. And it was she who helped him prepare his briefs, supported him, kept him organized. When she died, he was never the same. He...he had problems," Andy said, afraid now to go any further. He'd tried to protect her back then, and now he vacillated between coming right out and telling her the depth of her father's loss of control or continuing to gloss over that time of her life. He'd just moments ago thought of Ben Stuart as gutless, but perhaps he was becoming just as guilty. Besides, without Ben to corroborate his version of what happened, or unless Emma herself remembered, would she even believe him? Her mind had resisted the ugly truth once already. Would it continue to do so? And could he risk planting a seed of distrust in her at this juncture of their relationship?

"Emma..." he sat up on one elbow, facing her, his voice grim. "I really believe your father—just like my own mother—didn't want to continue on without your mom. He...he kind of lost control..." It had taken Andy years to get over his bitterness toward her father, forgive him for what he'd done, to accept the fact that he *wasn't* the same man Andy had looked up to and admired all his life, and even now he found it difficult to fight back the painful memories the total breakdown of a man he'd thought to be beyond reproach still seemed to generate in him. If he felt this horrible, he could only imagine what Emma must have experienced, could easily understand why she kept the memories suppressed.

Emma could read the turmoil, the indecision, the pain in Andy's eyes, and put her finger up against his lips.

"Enough," she sighed. "I've heard enough for one day. My head is starting to ache." They had all the time in the world to explore her past. She wanted a return to their earlier light, romantic mood. "But I know something that just might get my mind off my headache," she said playfully, boldly stroking him.

Andy's eyes widened with pleasure as he tried to block out his dark thoughts.

Later, with Emma fast asleep at his side, Andy's thoughts drifted back to Emma's last words.

Enough, she'd said. No—what he'd told her was not *nearly* enough, especially with Niles breathing down his neck, in hot pursuit of his records. He'd had his chance to tell her, and he'd blown it. But how does a person tell someone that one of the most admired men in the community, her father, had sought comfort from his daughter in the most perverse way a parent can?—that only months after his wife's death, he began to believe Emma was her mother, and had begun to force himself on her. And Emma had come to Andy for protection from the father she still loved, still needed, but loathed the sight of.

And Andy in turn had sought out Ben Stuart, not only a close friend of the family, but a noted psychologist.

But Dr. Stuart had delayed doing anything, afraid of damaging her father's sterling image, until it was too late.

Too late for Emma's father who lay dead in a pool of blood on the floor of Emma's bedroom, too late for Emma, hysterically crying in the corner of the torn bed, and too late for Andy, caught with his father's service revolver in his hand, standing over the unmoving form of the dying judge.

Twenty-Four

Neither one of them were anxious to leave the warm, comfortable confines of their cozy room, let alone their safe mountain haven, but Emma had an important morning shoot she couldn't miss the next day, and Andy needed to stake out the doctor's office where they'd discovered David Carlson was now employed. It wasn't enough he'd seemingly found David's place of business, he needed to locate the two boys—verify they were safe and sound before his work was done.

After reluctantly checking out of their room, they'd played around in the snow for a few hours, eaten dinner in the main dining room, then headed back to Portland.

Emma was in too wonderful a mood to want to face the possibility of squaring off with Niles again, so it was decided that they'd stop by her house, grab a change of clothes, then go back to Andy's hotel, thereby stalling, at least for one more day, a confrontation she was certain was awaiting her. She knew she was just putting off the inevitable, but she wanted to prolong the heady feelings she'd been experiencing ever since Andy had told her of their shared past. Not to mention the expectation of another night spent in his arms, making delicious love with someone who fired her to such a fevered pitch, every nerve in her craving him, sending her to heights of passion she'd never dreamed existed.

When they'd reached Andy's hotel room, they'd headed straight for the bed, and never once left it. Morning again rolled around much too soon for them. They'd held each other until the last possible moment, when finally Emma had to tear herself away from him with the promise that she'd join him on his stakeout later that afternoon.

"Karl? Niles. All you sent me was Andy Brannigan's current record. Did you check for a prior?"

"You got what I got. By the way, you know what 'mizpah' comes from? My secretary told me when she saw the stuff come off the fax."

"No, I don't know—"

"Comes straight from the Bible," he said, ignoring Niles' impatience. "It means, 'May the Lord keep watch between you and me when we are away from each other.' Funny, isn't it, how one word can mean all that. Niles?"

Niles was only half-listening to the other man's prattle. Instead, he was concentrating on the vital statistics of one Andrew Brannigan, noting that he had lived in Boston for a while.

Was there a connection, he wondered? The sketchy details Karl had been able to scrounge up on Andy Brannigan indicated he'd spent the majority of his youth there, just as Emma had—one of the few facts he *did* know about her—a definite connection to his growing suspicions. And the papers in front of him indicated Andy Brannigan was not only the head of this Mizpah Foundation, but one of its creators, not just one of the investigators. Could...could Andy possibly be someone out of Emma's past? he wondered, excitement coursing through his veins. If he was on the right track, it might explain Emma's strange behavior. But if this was so, why all the secrecy?

And could those words, that Mizpah thing Karl had gone on about, be a message, or a...a symbol? Niles wondered, determined to get to the bottom of it all, especially now that he might have found a link—a link that could possibly lead directly to Emma's mysterious, tragic past.

"Niles?" Karl repeated, "You still there?"

"Yeah," he said distractedly. "I was just thinking. Look, Karl, I need his juvenile records, if he's got any."

"Way ahead of you, buddy. I requested them, but what I faxed over to you is all they sent me."

"Then call them back, tell them you need a complete."

"I'll try, Niles. But you know, unless there's suspicion of a crime, they don't have to release them."

"Then tell them there's suspicion. Do whatever you need to do to get a copy, but get one. I need it—today!"

"I can't promise you—"

"Karl, you owe me. How many times have I come across when you needed me?"

"All right, all right," Karl sighed. "I'll do what I can."

"Right now?"

"Yeah."

"And you'll fax it to me as soon as you get it?"

"Yeah, yeah, you'll get it thirty seconds after I do," he said, then hung up.

Twenty minutes later, the D.A.'s office called Niles back.

"Jesus, Niles. You and I are even-steven in the favor's department starting right now."

"You get a complete?" Niles said.

"Yeah, it's coming. But some hard-ass back in Boston really put me through the ringer for it. He wanted to know what this Brannigan fella had done to make us want his file."

"What'd you tell him?"

"I gave him some crap about not being at liberty to discuss it right now, which, by the way, he didn't believe for even a second. Said he wanted proof of a crime before he'd send a copy. So then I got a little belligerent and told him I wasn't gonna let no desk jockey tell me what I could and couldn't have, and he better send me a complete, *pronto,* before I went over his head and requested it, from one D.A.'s office to another. The threat to leap-frog over him seemed to surprise him. Guess he didn't want to take the chance we weren't serious about the crime thing. He said he'd send it along today. Before the paper cools, I'll get it over to you."

"Thanks, Karl. I won't forget this one."

"You bet you won't, I won't let you."

Twenty-Five

"Goddammit! I told you to stall the guy, Dickie." Jack stormed around the room, threw his half-empty coffee cup in the wastepaper basket, then angrily grabbed his jacket off the coat rack.

"I tried," Dickie said, following the angry detective around the room. "The bastard threatened to go over my head."

"Jesus, Dickie, they all do. You know that by now," he raged. "You let some punk out there run your ass around in circles, asking for this, asking for that, next thing you know you're spending all your time filling requests for those creeps."

"He was from the *D.A.'s* office, Jack—I didn't have a choice. Where ya going?" he said as Jack headed for the door.

"Portland. You got a problem with that?" he glowered.

He'd virtually promised Andy a week, but that'd gone down the tubes in a hurry.

"No." Dickie Marshall, like most of the other guys at the stationhouse, knew anything that had to do with Dex Brannigan's kid, Jack made his business. Hell, they'd all done their part to protect the boy. But this time, his hands were tied. "Hey, Jack," Dickie said, following the angry detective out the door.

"What," Jack said over his shoulder, never breaking stride. He had a real bad feeling in the pit of his stomach and he was determined to act on it. He needed to get to Portland, and fast.

"I told him I'd send it to him today. But you know us desk jockeys," he shrugged, his voice deadpan, "we don't move too fast. Maybe I'll send it to him tomorrow, whadda ya say?"

Jack stopped, turned around and smiled at Dickie. It wasn't much extra time, but it was the best he could do, Jack knew. "Now that's the kinda news I like to hear," he said, cocking his head. "At least now I'll have a chance to get there before the sheet does."

"Hey, it's Dex's kid, right? We do what we gotta do."

Jack nodded, gave Dickie a thumbs up as he headed out the door, Dickie's words echoing in his brain.

We do what we gotta do, Jack thought sadly. Dexter Brannigan had taught his young son too well on that one.

Niles waited all afternoon in his office for the sheet on Andy Brannigan. He'd called the station half a dozen times looking for Emma and the last time he'd called, the receptionist had sounded irritated at hearing his voice yet again. He wanted desperately to go down to the station and wait for her there, but he was afraid of missing the fax when it came through. Instead, he called Karl again.

"I'm telling you, Niles, the rotten bastard's stalling. It's not like I'm not trying. First, I called him around one, wanted to know why he hadn't sent the sheet yet. He tells me he forgot. So then I call him about ten minutes ago and he tells me the computer's on the fritz, but promises me that absolutely, positively, it'll be sitting on my desk by morning. What can I do?"

So that was that. Niles had wasted the whole goddamned day waiting for the rap sheet, only to be told he'd have to wait one more day for it...maybe. He slammed the telephone down and grabbed his jacket off the back of his chair and left the office, hoping to catch Emma at the station.

"*Six times,* Emma," the receptionist said, wondering to herself what was going on between those two. There had been an edge to Niles' voice when he'd called, an air of desperation she'd never heard before. She handed Emma the messages and started to ask her what was going on. But her switchboard started ringing again, saving Emma from an embarrassing explanation.

And Emma didn't plan to stick around long enough at the office to receive, or return, any of Niles' telephone calls. She'd just dropped by to quickly finish her narrative for the evenings' show, then she was off to meet Andy. Just the thought of him, warm and waiting for her, brought a rush of desire. For someone who had been so disinterested in sex up until just recently, she seemed to be making up for lost time.

Niles missed Emma at the station by only a few minutes. If he hadn't stopped to make one last telephone call to her house, he'd have caught her coming out of the building.

When he approached the receptionist and was told she'd already left for the day, it took all his strength not to demand a look around, just to make sure she wasn't lying to him. Only the receptionist's genuine surprise at Niles' remark that Emma had never returned his calls made him believe she was telling him the truth. But his temper flared anew when Teddy emerged from the inner office, sidled up to Niles and asked him if he and Emma were going away for a few days.

"What do you mean?" Niles said, eyes narrowing.

Teddy immediately realized his blunder, but there was no

getting out of it now. "Emma's taking a few days off this week. I just assumed..."

Niles glared at Teddy, his eyes smoldering. Emma *never* took any time off. It was sweaty work just to get her to take a vacation.

"She what?"

"A...a few days," Teddy stammered. He'd never seen Niles angry before. He always seemed so calm, so controlled, but not now. "To...to straighten out a few things." Teddy had tried to get out of her what she'd meant by that, but she'd only smiled at him and told him it was none of his business. She'd said it with an edge of laughter to her voice, so he'd assumed it was nothing serious. She had been so animated today—so...*vivacious*—the whole crew had remarked upon the difference. Now Teddy had the sneaking suspicion that her cheerful, carefree mood had nothing to do with Niles Whitmann, and absolutely everything to do with Andy Brannigan. He thought it in Emma's best interest not to mention she'd added she wanted the film crew on call, just in case Andy's story broke within the next couple of days. Other than that little tidbit, she'd been happily silent about her plans.

"What things," Niles said slowly, his teeth clenched.

"I...I don't know—she wouldn't tell me."

Without another word, Niles left the building. Teddy heard his car peel out from where he still stood in the hallway, berating himself for his big mouth. He only hoped Niles didn't find her. But if he did, and Andy was with her...For some reason, Teddy had a sneaking suspicion Andrew Brannigan would be quite capable of holding his own against the wily attorney.

Twenty-Six

Andy Brannigan was in a fantastic mood. Not even the long, boring stakeout dampened his high spirits. Coming off the greatest weekend of his life, he was overjoyed at not only Emma's acceptance of him back in her life, but of the fact that even now, Karen Carlson was on her way to Portland. The sound of her voice when Andy had told her he'd found her ex-husband had brought tears to his eyes. He had cautioned her he hadn't made visual contact with her two boys yet, but she was so anxious about them, he hadn't had the heart to talk her out of coming until he could confirm their presence.

Instead, he'd wired her the money for a ticket, made reservations for her at the same hotel he was staying at, and made arrangements to pick her up at the airport later that same evening. Even the thought of Niles digging into his past did little to dampen his soaring mood.

His eyes lit up when he saw Emma's white Camaro round the corner to his left. As he'd instructed her to do, she parked a few blocks down from him and walked quickly back to the waiting rental car.

She slid into the seat next to him, a wide smile on her face, her expressive brown eyes brimming with happiness. After exchanging a long, lingering kiss, she asked him if she'd missed anything.

"Not a thing. It's been pretty quiet. A few people left the building at lunchtime, but I didn't see David." Glancing at his watch, he said, "I can't imagine they'll be open much longer, it's almost six o'clock. I've seen a couple of people leave already. Wait a second," he said, sitting up straighter in his seat. "Is that him?" He pointed to the figure leaving the building, an overcoat with the collar pulled up obscured his face, making it difficult to identify the man. But a gust of wind pulled the collar away from the face for just a second or two, enough to give them a positive I.D.

"It's him!" Emma said. Andy started the engine, ready to follow their quarry. "It looks like I got here just in time," she murmured.

"You must be my lucky charm," Andy said, bestowing a quick kiss before returning his concentration to David Carlson. "As soon as he pulls out, I'll try to get us as close to him as I can without calling attention to ourselves. There's a pencil and paper in the glove compartment. We need to get his license plate number down, just in case we lose him or it gets too obvious for us to keep following him."

David Carlson unlocked the door to a two-tone gray Chevy Blazer, and pulled out into traffic a block away from them. Andy pulled as close behind him as he dared, and Emma quickly jotted down his license plate number. With that small feat accomplished, Andy dropped further back in traffic, able to relax a little.

Emma had originally suggested they get a film crew in

place, record Andy tracking David for the story they were doing, but Andy had been afraid of the crew being spotted, instead hoping to arrange the filming of the reunion of Karen and her two sons, if everything worked out as they envisioned. This reunion, they'd both decided, would be the focal point of the whole story. They'd tell the story backwards, from the reunion, if Karen had no objections. And if they needed to, they could always reenact this part of his investigation, *without* the worry of being spotted.

Andy followed the Blazer, careful to stay a few car lengths behind, then had a brief scare when David pulled abruptly into the parking lot of a Safeway store. At first, Andy was afraid he'd been spotted, and David was trying to duck his tail. But when he parked the car and went into the store, coming out a few minutes later with a small bag of groceries, they both breathed a sigh of relief and resumed the tail when he pulled the Blazer back out into traffic.

After several minutes, following at a discrete distance, David finally turned into the driveway of a small, well-kept house. Andy swung over to the curb a few houses back and kept the motor running.

"Write this address down," Andy instructed Emma as he read the address out loud to her, closely monitoring David as he made his way to the front door and knocked. An elderly woman stepped to the door, exchanged a few words with David and motioned him inside.

"The baby-sitter?" Emma said.

"I think so," Andy squinted, a frown on his face. "We'll know in a minute." Just then, the door opened and David emerged carrying his younger son, Jacob. Andy knew it was him from the shock of red hair his stocking cap didn't completely cover. Andy grinned widely at Emma. "One son located and accounted for," he said.

As David was getting his son settled into the front seat of the Blazer, the door opened again and a young boy came bounding out to the curb. He didn't have the tell-tale red hair his brother had, but he had more than a passing resemblance to his father.

"Number two located and accounted for," Andy said, not even trying to disguise the smugness he felt.

After helping his other son inside the Blazer, David pulled out of the driveway and turned back toward where Emma and Andy were parked. Just before David and the two boys passed by their vehicle, Andy pulled the collar of his jacket up to conceal his distinctive hair color and quickly told Emma to slink down in her seat. Seconds after David passed them, Andy had the car turned around, following him again.

Just a few blocks away, David turned off the main street and into another residential area. Andy let him get even further ahead of him, conscious of the fact that he'd be much more visible to David now that they were off the main arterials. From a distance they could see David turn into the driveway of a light brown, neatly kept split-level home. David and his two sons got out of the Blazer and disappeared into the house.

Andy and Emma looked at each other and smiled. Karen Carlson's ordeal was almost over. When she arrived in Portland, they'd have wonderful news for her.

Twenty-Seven

Since they had a few hours before they were to meet Karen's airplane, Emma and Andy decided to celebrate the near end of his investigation by treating themselves to an expensive, leisurely dinner. At Emma's suggestion, they drove over to her house, made reservations at Atwater's, a popular eatery located on the thirtieth story of the U.S. Bancorp Tower in the middle of downtown Portland, and started to change for dinner.

Emma had been a little nervous when they'd pulled up to her house, but relaxed when she saw the empty driveway. She was still a bit jumpy about running into Niles, and Andy was quick to notice her unease.

Dashing around her room, grabbing things to change into

for dinner, Andy finally stopped her mad rush, pulling her down next to him on the edge of the bed.

"Emma, you're going to have to face him sometime," Andy said, reading correctly the reason behind her apparent nervousness. He, too, was afraid of another confrontation with Niles, but for a completely different reason. For three days now, Emma had avoided spending any time at her place—but it made no sense to feel shut out of her own home. And Niles wouldn't have anything on Andy for at least a few more days, so as far as he was concerned, neither one of them needed to rush around, afraid of running into her former fiancé. Andy was there—he wasn't about to make Emma face him alone, and he told her as much.

"I know," she sighed in agreement. "I know I need to quit avoiding him," she added, with little conviction, flopping back onto the bed. "It's just that...everything's been so wonderful the last few days, I don't want anything—*any-one*—to spoil it. I've already told him the engagement is off. I just don't see any need to rehash everything."

"And you won't have to," Andy said, laying back beside her. If he calls, don't avoid him. If he comes over, talk to him. I'll be here. The sooner he accepts the fact that you're with me, the better for both of you."

But he would never accept the situation, not without a fight. He had too much pride to just give up on her, she was sure of it. But she was afraid to tell Andy this, afraid of putting a damper on their wonderful day.

"Now," Andy said, stroking her hair, "go in there, and take a nice, long, hot shower. We don't have to be at the restaurant until eight. You've got plenty of time."

"But what'll you do?" she said, warming to the idea.

"Me? Oh, I don't know," he said, kissing her, caressing her. "A long, hot, leisurely shower sounds awful good to me, too..."

They never did make their dinner reservation. As it was, they barely made it to the airport to meet Karen Carlson's plane.

Karen and Emma took an immediate liking to each other,

chatting away as if they were old friends. Despite the desperate strain she'd been under, Karen looked a great deal better than the last time Andy had met with her. Obviously, the knowledge that her ex-husband had been located after all these agonizing months had done much to change her perspective on things. And when he told her the children had been found, safe and sound, she burst into tears of joy. For the first time since taking her case, Andy saw her smile, really smile; not that nervous, forced, just-to-be-polite smile he'd glimpsed in the past, but a genuine smile that even reached her eyes.

It was quite late by the time Andy got Karen settled in her room for the night and updated on all that had happened in the investigation since he'd arrived in Portland. The three of them agreed to meet in the hotel lobby at eight the next morning, then proceed together to the police station, all documents in hand.

Andy was pleased Emma had arranged to take the next few days off. He suspected this was something new to her, taking time off on the spur of the moment. But she'd wanted to be there when Andy wrapped his investigation up, not only because her personal involvement would play better on television when they finally got around to filming the segment for her show, but because she now felt as if she was an integral part of the investigation—that she'd earned the right to witness the end of it.

When they finally retired to Andy's room, they didn't immediately fall asleep. Too keyed up over the events of the day, they spent the next few hours discussing their future, now that this case seemed to be near an end. It was then that Andy told Emma his plans of moving the Mizpah Foundation's headquarters to Portland. She'd been surprised to find out he was not just an investigator for the organization, but the head of it. He told her there were four other investigators besides himself, but only he and one other were actually based in Washington. The others were strung out over the country, so moving the office to the Portland area would cause no major problems for any of the people involved, he was sure of it.

He then shared with her how the organization was started in the first place; how it had been Jack's idea, and how Jack had gone to his brother, and they'd talked his church into becoming involved financially. What he didn't tell her was how the organization turned out to be Jack's way of getting him involved in something worthwhile in his pursuit of Emma's whereabouts; or that it was Andy's money, money from his father's pension, that kept the organization afloat, along with a sizable amount from the Catholic Church, plus private donations from some of his father's buddies, like Jack and Dickie.

Andy's dream had always been to follow in his father's footsteps, become a cop, serve the people. But that dream had been shattered the day he'd been found standing over Emma's father's body. With his record, he wasn't allowed to carry a gun, or even own one for that matter. His father's gun, the one used to kill Malcolm Nash, Emma's father, was now in Jack's possession, for safekeeping. Jack had pulled a lot of strings just to get a hold of it, and then only because he knew how Andy had felt about his father's gun. It had been the only gun his father had ever carried in all his years as a Boston cop. To Andy it had symbolized everything his father had stood for; that and his father's badge had been the only concrete things he'd kept to remember his father by.

And now, all he was allowed to keep was the badge.

They talked about getting married as soon as everything could be arranged, and about Emma staying with the evening show she loved so much. They even talked about the separations they might have to suffer through if Andy continued as an investigator. Emma was selfish enough to want Andy with her always, but after meeting Karen, realizing firsthand the impact Andy had made on this woman, who she could easily see thought the world of him, she knew she couldn't allow him to give up what he did so well just to be with her. She needed him—desperately—but his wonderful talents had to be shared. Just knowing he would always return to her would have to be enough.

Emma brought up her stepfather's name again, and Andy still found it difficult to hide his dislike of Ben Stuart, even though things had turned out all right after all—no thanks to him, however.

What was worse, Emma wanted to invite the old man over to her house for dinner tomorrow evening, surprise him.

At first Andy balked at the suggestion, but immediately backed down when Emma's questioning gaze required an explanation from him as to why he didn't want to see him again. Andy had once sworn revenge on the old man, and now, if he really wanted, was his chance to follow through on his vow—give the old geezer the shock of his life. But he found he just didn't have the desire anymore. He had what he wanted—the only thing he'd ever really wanted, besides being a cop, and even that dream he'd unselfishly given up for Emma.

And there was absolutely nothing Dr. Stuart could do this time, to prevent them from being together.

In the morning, Emma, Andy, and Karen ate a light breakfast in the hotel restaurant, then made their way to police headquarters. Andy had done this many times before, so he knew the procedures to go through. He asked to speak privately with a detective, keeping to a minimum the people involved, thereby reducing the chance that somehow, some way, word might get back to David Carlson that he'd been fingered before the police had a chance to act on Andy's painstaking information.

The detective listened patiently to Andy's discourse, read over the divorce decree placing Karen Carlson as the custodial parent, verified in his computer that there was an outstanding warrant for David Carlson's arrest, then took down David's current address and place of business, along with the babysitter's address.

Everything seemed to be in order, the detective said, impressed by the thoroughness of Andy's investigation. Little was left to be done by his department but verify the man's and the children's identities and pick them up. The detective assured them they'd be able to make verification quietly, and if everything was in order, Karen would probably have her children back in her possession by tomorrow afternoon.

Then, in deference to all the work he'd done, the detective asked Andy if he'd like to accompany them on the arrest. Andy immediately accepted, then requested Emma and a two-man crew be allowed to shoot the reunion of mother and sons when they returned to the station.

The detective was a little hesitant until Emma promised him that he, too, would be captured on film. After that, he'd been putty in her hands.

If it wasn't for the fact that there was a chance the arrest could turn dangerous—although both Andy and the detective didn't really believe it to be an issue in this instance—Emma might have been able to talk the stalwart detective into letting her in on the arrest, too. But he drew the line there; it was going to be hard enough to talk the station chief into letting her film crew in the building.

After their meeting, Emma and Andy escorted Karen Carlson back to the hotel armed with the detective's number, along with Emma's home number, just in case she needed to get in contact with either of them for any reason. As soon as Andy deposited Karen and her two children safely on the plane for home, he was checking out of his room and moving in with Emma.

They'd already discussed flying back East together over the upcoming weekend to pack up his sparse belongings, close up shop in Washington, and say good-bye to his few friends. Except for the fairly close proximity of Jack and his cronies, there was very little in Washington Andy would miss.

Then Emma called Ben and invited him over for dinner, which he promptly accepted. She didn't mention she had a surprise in store for him, a much bigger surprise than even she was aware of, and Andy toyed with the idea of calling the old man at his office and tipping him off, lessen the blow a little, but then decided against it. The old doc was too cunning, and

Andy didn't want to give him an opportunity to stir up any additional trouble. He was already up to his neck in problems, he didn't need any more worries from a new source.

Besides, he reasoned to himself, he owed the slippery, deceiving doctor nothing, nothing at all.

Twenty-Eight

Around mid-morning, Niles finally received the eagerly awaited juvenile sheet on Andy Brannigan, and even though there had been a delay in getting it, it turned out to be well worth the wait. With a smile on his face—his victory smile—he re-read the paper in front of him.

Up until the time he was sixteen, Andy Brannigan had been clean, squeaky clean. But not long after his sixteenth birthday, he turned dirty, as dirty as a man could possibly get.

At sixteen, Andy Brannigan became a murderer. And what was worse, he'd murdered a public servant, a popular judge by the name of Malcolm Nash.

What Niles couldn't understand—what puzzled him the most—was why, considering who he'd murdered, he'd been allowed to be tried as a juvenile, instead of as an adult. State law said that, starting at age fifteen, a juvenile could be remanded to adult court.

But for Andy Brannigan, that didn't happen.

After murdering a *judge,* that didn't happen.

Instead of spending years locked up as normally expected for such a heinous crime, Andrew Brannigan spent no time whatsoever in prison; instead, he spent a couple of years in reform school—a relatively light sentence, all things considered.

Reform school, then parole—for murder.

It just didn't add up.

And how did Emma come into play? he wondered, staring straight ahead, deep in thought. Was he wrong in believing Andy was somehow connected to Emma's past? He shook his head in frustration. It was there, right in front of him, the puzzle waiting to be solved, he just knew it was. What...was...it?

Niles picked up the sheet of paper again, studying it. Andrew Brannigan had been arrested for the murder. He'd confessed to the crime, had undergone psychiatric examination. And the D.A.'s office had cut a deal with him. But why? Psychiatric examination...Ben Stuart was a psychiatrist. And Malcolm Nash...could he, could he possibly be Emma's father?

Niles thoughts were whirling, probing as he tried to get it all to come together the way he wanted, *needed* it to. Emma had experienced some trauma in her life, a trauma revolving around her father. Andy just might be someone out of her past. And Ben Stuart *was* from Emma's past...and perhaps Andy's too. It was all there in front of him, ready to come together.

Should he risk calling Ben and just asking him outright? he mused. With just conjecture, and a lively imagination, without proof positive, would Ben even tell him if he was on the right track? Niles shook his head.

No, he was sure Ben wouldn't tell him anything, not if it could possibly hurt Emma. Getting his answers out of Ben was the quickest way, if he was willing to cooperate, but it wasn't the only way.

Niles set the juvenile sheet aside, then placed another call to his friend at the D.A.'s office.

"Karl...who do we know at the D.A.'s office in Boston who's been around, say, ten years or so, who I can talk to?"

"Quite a little kicker on that juvvie sheet, eh?" Karl snorted.

"Do you know anybody?" Niles repeated, in no mood for small talk.

"Hey...I thought we were even—"

"Then this puts you one up on me."

Karl liked the sound of those words.

"Lemme think," Karl said, leaning back in his chair, drumming his fingers against the edge of the desk. "Tell you what, let me call you back. Georgia's from the East Coast, she just might have a name."

"Karl—"

"Yeah, yeah, I know. You want it yesterday. I'll do my best," he said, hanging up.

True to his word, Karl called Niles back twenty minutes later with a name. Forty-five minutes after that, every piece to the strange and twisted puzzle was neatly in place. And with the completion of the puzzle came the opportunity Niles had been looking for—the destruction of Andy's image—of Andy's *presence*—in Emma's life.

Niles strode out of the office, determined to find Emma, wherever she might be. He was done with trying to get through to her by telephone. Instead, he was going to drive out to her house, see if she was there. And if she wasn't, he was prepared to camp out there, waiting for her return, if need be.

Twenty-Nine

Earlier in the day, Emma had been a little surprised at Andy's reluctance to see Ben after all these years. He'd made some comment about springing that kind of surprise on an old man, but she'd poo-pooed the idea. Ben had never pressed her to remember the events that had sent her into a bleak vacuum of nothingness for two long years, rationalizing she'd remember when she was good and ready to. The memories, dimmed by time, he'd said, would not be as painful as they'd once been; that she'd met someone so pivotal to her past and not been adversely effected by it would please Ben tremendously, she was sure of it.

Now, cutting up fresh vegetables for a light snack before dinner, she said as much to Andy.

"Maybe he should have gotten you to face your past, Emma, instead of just playing a waiting game," Andy said quietly, his eyes transfixed by the slicing knife.

She paused in her cutting, looked up at him quizzically. "But what good what it have done, if I wasn't ready?"

"Then maybe he should have prepared you," he said. Why was he pursuing this? Was it because Niles was breathing down his neck, or because Ben would soon be there and Andy had no idea how the *good doctor* would react to his presence?

"Prepared me how?" she asked. She pulled a plate out of the cupboard and started arranging the cut up vegetables on the plate.

"I don't know. Filled you in on some of the details maybe."

"But he did, a little," Emma shrugged.

But not the important ones, Andy thought grimly.

"What's wrong, Andy?"

"Nothing." She arched her eyebrows, waiting for a response, some explanation from him. "I don't know," he said uneasily. "I guess...I guess what I'm trying to say is that...that sometimes things happen you just can't control. And...and no amount of 'I wish I could haves,' or...'I should have done this' type of...of excuses can change what's already been done. The best you can try to do is...is try to outlive your past, make up for it in other ways..." He knew he wasn't really making sense, but he didn't want to just blurt the truth out to her without trying to prepare her a little.

"Andy," she said, "Ben isn't going to bite you. If you're worried he—"

"No, that's not it at all," Andy interrupted, determined to have his say, tell her about her father. But just then the doorbell rang, forestalling any further confessions.

"That must be Ben." She arranged one last piece of vegetable, then wiped her hands on her apron. "*Relax*, Andy," she said, then gave his clean-shaven cheek a fleeting caress, trying to relieve the tenseness she saw there.

Andy sighed unhappily as he watched Emma's retreating back. From his spot near the kitchen door, he could hear her greet her stepfather warmly, mentioning she had a wonderful surprise in store for him.

Wonderful indeed, Andy thought wryly. He took a deep breath and rounded the corner of the kitchen.

"You!" Ben Stuart gasped, the color draining from his face.

"Isn't it fantastic, Ben? Andy Brannigan—you remember him, don't you?" Emma said enthusiastically, unaware of the profound shock Andy's unannounced presence was causing the seasoned doctor.

Before Ben could reply, the oven timer in the kitchen went off. Emma reluctantly pulled herself away, promising to be right back.

The pained expression on the doctor's face gave Andy little pleasure. For the first time in his life, Andy almost felt sorry for his scheming nemesis. But his next words erased Andy's moment of weakness.

"What are you *doing* here?" Ben seethed. "You…you *promised—*"

"I promised not to hurt her, that's all. As you can see, she's quite happy."

"Stay away from her, Andy, or—"

"Or what?" Andy smirked, in control.

"I'll call the police," he said, trying desperately to come to grips with his sudden frustration and rage at seeing Andy standing so calmly in Emma's home.

"Go ahead," Andy challenged. "Call your cronies. I did my time. Only Emma has the power to send me away this time. And as you can see, she's quite content having me here."

"Why did you have to interfere? You ruined her life once. If you loved her as you say you do, how can you risk doing it again? She's happy here."

Andy could see he was scared, but of what? Was he scared of what Andy might say, or scared of what Emma would remember? Or was he scared she'd plunge back into her netherworld, never to regain consciousness again if pressed to remember details of her tragic past?

"Is she? Living vicariously in front of the camera, her only *real* life, played out nightly in front of thousands of people tuned into just the right station? You're a *doctor,* you saw how much she worked, keeping busy so she wouldn't have to face what her life was really like. You told me earlier that her life was full, but you were wrong, Ben. Her life wasn't full—it'll never be full again until she can drink in all her memories, good *and* bad. And as for ruining her life," Andy said nastily, "I think you can share a good part of the blame, don't you?"

Ben gasped, that last remark hitting its mark. Andy could see he was afraid to acknowledge the truth of it, even to himself.

"But she's not strong enough—"

"How do you know? She was strong enough to survive the first time."

"We were lucky the first time," Ben said, his mouth set in a thin line of defiance as he tried to regain some control, the shock of Andy's presence in Emma's home still roiling through him.

"You continue to take credit for something you had no real control of, *old man.* That's all it is for you, isn't it?—control. Like tonight—it galls you to realize you can't control who she sees, what she remembers, how she acts. You're pathetic—" Andy bit off his last words as Emma entered the room again. With her eyes on the tray of drinks balanced in her hands, she was unaware of the combative stance of the two men exchanging heated barbs with one another. She set the tray down on the coffee table just as the doorbell rang again.

"Now who could that be?" she said distractedly, wiping her hands on her apron. The two men watched silently as she moved to answer the door.

"Niles!" she gasped, startled.

"I've got to talk to you, Emma," Niles said determinedly, noting the unfriendly look on her face.

"I'm busy right now, Niles," she said through the half-opened door. "Can it wait until tomorrow?"

"No, it can't," he said, pushing his way through, bent on having his say. This time, he wouldn't be put off. He glanced around the room and smiled maliciously at finding Andy there.

Andy's eyes narrowed. The look of triumph on Nile's face was not lost on him. Could he have gotten his juvenile record already? Not possible. Jack promised he'd hold them off for at least a few more days. And what Jack promised, Jack delivered. Unless...unless the bastard went over Jack's head to get them. Shit! All hell was going to break loose in a minute, and there was nothing he could do to stop it.

"Niles, you're interrupting—"

"Emma, this man is not who you think he is," Niles said, pointing an accusing finger at Andy.

Emma glared at Niles. "I don't know what you think you're going to reveal to me, Niles, but if it's the fact that I grew up with Andy, then you're too late. He's already told me."

"But has he told you the rest?" he said snidely, eyebrows arched.

This time Ben spoke up. "Niles! This isn't the time or the place to discuss this—"

"Oh, so now he's got you protecting him, is that how it is?"

"Protecting him—from what?" Emma said, confused.

"He's going to tell you about the day your father was killed," Andy said quietly, his gaze never leaving Emma. "And my role in his death."

"You're starring role!" Niles shouted. He wasn't going to allow Andy to steal his thunder by softening the blow any. The truth was going to be painful for Emma to hear, but better she learn it now, before Andrew Brannigan became so completely entangled in her life he ruined it again, along with her lucrative career.

"Niles," Ben warned, at a loss as to how to stop the awful confrontation taking place around him.

"What's he talking about, Ben?" Emma asked, turning to her mentor for support, her brows creased in puzzlement. "Andy?"

Andy felt like his heart was being torn from his chest; the pain, the humiliating memories long buried were rising up to destroy him yet again, and just like before, there was absolutely nothing he could do—would do—to stop it from happening.

"Emma," he said, his low, husky voice barely audible. "I...I...he's here to tell you that I...I killed your father." The anguish in his eyes was so deep, it took Emma a full minute to comprehend what he'd just said.

"*What*?" She was staring at him in complete disbelief.

"He murdered your father, Emma. He shot him, in your bedroom. I've got the police report right here," Niles said, waving a sheaf of papers in her direction. "He spent two years in a juvenile delinquent hall and another three years on probation *for killing your father!*" Niles was too wrapped up in his own victorious revelations to notice how pale, how shaken Emma had suddenly become.

"What?" she said, her voice faint. She turned to Andy, her mind reeling. "Andy?" She looked up at him with eyes filled with anguish and confusion. What was Niles saying? That Andy killed her father? But it couldn't be true. She would know, she would have *felt* it, wouldn't she? Just like she'd felt her love for Andy. But why was he standing there so woodenly, staring at her with tears in his eyes. Why didn't he defend himself? Why wasn't he rushing to her, telling her the vile things Niles just shouted weren't true? "Oh God, Andy," she said, her body beginning to shake uncontrollably. "Say it isn't true," she pleaded.

Andy stood still, his feet rooted to the ground, unable to answer her pleas. He couldn't, not without telling her all of it, and he wouldn't do that to her, not even if it meant losing her again.

"Your father trusted him, Emma, and he returned his trust by killing him," Niles said, twisting the knife.

"Shut up, Niles," Dr. Stuart repeated, but Niles simply ignored him again.

"Ben...is he telling the truth?" Emma said, still unable to

comprehend the magnitude of what Niles was so anxious to drive home to her.

Before the doctor could answer, Andy cleared his throat. "Emma, your father was a very sick man—"

"Sick?" Niles said. "He wasn't sick. He trusted you with his daughter and you ended up killing him in cold blood."

With a deadly edge to his voice, Andy said, "You were told twice to shut up. You weren't there, you don't know what happened."

"I didn't have to be there. I talked to one of the prosecuting attorneys involved in the case," he said, ignoring Andy's warning.

"But that's not the way it happened," Andy said, turning to Emma. "Emma, please, that's not the way it happened. I'd never do anything to hurt you, you know that."

"Did you kill him, Andy?" Emma said, her voice cracking, barely audible. She felt faint, her world was turning too fast for her to understand all that was being said around her.

"Emma—"

"Did you, Andy?"

Niles stood smugly by, his arms crossed, his body tense with emotion as he waited for Andy to try and excuse his role in the Judge's death.

"Emma, we chose each other, you and I," he pleaded, avoiding the question. "Nothing else matters. That choice was the only decision truly our own so very long ago, don't you see? It was the single most important happenstance in our own painful childhoods that was of our own making. Remember? With everything else you're being told…remember that one important fact." His eyes pleaded with her, begging her to understand.

"Just tell me you didn't kill him, Andy, and I'll believe you. I don't *care* what those papers have to say."

Andy clenched his teeth in a effort to hold back what he wanted so desperately to tell her. Instead, he said, "I'm not going to start lying to you now, Emma. What we've shared, you and I, is too important, too strong to be denied, no matter what else has happened." He'd lie for her, and yes, he'd even kill for her, but he'd never, ever lie *to* her; he never could.

"Oh God, Andy," she begged, desperate now. "Just say it…say you didn't do it…," she pleaded. She took a deep gulp of air, afraid she was going to pass out.

Andy's chest was heaving in unspent emotion. Something beautiful between the two of them was dying, he could read it in her eyes, and there was nothing he could do to prevent its tragic death.

"Emma," Andy's chin quivered, "Don't make me…don't let our love for each other slip away."

"Love!" Niles interjected harshly. "Look what your *love* has done to her."

Andy jerked his head in Niles direction, eyes narrowing. He took a menacing step toward the gloating attorney. He wanted to pound something, *anything* to release the unbearable pain in his heart, and Niles was conveniently close at hand.

"I'm warning you for the last time," Andy whispered, through clenched teeth. "Stay out of this!"

Seemingly unafraid, Niles said, "Look, Emma. Look at this man. He has a history of violence that didn't stop with the murder of your father. It's all here in this file." He waved the papers again as he moved to stand near Emma as if it was she who needed protection, not himself.

Emma stared at Andy, her tortured eyes wide with horror at Niles' accusations, tearing him up inside. He shook his head slowly, "Emma, I can't change what happened ten years ago. I just ask you to search your heart for the answers and try to remember what we had together."

Emma's world was falling apart. If someone touched her she'd shatter into a million pieces. Andy stood before her, trying to convince her that the love they felt for each other should override all else. But her father! *He'd murdered her father!* How could she live with Andy knowing he'd done such a heinous thing?

Emma staggered to the couch, her legs like rubber as she

sank heavily down on the cushions, her emotions raw, an aching void in her chest. No one knew the agony of despair she was feeling. She was being ripped apart inside and her head felt as if it would explode.

"You'd better leave, Andy," Ben said, pulling Andy toward the door.

"No," Andy said, angrily brushing aside the doctor's arm. He rushed over to the couch, grabbing Emma's cold, lifeless hands in his own. "Emma, please," he murmured, squeezing her hands, trying to get a response."

"Go, Andy," she said, her voice flat, devoid of emotion. Shock had finally overcome her, numbing her.

"Emma—"

"You heard her," Niles said, approaching the other man. Andy ignored him. "Emma, *please.*"

"Go," she said, more firmly this time, pulling her hands away. "You murdered my father. And when you did that, you killed any chance for us, Andy. Now go," she said, her eyes averted, her voice tired, tears spilling onto her blouse, leaving long, dark streaks on the silken material.

Andy gazed hard at her for a long moment before standing up, then he smiled down at her averted face; a small, lonely smile. Unspent tears, burning to be let loose, were making his eyelids ache.

"It took me ten years to find you, Emma; I'm not going to give up. It won't be me to walk away this time. You'll have to do it," he said sadly, his voice shaking. Ben grabbed his arm again and guided him unresisting to the front door. "I'll be here, Emma," Andy whispered as he left, the tears now rolling unchecked down his cheeks, his voice echoing back, flowing over her still-averted face.

How he made it back to his hotel without getting into an accident, he'd never know. He couldn't even remember parking the car. The only thing to sink through his hazy pain-filled mind was the few words he'd read on the note the desk clerk has given him as he passed by the front desk.

Jack was in town, wanting to see him.

Zombie-like, Andy rode the elevator to Jack's room and knocked on the door.

Thirty

Jack opened the door to his room, surprised to find Andy sitting on the couch, his hands folded in his lap, staring intently at the gun resting on the glass coffee table in front of him.

Without breaking his concentrated gaze away from the gun, Andy said, "You weren't in, so I just decided to wait. It's funny, isn't it? I just knew you'd bring it along," he said, nodding at his father's service revolver.

Dropping his keys into his jacket pocket, Jack slowly approached Andy, wary of his strange, emotionless tone. He took the seat opposite him, the gun between them.

"Odd, wouldn't you say? How a cold piece of metal could have such a tragic impact on people's lives. A cold, impartial object, a taker of dreams, of hopes, of desires, indiscriminately changing the course of people's lives forever." He finally looked up at Jack, and the older man was startled at the look in the other man's eyes. There was such unadulterated grief staring back at Jack, it made the hair stand up on his burly arms.

"What happened—"

"What the fuck do you think happened, Jack?" Andy said, suddenly breaking out of his trance-like state. "She threw me out of her life."

"Your record," Jack snorted in disgust. "We tried to suppress it, Andy. Even so, you were just putting off the inevitable, we both knew that."

"Why are you here, Jack? To get me through this again?" he said sarcastically.

"No," Jack said, taking no offense. "I'm here to make sure you finish up your investigation." And hustle you out of town in one piece, he wanted to add.

"That part's over." Andy leaned back against the couch, covering his eyes.

"The boys are in custody?" Jack asked, trying to get Andy's mind working on something else.

"Not yet. Tomorrow probably."

"Then it isn't over."

"It is for me."

"It isn't over till the mother and the kids are on their flight home, Andy," Jack said stubbornly.

Andy leaned forward, his eyes hard. "I can't do it, Jack. You do it. Make yourself useful instead of babysitting me. You go with the officers tomorrow, you make sure they get on the plane. I'm out of it."

Angry now, Jack said, "Goddammit, Andy, pull yourself together, finish your job—"

"Don't you see? I can't…I can't do it," Andy said, despair overcoming him again. "I can't…I can't leave her, Jack."

"You've got to let her go, Andy—"

"Don't you *understand*, Jack? She's all I've ever wanted. The hope of one day getting her back was all that kept me going. She took my heart, my *soul*, I don't have the strength to continue with that hope stripped away from me."

"Then tell her. Tell her what really happened, Andy. Why you did what you did that day. It's the only option you have now, other than simply walking away from it all."

Andy sat silent. He couldn't tell her. She probably wouldn't believe him anyway. No—unless she remembered on her own, when her mind was strong enough to accept what had happened, he would remain silent.

"Goddammit!" Jack railed at the sullen figure opposite him. "When are you going to stop protecting that girl at the expense of your own life! She ruined you once, are you going to let your stubbornness and your misguided sense of what's right destroy you again? Are you going to let your dreams die again? Are you going to let your reputation be ruined again by some smart-ass lawyer who doesn't have a *clue* as to what he's got his fingers in?"

Andy continued to stare straight ahead, his jaw set in a firm line, his teeth clenched tight.

"There you go," Jack said, righteous anger propelling him forward. "I went through this silent act of yours ten years ago—don't pull that shit on me again. Just because you wouldn't tell me the truth about what really went down that night doesn't mean I don't know. Her fingerprints were all over your dad's gun."

Andy's head jerked up, eyes narrowing at Jack. This was old territory for them both. He wouldn't let Jack goad him into admitting anything. As a young, scared sixteen year old, he'd withstood Jack's badgering, his threats. He could do it again.

"Admit it, Andy," Jack continued on. "There's just you and me in this room. Admit to me here, now, how she took the gun from your room and hid it in her own, bent on threatening her father with it if he tried to touch her again. Tell me! Tell me how he entered her room, tried to rape her, how she struggled desperately to fend him off, and when that didn't work, she grabbed the gun and shot him. And how you heard the noise from your own bedroom and recognized it for what it was. Tell me!" Jack spit out, leaning across the glass coffee table.

"Tell me how you rushed over there, found her hysterical, cringing in the corner of her bed, her nightgown torn and bloody, the gun still gripped tightly in her hand. Tell me!" he shouted, just inches away from Andy now, his hot breath striking Andy's face like a furnace blast. "Tell me how you took the gun from her and waited for the police to arrive, taking the blame for her in a misguided attempt to keep her from going to jail. Tell me!" he shouted, rocking the room.

But there was nothing for Andy to tell. All he could do was confirm what Jack said. And he could, because every word Jack had just uttered was true, except for the fact that he'd returned home late from his night job and had discovered the gun missing, realizing immediately what must have happened to it. He'd already been heading in the direction of Emma's house when he'd heard the gun go off. But by the time he'd reached Emma, it was too late. Her father lay dying and Emma was a shaking, bloodied mass in the corner of her bed, in shock. Andy'd had to pry the gun out of her hand, all the time repeating to her that he was going to tell the police he'd pulled the trigger, all the while worried Emma would confess to the crime anyway and he'd have to convince the police otherwise.

But all that had gone by the wayside as Emma retreated into an impenetrable shell of silence from which, eventually, she'd emerged memoryless.

But at least she'd been spared being the center of a scandalous trial she would never have lived down, of being jailed, or perhaps even institutionalized with criminally insane inmates.

He'd given her that at least. He'd paid the price for his unselfish act, but even now he didn't regret it. Even if it meant losing her again, he didn't regret it.

Andy's eyes clouded over as his mind drifted back to the horrible scene with Jack at the station house after his arrest. Jack hadn't believed his version of what had happened, not even for a minute. And when forensics had come back with the fingerprint report, Andy thought for a while there that Jack was going to beat the truth out of him.

Instead, he'd stuck to his story, how he'd heard Emma's screams, had picked up his father's gun and gone racing over to the house, knowing the cause of her screams, and how he'd struggled with Emma's father, pulling him away from her, and how the Judge had in turn lunged at Andy when he saw the gun in his hand, and the gun accidentally going off. He told Jack how Emma's father had been molesting her and how he'd tried to help her by going to Dr. Stuart, a man not just well-known in his field, but also close friend of Emma's father, a man Andy was sure could help them. But when Jack had called Dr. Stuart in to confirm the fact that Andy had gone to him for help, he'd categorically denied knowledge of the Judge's perversities.

At the time, Andy had been devastated that Dr. Stuart, a trusted family friend, would out and out lie to protect both himself for not acting on Andy's information and also the popular Judge's sterling reputation. That he tried to make up for his rotten deed by taking Emma in and tending to her himself did little to assuage Andy's bitterness over his apparent betrayal.

Even now, Andy was reluctant to give the doctor any credit for Emma's apparent recovery.

Unable to corroborate Andy's story that he was just protecting Emma, thereby giving him *some* credence for shooting the Judge, Jack had been at a loss as to what to do with Andy. He knew Andy well, knew if he said he'd gone to Dr. Stuart for help, then by God he had. But the doctor stubbornly denied the whole thing. However, behind closed doors, in an effort to hold down the scandal threatening to erupt because Andy categorically stood behind his charge that the Judge was sexually attacking his young daughter, the three of them cut a deal. If Andy would change his story slightly, Jack and Dr. Stuart would see to it that he wasn't tried for murder as a adult, thereby allowing Andy to avoid being sent to prison. Instead, it was determined he would go to reform school, then be put on probation for the murder of Malcolm Nash, thereby completely bypassing a criminal trial. Andy learned quickly, however, that reform school was prison enough.

The story released to the papers was that of a tragic misunderstanding. Andy Brannigan, next door neighbor to the popular Judge and boyfriend of his pretty, fifteen-year-old daughter, was lying in his bed when he thought he heard screams coming in the direction of the Judge's home. Grabbing his father's service revolver, he quickly rushed to his girlfriend's aid. Following the sounds of her struggle, he'd entered the dark house and ran quickly to her bedroom. The bedroom had been dark and she'd looked to be struggling against some unknown assailant. Without thinking clearly, Andy had fired the revolver, instantly killing the Judge, her father, who had just been trying to console an overwrought daughter still grappling with the painful loss of her mother less than a year before.

That was the story the papers received, the version Andy had had to live with all these past ten years. And only he knew the whole truth—he and Emma. Jack suspected it, was fairly certain what'd happened, but without Andy's confession, it was all he had—conjecture.

And it was all he'd ever have.

From the moment Andy confessed to a murder he didn't commit, his goal had never wavered. Even in reform school, and the years afterwards spent on probation, the one objective that never changed for him was to reunite with Emma again.

Jack had originally filled him in on her condition, but being young and stupid, Andy had been sure at the time that it was just a temporary thing. He wrote to her, almost daily, never once getting a response, until finally Dr. Stuart had come to visit him, bringing along the packet of letters that had been stacking up, unopened, to a young girl who would never answer a single one of them. Dr. Stuart explained Emma's current state of mind, her nearly hopeless situation, but Andy again refused to believe she wouldn't recover. Still, he was powerless where he was, and therefore tried to keep the lines of communication open with Dr. Stuart, despite his betrayal, because he was his only real link to Emma.

For a few months, Dr. Stuart was even pretty good about

keeping Andy apprised of Emma's condition, but eventually Andy stopped hearing from him. Although Andy wrote time and time again, Dr. Stuart had, for reasons only he could answer, decided it was no longer important to keep Andy informed of Emma's progress, or lack of it. Frustration over the doctor's silence, and the return of his last letters sent, drove Andy to go to Jack for answers. All that Jack had been able to learn was that the doctor, along with his young patient, had left town with no forwarding address.

The news had devastated Andy, and he'd felt his imprisonment in reform school tighten around him like a noose, stifling him, killing his one hope, the driving force keeping him on the straight and narrow. He'd nearly taken off then, set out to find Emma, steal her away from the doctor who'd grown to evil proportions in his young mind, determined to make her better himself. He was so sure he could cure her, given the chance. Surely she would remember *him.*

It wasn't till years later, when Andy delved into the subject of sexual abuse that he really understood what must have happened to Emma. It wasn't just a person's mind that could virtually shut down to survive these horrific attacks, there were other symptoms as well, symptoms Andy had no way of knowing whether Emma suffered through.

He'd found that literally millions of adult men and women suffer from sexual abuse; most often from someone within their own family. Not only do some react as Emma did, but others suffer nightmares, or worse, have no memory of their abuse, yet their symptoms indicate it happened. Oftentimes, they become sexually promiscuous, or, at the other end of the spectrum, completely avoid sex. Others turn to other mind-numbing behaviors such as drug or alcohol abuse, overwork, compulsive exercise, even eating disorders. The list went on and on.

That Emma's condition could be statistically proven did little to ease his worries. And he hadn't known all these facts when he was in reform school; he just needed *out.*

But Jack must have recognized at least some of the

thoughts rolling around in Andy's mind, because from then on he was on him like a shadow, and when he wasn't around, he made sure someone else was.

If Andy'd really wanted to get out—escape—he probably could have. But his better judgment finally broke through the angry haze of his frustration and fear for Emma, and he realized he didn't have long to go before he'd be out of the stifling reform school for good, free to find her on his own without someone dogging his trail.

Besides, if he left the school before his time was up, he'd be breaking his probation, and if he was caught, he'd go to prison for sure, no matter what Jack tried to do for him.

No, he didn't want to risk losing even more of his life to the system, he just wanted out. He wanted out—*needed* out desperately—needed to find the only thing that mattered to him, the only person left in his life, save Jack, who held any real meaning to him.

And finally, the day had come. He'd graduated from reform school, the ceremony a far cry from what he'd have gone through if he and Emma had been able to finish out their high school years like normal teens; but at least he had a diploma to show for it. He still had probation to go through, but from the sound of it, probation would be a piece of cake compared to what he'd gone through the last two years. And even on probation, he could search for Emma. All he had to do was make sure the probation officer knew where he was, check in with him on a regular basis, show him he was staying out of trouble.

No problem, especially since Jack had somehow finagled the role for himself—the mighty detective lowering himself to probation officer status, just in this one instance.

Jack O'Malley was not without influence in his own little world, and Andy was infinitely thankful for his influence many times throughout the coming years; was especially grateful when Jack had come to him just months before his release and told him of his plan to start an investigative service, a missing person investigative service, to be exact, sort of on the side. He and some other fellas had been tossing the idea around for years, and now the time had seemed ripe, especially since they'd talked Jack's brother's church into sponsoring the idea. And Andy would dovetail nicely into their plans, Jack had told him.

It didn't take a genius to realize Jack and his friends were doing this solely for Andy; were in fact relying heavily on the fact that Andy would jump at some chance to learn the investigative business, get in with the contacts, procedures, all the nuances that could help immensely when searching for someone, and he could combine this job with his efforts to find Emma. Part of his probation required he have a job, so again Jack was covering his bases for him. Jack had tailor-made this one to fit Andy's needs, and Andy had repaid Jack by keeping the program afloat with the money he'd finally received from his parents' insurance policies when he turned twenty-one. By that time, he was hooked on the business, and still looking for Emma every spare moment he had.

It'd taken him nearly a year to track Dr. Stuart to Dallas, Texas. It'd been three years since Emma's father's death and her demise into a world of her own. Three years of wondering where she was, worrying about her, aching for her presence, her soft, gentle touch; of gazing upon the knowing smile that touched her face, lighting up at the sight of him.

He'd immediately flown to Dallas, only to be told by Dr. Stuart that Emma had never recovered from the tragedy of her father's death, that she still remained catatonic, staring out at the world from unseeing eyes. Andy had insisted on seeing her, and only then did Dr. Stuart admit that Emma was no longer in his care, that he'd been unable to continue care for her in the way she most desperately needed it.

It had taken much cajoling, and finally threats to get Dr. Stuart to tell Andy where she now was. Andy had been heartbroken to find she was no longer even in the country, but instead at a very specialized sanitarium in Switzerland, getting the needed care her damaged psyche still required.

It wasn't until several months and several thousand dollars

later that Andy found out the doctor had lied to him; not just about Emma's whereabouts, but everything. He discovered that Emma had been in Dallas all along, still in Ben Stuart's care, but not before he had spent precious time and money scouring Switzerland for her. He'd been devastated to learn of the doctor's treachery, and even more determined not to let the scoundrel get away with it. But by the time he'd returned to Dallas, Dr. Stuart, and Emma, were gone.

They'd disappeared without a trace, again.

Andy had wanted to scream in frustration and anger as feelings of defeat threatened to overcome him.

But with a stubbornness and determination he never knew he was capable of, he continued on with the search. He even had Jack looking for the doctor from time to time, but Ben Stuart seemed to have just dropped off the face of the earth.

Andy picked up his trail once or twice by hooking into the IRS computer and tracking where he filed his taxes from, but by the time he was able to zero in on him, he'd be gone again. Andy was afraid to use that method of trying to find the doctor more than once or twice; the penalty for breaking into the IRS computer system was probably worse than the Internet one. He didn't want to risk finding out for sure, couldn't afford to spend time in jail—time away from finding Emma.

But Andy had just discovered that the reason he'd had no luck in finding any further traces of the doctor until just recently, was because Ben Stuart had stopped practicing for a few years, concentrating instead on his thesis on catatonia and its effects on the human psyche. This Andy learned from one of Dr. Stuart's old cronies who'd stumbled on the write-up in a medical journal, a gentleman who knew of Andy's plight and sympathized with him, passing along the information to him. It had been on Andy's agenda to get in touch with the magazine where the write-up had appeared, and try, through them, to get a line on the doctor's present whereabouts when he'd had to leave town on his current investigation, head out to the West Coast.

Imagine how he'd felt when, out of sheer, unadulterated

luck, he'd stumbled upon, not the doctor, where his efforts had been concentrated, but Emma herself. No hard investigative facts leading up to the discovery of their presence in Oregon, just a lucky break.

And maybe that's the way it should have come about, after all. Maybe, just maybe, his luck was changing on him. After such a long string of bad, perhaps it was finally turning. Andy liked to think it was finally full-circle time—that the sacrifices he'd made, the miles he'd covered, the tears he'd held back unspent, refusing to acknowledge the futility of his dreams, were all going to be rewarded with the discovery of his lost, but never, ever forgotten, one true love.

And it had turned out to be even more simple than he'd ever dreamed possible, after all this time. Divine justice—something else he liked to believe in. So very, very simple. So simple, in fact, he hadn't believed it at first, thought his eyes were playing tricks on him again.

Two years in reform school, a year searching for Dr. Stuart's whereabouts, only to be thrown off the track for nearly seven years, just to discover the visage he'd dreamed about every day for the last ten years was staring back at him, talking to him, from the small television screen in his hotel room—looking robust, healthy, *beautifully normal,* just as he remembered her to be. And now the dream was shattered again…shattered into a million jagged pieces. And with that dream went Andy's desire to even exist, let alone pick up those pieces and go on.

"You're still not going to tell me, are you?" Jack said, disgust ringing in his voice.

It took a full minute for Andy to realize Jack had spoken to him, so caught up was he in his own sad recollections, the path that had led him to this devastating moment in time.

"No," Andy answered, his husky voice barely audible, pain wracking his mind, his body, sickening him.

"Then I'll go to Dr. Stuart, make him tell Emma. He knows the truth, just like I do."

"He won't say anything, Jack, you know that. Just let it

be," his voice cracking at the exertion of spitting out those few words. He'd long ago stopped looking in Ben Stuart's direction for any kind of help. Jack knew it, too, but was unaware of the full extent of the doctor's treachery. "All right. Then what about your investigation?" Jack said, switching tactics again as he tried to get Andy to care about something besides his own miserable self-absorption.

"You do it," Andy said, hanging his head in despair.

"I can't, I have other things to do." Whether Andy liked it or not, he was going to have it out with Dr. Ben Stuart. Ten years too late, but what the hell. He was spoiling for a fight and that slick son-of-a-bitch was the perfect target.

"Like what? Making sure I don't do something foolish again? Just leave me be."

"You just get Karen and her two boys on that plane. This thing with Emma—"

"This *thing* with Emma?" Andy repeated, a strange note in his voice. A new wave a nausea swept over him at the thought of his loss. "You just don't *get it,* do you Jack? After all this time," he said, incredulous, his voice strained, yet gaining in strength.

"I know how much the girl meant to you, Andy, but—"

"But what? Time to move on? *Goddammit,* Jack! Don't you think I've tried? Love isn't like some fucking blues song you sing about! You don't just shed a few tears, then move on in search of somebody else! *It's real*—so real that what I feel for Emma I feel with every nerve in my body, and it's tearing me apart. Can't you see?" he pleaded, trying to get Jack to understand the bottomless depth of his misery. "Emma and I together again was the only dream I had left. The rest are gone, blown away forever with a single bullet. How...," his voice quavered, tears standing out in his eyes, ready to spill over, "how am...am I supposed...to go on...without a *dream,* Jack? The only dream that gave my life meaning?"

Jack swallowed down the lump in his gruff throat and approached Andy's heartsick pleas the only way he knew how. He said, "You think you're the only one in the world who's had a dream shattered? You've come closer to out-and-out misery than most people could ever even think of trying to understand in their lifetime, yet look at you," he said, arms waving. "You've come face to face with killers and come away with your *life*, boy, which is more than a lot of the poor souls we've been looking for can brag about. What about *their* dreams? You don't think their dreams were shattered the day we had to tell those families the news? Way I look at it, you're life ain't so awful, not compared to some. You lost your dad, you survived it. Your ma drank herself to death right before your very eyes, and you made it through that, too. You sailed through reform school without hardly a scratch on you.

"And now Emma. You can make it through this, Andy. You've got a job to do. Why don't you pull yourself together and get this thing finished?" he groused, getting on Andy with more roughness than he felt, but the boy needed to see the sense of what he said.

Andy just shook his head, Jack's words having no effect on him. He picked up the gun lying between the two of them, caressing the metal between his two hands as if he were trying to bring some warmth to the cold, hard, unfeeling surface.

"I said I can't," Andy said, his voice again flat, devoid of emotion as he contemplated the heavy revolver in his hand. Jack just didn't understand. Maybe he never would, not the way Andy wanted him to. Maybe nobody would understand, not even Emma, with the news of her father's death tainting all her feeling for him right now, maybe forever.

He focused in on the hard object in his hand. "This gun meant so many things to me," he murmured softly, "the career of my father, a father I idolized and wanted to spend my life emulating, the ultimate compliment a son can give his father. It was a symbol I kept tucked away in the drawer I reserved for all my most important treasures. Dad's badge, the book of poems my mother had written, Emma's love letters to me, memoirs from proms we'd gone to and dates we'd been on, the flag from dad's coffin, his medals, the story written up about him in the paper when he died." Andy stopped stroking the gun, looked up into Jack's wary eyes.

"And then it turned into something ugly, something hated," Andy continued on, "a destroyer of life, a killer of not just one sick and deranged man, but three people. Three people with one single bullet," he said softly, tears finally spilling out of his eyes, coursing down his cheeks unchecked, splashing off the metal held tightly between his two hands.

"Maybe there's just one way this story was meant to end, after all," Andy said, lifting the heavy revolver to his temple, a proud symbol of his father's illustrious career for so many years, but now the tragic embodiment of all Andy had lost.

Before Jack could lunge forward, stop him, Andy pulled the trigger for the very first time in his ill-fated life.

Thirty-One

Click.

The sound reverberated in Jack O'Malley's head, over and over again. He couldn't seem to get it out of there, no matter how hard he tried.

Shit!

He knew the gun hadn't been loaded, but he'd still reacted with an instinct years and years of police training had instilled in him. And he also knew Andy wasn't the sort of guy who blew his head off, for any reason whatsoever, even the one he was struggling so mightily with right now. He just wasn't the type.

He knew all that.

And still it hadn't stopped him from lunging for the gun

anyway, like a big-assed jerk sucked into the moment.

Okay.

So Andy'd made his point.

Loud and clear.

But now it was time for Jack to make his own point, starting with one Doctor Benjamin Stuart.

He gripped the steering wheel tightly between huge, callused hands, swinging the car back and forth in traffic. So Andy still wasn't going to come clean with him. But then Jack hadn't really expected him to. Hell, he hadn't been able to scare it out of him ten years ago, no way was he gonna be able to now. He'd just thought, what with the state of mind he'd been in, Andy might finally spill it all out. But the boy was tough, tough as nails, just like his old man. And Jack should've known better, backed off, really listened to the boy before he'd found it necessary to get his undivided attention with that scary, stupid stunt.

But it'd had its desired effect, Jack smiled admiringly to himself. He'd pulled the gun away from Andy and talked quietly with him, sympathized with him, told him ultimately he could do whatever he wanted. But then he'd told him that sitting there and feeling sorry for himself like nobody else in the world mattered, well, that just wasn't Andy. Instead, he needed do what he'd always done: pick up the pieces and start over. Oversimplified, maybe. But it was the unadulterated truth of it.

He'd left Andy with that thought, having enough confidence in him to know he'd do the right thing. And in return, even though he wouldn't want him to, Jack was going to clear the air, once and for all, between himself and Ben Stuart. Ten years late—too late maybe—but there you go.

A quick stop at the police station flashing his badge had gotten him Ben Stuart's home address. He'd tried the telephone book first, knowing it was an effort in futility, but tried anyway.

All he got for his brief trouble was the doctor's office address.

Not good enough.

He needed to see him today, now, while his mind was made up to do something about all this old shit. Jack figured the doc still had police contacts, what with working in the field for so many years, and he figured the station would have his home address.

Right again, he thought smugly, on his way to confront a man he hadn't seen, hadn't spoken to, hadn't *wanted* to, in nearly ten years.

Jack was right. Andy knew he was right, but it didn't make things any easier, less painful. Jack thought he knew him so well, but Andy wasn't even sure himself if he wouldn't have pulled the trigger if the gun had actually been loaded. He felt so out of control right now, so purposeless. For the first time in his life, he had absolutely no mission, no goal in which to lose himself, and it left him feeling desolate. Always before, when he'd felt this way, he'd at least have the thought in the back of his head that it wouldn't always be this way, that he'd find Emma and life would be good, really good, again.

But he could no longer cling to that dream. It was gone, forever, the key to everything—their love, their lives, the true events of that awful day—locked away in a mind that refused to remember, and there was absolutely nothing he could do to change the situation. He was the one with full disclosure, but the knowledge was locked away just as tightly, just as assuredly as Emma's repressed, agonizing memories, and until hers were freed of their own accord, his would remain as they'd always been, close to his heart, tucked away tightly from exposure to all outside forces.

It'd taken all his strength to pull himself up from the couch after Jack had left, drag himself back to his own room. He'd thrown himself across the bed, not even bothering to undress, pulling the pillows down around his ears in an effort to block out his pain-filled memories.

But no matter how much Jack tried to instill some will in him to go on, giving him the 'don't try to make life worth living, *make it that way'* routine, Andy just didn't have the reserves to pull from anymore. They were all gone, drained from him the moment Niles had shown up with his untimely news, the half-truths and innuendoes driving Emma away from him forever.

Life had been brutally unkind to him so long ago, but the last several years had been pretty good, even without Emma's physical presence by his side. But then, he'd always known in his heart he'd one day find her. Now he didn't even have the benefit of peace of mind anymore. It would be worse now, much worse, because he'd know the extent of what he would be missing. They'd both experienced the full measure of their love for each other, and neither of them would ever be the same again.

Thirty-Two

Emma finally quieted down, but only after Ben talked her into coming home with him, away from any unwanted interruptions. He gave her a strong sedative, and she was upstairs in the bedroom, lying quietly now, after an outpouring of grief that not only left her stepfather shaken, but her own spirit totally drained.

Before they'd left, Niles had tried to comfort her, but she would have none of his unwanted ministrations. Pushing away his offer of comfort, she'd withdrawn even further into her own misery until Ben finally insisted Niles leave them alone. It was after Niles had reluctantly left that Ben had quickly moved her to his own place.

It was all such a horrible mess, and Ben knew of no quick

fix for the awful situation.

That Andy, not Emma, was the ultimate victim in this whole mess was something Ben hadn't been able to help or rectify, not ten years ago, and not now. He'd done a terrible thing back then by not coming to Emma's aid sooner, but he had been certain at the time that Andy was overstating the problem between Emma and her father.

But he'd been wrong, dead wrong, and Andy had turned out to be the fall guy for everyone. That Andy chose to do so was his own decision, but perhaps if Ben had admitted to the authorities the Judge's precarious state of mind, both Andy and Emma would have been spared, instead of just Emma.

All he'd been concerned about at the time was his own reputation and the resulting furor if his hesitation in coming to the aid of the young, helpless girl was uncovered, not to mention his reluctance in confronting the Judge, his friend, when he'd been silently crying out for help. Ben had vacillated just long enough to allow the whole situation to escalate into a tragedy that could have been avoided if he'd only moved sooner.

And he'd had to live with that fact.

For ten years, guilt had been eating at him, sticking in his craw like a bad piece of meat that couldn't be dislodged. And when Andy had shown up seven years earlier while he and Emma had been in Texas, he had again passed up the chance to make things right with the boy. He could rationalize all he wanted that it was for Emma's own good, but he knew, again, that he was protecting himself, his reputation, more than her vulnerable, still tender state of mind.

Ten years ago, he had made the determination that Andy was expendable.

Three years later, he made that same determination.

Now, as inexcusable as it seemed, he had done it to the boy again. And this time, it appeared, for good.

Moving like the old man he was, Ben Stuart descended the stairs, wondering again how in God's name he'd ever let this whole mess get so out of control.

A rap on the front door brought the doctor out of his painfully truthful introspection. He moved slowly to the door, afraid to answer it, afraid any further confrontation with anybody would break down the wall of resolve he'd spent years and years building up within himself to counteract the dreadful feelings of failure and inadequacy haunting him since the day he'd betrayed a young man of sixteen.

He opened the door and the blood drained from his face. He was staring at his greatest nightmare, the one man, besides himself, who knew—or at least suspected—Andy's innocence in the whole affair. His worst nightmare had been realized, come back to haunt him. He couldn't face him, he just couldn't.

The door open just a crack, he said, "I'm sorry, Detective, but I can't see you right now."

Jack shoved the door open, sending the doctor back on his heels. Snarling, he said, "You see a permission slip in my hand, Doc? I don't care what you want, you're gonna talk to me, right now!"

"I'll call the police," the doctor said, then immediately realized the foolishness of his remark. Twice in one evening he'd made that mistake—

"Buddy, I *am* the police, and unless you want a bunch of strangers listening to the shit you pulled ten years ago, I suggest you sit down, shut up, and hear what I have to say."

"All right, just keep your voice down," Dr. Stuart conceded, backing away from the belligerent detective.

Eyes narrowing, Jack looked around. "Is she here? I want to talk to her."

Trying to fight down his rising panic, the doctor said hastily, "I've just given her something to help her sleep. She was overwrought with grief. She's upstairs, resting peacefully now. Let her be." Reading the momentary indecision in his eyes, knowing with the mood he was in that he just might march up the stairs anyway, he added, "In here," indicating the living room and steering the burly detective away from the stairs. "We can talk in here."

Jack reluctantly allowed the doctor to lead him into the other room, but not before hesitating at the bottom of the stairs for a moment or two, glancing upward. If she was truly sedated, then she'd be of no use to him right then anyway. Sighing, he turned his attention back to Benjamin Stuart.

"You've had nearly ten fucking years to tell her what happened," Jack said, launching his attack before they'd even seated themselves. "Now tell me why you didn't," he said, tightly controlled anger surging in every word.

"I didn't feel it was necessary. She was functioning normally—"

"Normally? Is that all you care about—whether she *functions normally?* Jesus Christ, you're something else. I've got a boy sitting back at the hotel who feels like his life is over, and you talk to me about *functioning normally!*"

"Just listen to me—"

"Listen to you! I listened to you ten years ago, and look what a mess it caused. I let you talk me into sacrificing a scared and defiant boy just to save your ass and the reputation of some *pervert* who was better off with a bullet in his head. You and I both know Andy didn't pull that trigger and if the Judge hadn't been killed, more than likely he'd have put a gun up to his head and buried a bullet there himself. He was heading in that direction—you know it, and I know it," Jack said, pointing an accusing finger at the doctor, challenging him to deny what he said.

Dr. Stuart sat silent in the face of the detective's accusations, infuriating Jack even further.

"Now don't you start with this silent bit. I've had just about all I'm gonna take in that direction."

Eyebrows raised, Dr. Stuart found his opening, and perhaps the only way to take the heat off himself. "There you go. If even Andy is unwilling to say what really happened, what good would telling Emma do? And if Andy won't tell you, how do either one of us really know what happened that night?"

"Goddammit!" Jack roared. Dr. Stuart winced at the fury

that one word contained, then glanced fearfully at the stairs, afraid Jack's voice would carry to the fitfully slumbering Emma, waking her again to the nightmare that was such an integral part of her life, albeit a forgotten one.

"You're gonna tell her—or *I* will—what happened to her father, you hear me?" Jack said, pointing a menacing finger at the other man. "How screwed up he became, how it was Andy who tried to protect her, and how you let them both down."

"Do you really believe telling her will change her mind about how she feels about Andy? She'll still think he killed her father."

"It's a start anyway. And maybe, just maybe, if someone starts telling her the truth behind her father's death, the rest will fall in place for her."

Dr. Stuart shook his head in disagreement. "She's not *ready* for those revelations yet." At the detective's heavy-handed look, he said, "If you'd seen her tonight, you'd believe me when I tell you she's not strong enough to hear about her father."

"Andy gave you ten years to straighten out the mess you made, I'm not giving you any more time. Either you tell her, or I will—"

"Tell me what?" a sleepy Emma said from the top of the stairs, trying to place the man in the living room. He looked vaguely familiar to her, but her mind seemed to be full of cobwebs, no doubt caused from the strong sedative Ben had given her; her eyes felt grainy and swollen, blurry from the intense crying of a few hours ago.

Both men looked up, startled, coming instantly to their feet. Ben was the first to recover. "Go back to bed, Emma, let the sedative do its work."

"No!" Jack shouted, pushing himself in front of the doctor. He'd just warned Ben he wouldn't be put off any longer, and he meant it. "Do you remember me, Emma? I'm a friend of Andy's," he said, deliberately omitting his name.

Emma stared intently from the top of the stairs, never taking her eyes away from the tall, imposing figure walking toward her. She put her hand up to her forehead, squinting with concentration, trying to recall…

"Jack…Jack O'Malley, isn't it?" she replied hesitantly. She didn't know if it was the effects of the sedative Ben had administered that seemingly allowed her mind to relax enough to push forth some of her lost memories or if the trauma she suffered earlier in the day had been the catalyst. All she knew was that, lying upstairs, not asleep, but not totally awake, she'd begun to remember bits and pieces, and suddenly, what she'd heard earlier in the evening about Andy's role in her father's death had not quite rung true to her. Suddenly, in the hazy recollections of her damaged mind, she'd begun to sense that there was much, much more to the story than had earlier been revealed. And when she'd heard the voices downstairs, she'd been drawn to them like a magnet, unable to stop herself from getting up out of the comfortable, safe, secure confines of the warm bed, hidden away from conflict.

"That's right," Jack nodded, smiling. He glanced in the doctor's direction, a look of triumph on his face.

"What did you mean about the truth behind my father's death?" Her eyes were wider now, her muted emotions slowly dissipating the effects of the strong sedative.

"Emma, Andy didn't—" Jack started to say.

"What he's going to tell you," the doctor interrupted hastily, still unwilling to let the whole, unadulterated truth be told so starkly, "was that Andy was just trying to protect you the night your father was murdered."

"What?" she said, uncomprehending.

Jack shot the doctor a look of disgust. He couldn't believe he was going to continue to try and lead her on with select portions of the truth. He might try, but Jack was going to have no part of it. He was tired of everyone pussy-footing around the girl as if she were made of glass. She had a right to know what happened, all of it, and he was going to tell her.

"Shut up, Ben," he cut in unceremoniously. "You've had plenty of time to deal out the truth, now it's my turn," Jack said, never taking his eyes off the girl at the top of the stairs.

Dr. Stuart went ghost-white, his face suddenly covered with a thin film of perspiration. He stood there, motionless, helpless—the detective's command brooked no nonsense out of him. He'd lost control of the situation and there was no going back now. The best he could muster out of it all now was to try and control the damage a bit.

Emma's feet were firmly rooted to the space at the top of the stairs. She'd never heard anyone talk to Ben so roughly, and it frightened her. Not because he'd suddenly seemed so weak, so...shaken, but because she knew instinctively that his apparent fear had something to do with her. Was he afraid she'd slip back? Was *she* afraid, too? *What was going on?* Why was Jack O'Malley there?—on Andy's behalf?—to convince her to accept him even in the face of the fact that he'd killed her father?

Even when she rolled those thoughts over in her mind—Andy murdering her father—they still didn't seem to stick—continued to unsettle her in a way not related to the bare facts. It was as if...as if her mind was trying to accept the fact, but her heart told her otherwise. Did she want Andy so badly she was trying to convince herself he didn't pull the trigger? But he was convicted of the crime—Niles had said so, and Ben hadn't denied it. Most important of all, Andy hadn't denied it.

She put her hand up to her head, the throbbing had started anew at the confusing thoughts jumbling around in her mind, the unnamed anxiety welling up in her again, unbidden, seemingly uncontrollable.

Jack moved to the bottom of the stairs, clutching the banister tightly in his hand, holding himself back, afraid that if he rushed up the stairs, he'd try to physically shake her memory back, force her to remember.

Instead, he said, "Emma, your mother's death caused horrible changes in your father. He began to experience mental instability. Andy was just trying to protect you." *Shit.* Now even he was waffling over the truth. Why didn't he just say it—*Andy didn't kill your father.* Because she'd ask him who did, and he'd have to tell her, that's why, Jack thought disgustedly to himself, exasperated that Ben Stuart had instilled just enough fear in him to prohibit him from blurting out the whole truth, maybe end up being responsible for sending her back into that horrible black void again at the shock of it, possibly forever this time. And Jack knew if that happened, it would completely destroy Andy. Right now he still had a good chance of pulling Andy out of his deep depression. If something happened to Emma, Jack knew it would be all over for Andy, too.

"What do you mean?" Emma whispered. The throbbing was getting worse, yet she couldn't stop. Like a runaway freight train, the pounding kept coming, coming, coming, yet she didn't fight it. She needed to hear the detective's words, needed to understand what really happened so many years ago.

Dr. Stuart came up next to Jack, started to ascend the stairs as he saw the look of anguished realization pass across Emma's face, but Jack blocked his way easily with his big, beefy forearm.

"No. She's got to hear this," Jack said.

"But look at her, she's in pain," the doctor said, trying to appeal to the sympathetic side of the determined detective.

"No," Emma said faintly, moving her hands away from her eyes. "I...want to hear it, Ben." She glanced back at Jack, staring at him with slowly comprehending eyes.

"He...he never got over my mother's death," she whispered, her eyes clouding over, memories beginning to wash over her like a huge, crashing wave—strong, lucid memories of herself, her laughing mother, her father, Andy. She squinted, concentrating on the bits and pieces coming back to her, the thundering in her head growing ever louder. She had to ignore the pain, had to get it out, all of it before the pain overtook her and blotted everything out.

Through a red haze she could hear the detective's voice, as if it was tunneling in to her from a great distance away.

What was he saying?

No, oh, God, no, it couldn't be true. He was saying her father was...was...no, it can't be true—but it was!

The pounding was getting stronger and stronger, the red haze spreading, yet she needed to say it, she needed to shout it out for all the world to hear. She had to…get it out…before she…she went under again. She was slipping away, could feel it in every inch of her being, but with the strange, yet familiar sensation also came the words she'd held back so very long—forever it seemed.

With a mad rush of air, she screamed it out, then collapsed in a heap at the top of the stairs.

Thirty-Three

"I killed him! Oh my God, Annn-ddee—"

Both men rushed up the stairs before the last echo of the anguished confession stopped reverberating down the stairwell and past the two fast-moving men, their attention riveted on the collapsing form at the top of the stairs.

Ben reached her first and grabbed her hand, searching for a pulse, then looked accusingly at Jack hovering over them both.

"She's got a pulse, but it's weak. Help me get her back into bed." They gently picked her up and moved her into the waiting bed.

"Get me a cold washcloth," Ben said over his shoulder, once again in control, rearranging the comforter around the immobile Emma.

Anxious for something to do, Jack raced down the stairs and grabbed the washcloth sitting on the kitchen counter. The doctor had warned him this could happen, but he'd been too stubborn to listen. He'd let his feelings of anxiety for Andy override any concern for the girl lying unconscious a floor above him.

He felt like a murderer himself now for pressing the facts surrounding her father's death onto her.

Even her confession held little triumph for him, not now. He didn't even want to think about what Andy was going to do when he found out what he'd just done.

He ran back upstairs and handed the doctor the cold washcloth, trying to push back the growing seeds of panic.

Emma was struggling mightily to lift the leaden burden seemingly entrapping her entire body, her treacherous mind. She felt as though she were in a deep well, unable to scramble out to the surface. Every time she seemed to come close to the light, the pain would drop in on her again, causing her to lose her grip, fall back into the safe haven, the comfortable silence.

But no...she had to get out, had to return to...to someone...someone who loved her, cherished her, *needed* her as she so desperately needed him. And he would protect her, just like before. But her father—the shame, the humiliation, betrayal, pain. So much easier to stay there in the dark, forgiving, all-encompassing silence.

But no—he was pulling her back—the familiar, adoring face of the man who'd never given up on her, had never stopped searching for her. If he could be strong for her, she, too, could be strong.

Again, resolve took a mighty grip on her fears, pushing them out and away from her as she began the climb again, away from the warm nothingness, toward the beacon of light that signaled pain and anguish to her, but also brought an almost overwhelming, deep blanket of love and urgency to her, calling to her, begging her to come back, to be released finally from a world that both protected and slowly decimated her.

Suddenly, Emma felt something cool and soft touch her mind, further distancing her from the darkness, pulling her toward her true salvation.

As Ben Stuart laid the cold compress gently across Emma's forehead, he was startled when she stopped her desperate thrashing and rewarded him with a small moan. He leaned forward, his ears close to her slowly moving, cracked lips.

"Andy," she whispered, her eyes shut tight.

"Emma…Emma it's Ben. Can you hear me?" he said, trying to keep the urgency out of his voice. He glanced over at Jack, a flicker of hope in his eyes, then turned his attention quickly back to Emma. "Can you hear me?"

Emma licked at her parched lips, trying to work them. "Yes," she managed to croak out, stretching out the word as if she, too, didn't believe she was coherent. She raised her hand and touched the cold rag on her forehead, shifting it a little, then slowly opened her eyes.

Ben was thrilled by the fact that her eyes seemed to be lucid and clear. There would be no slipping back this time, he was certain of it now. Perhaps the sedative she'd been given had something to do with it. Perhaps it'd taken enough of an edge off the impact of the truth of her lurid memories to help her survive the onslaught of agony such revelations had obviously caused in her. He'd have to mull those thoughts, this new theory of his, over later. For now, he was just so grateful to have her lying there awake, seemingly coherent.

She gingerly moved her head, afraid the throbbing would start anew, then turned her focus on Jack for the first time since breaking out of the netherworld that had almost claimed her again.

"I remember it all," she rasped out, her voice betraying the depth of her emotions. "Why did he do it, Jack?" Tears began to well up in her eyes.

Jack wasn't certain if she was talking about her father doing what he did to her, or Andy's role in everything. Before he could answer her, she cleared her throat and began to talk of the events that had taken place so long ago, forever changing the course of two young lives.

She squeezed her eyes shut again. "We…we both took her death so hard. But daddy, he…he never really accepted it. He…he changed. Not overnight, but slowly." She shifted slightly, her eyes opening again, wanting something, *someone* to focus on, to share the nightmare she'd lived through with her. "First he…he just wanted to have me near him…you know…stay home with him instead of going out with Andy or my girlfriends. There…there were times when he'd look at me and call me Suzanna, but I just thought it was…was because I looked a lot like her. But then when he…he started to…" She shut her eyes tightly, humiliation and disgust taking a firm grip on her emotions again.

"Emma, you don't have to go on…"

"No," Emma said, her voice gaining in strength as her eyes flew open. "No," she shook her head. "If I don't tell it now, it'll never really be over with. I…I know I can't hide from it any longer. Andy tried to tell me, you know. But I thought he was talking about himself. He…he said that a person should be able to outlive their past, make up for it, forgive themselves and go on." She started to cry again, softly this time, remembering Andy's gentle words.

"All…all that time I thought he was talking about himself, when he was really trying to tell me that no matter what I'd done, and the…the ordeals he'd suffered through over me, he still loved me." She looked solemnly up at Jack. "He took the blame for me, didn't he?"

"Yes," Jack nodded, a sad smile on his face.

Emma sighed, then began again. She told both men how her father's behavior began to escalate to a more perverse nature until she was afraid he would eventually try to rape her. She'd gone to Andy, who'd himself noticed a marked change in her father. He'd been horrified by her father's actions, but had tried to keep a level head in the face of her father's growing obsession with her. She was becoming more overwrought by the day, and Andy had urged her to go to Dr. Stuart about her father. She had been too mortified and scared to, so Andy had seen to it himself.

Emma stopped her narration for a moment, looked quizzically at her stepfather. "What happened, Ben? Andy came back from his meeting with you so sure you were going to help my father and I."

Jack's eyes narrowed, but he kept silent. If there was ever a time the doctor would come clean in his role in this whole affair, make up for the years of silence, now was the time he'd do it.

Ben hung his head, afraid to look into Emma's questioning gaze.

"I…Emma, I'm afraid I did both you and Andy a great disservice…" he started, then more firmly, "Actually, it was more than that. Perhaps I could have prevented what happened that night if only I acted on what Andy had told me, I don't know," he said, shaking his head in regret. "But I'd known your father for over twenty years, I'm afraid I just didn't believe what Andy was telling me. And then…then it was too late," he finished, his voice trailing off.

Emma stared hard at her stepfather, silently disseminating his belated confession. Too late. Was that all he could manage to say?—*Too late*! There was much more to be said—she could read it in his eyes—but she had to get through the other memories crying to get out before she could pursue Ben's role in the whole mess. Disgusted at his apparent lack of courage, she turned her attention to Jack and continued her remembrances.

After Andy had come back from speaking to Ben, she said, he'd told her he was going to take her to the police if the doctor failed to contact her father within the next day or two. Emma had fought the idea, but Andy had convinced her that her father desperately needed help. But before they could follow through, disaster had struck. That very night, Emma's father came into her bedroom and raped her. She'd been so sickened, had felt so degraded and despoiled, she couldn't even tell Andy of the attack. Instead, she promised herself she would not let it happen again. She remembered Dexter Brannigan's gun, sitting in the dresser drawer, so close at hand.

It was then she knew she'd never let her father touch her again.

As if in a trance, she'd drifted over to Andy's house and sneaked in the back door while Andy was at work and his mom lay in a drunken stupor on the living room couch. She'd gone into the familiar bedroom, opened the drawer and pulled the gun out. She knew it wasn't loaded, but she also knew where Andy kept the bullets. She rummaged around in another drawer until she came up with the needed bullets, then she'd taken both the gun and the bullets and returned home and sequestered the items under her pillow. She only meant to scare her father, ram home to him a message that she was at the breaking point, that she would do *anything* it took to keep him off her.

In the end, she'd taken the only option she felt was open to her anymore.

"It was as if...as if my father *wanted* me to do it," she said, her voice quavering in incomprehension. "Even when I'd pulled the gun out from under my pillow, my hands shaking with fear and revulsion when I heard him moving slowly down the hall, calling me by my mother's name, I begged him not to come into my bedroom, but he wouldn't *listen*," she said, a look of terror in her eyes.

Instead, she'd watched in horrified fascination as the doorknob slowly turned and the door opened inward to her room, his silhouetted face blank except for the dark, heavy brows that seemed to glisten menacingly in the half-light. She'd screamed at him, waving the gun, but he'd kept coming at her, at her, at her, daring her to use it on him. It was then that she'd realized that he wanted her to shoot him, that he wouldn't stop until the deed was done. Infinitely wise and tragic at the young age of fifteen, Emma had seen the look in her father's eyes, begging for death as he approached her cringing form on the bed. And still she wouldn't pull the trigger.

He continued his slow, almost mechanical descent upon

her, her pleas falling on deaf ears as she backed further and further away from him until the hard wall against her back stopped her trembling form from escaping. It wasn't until he'd torn the nightgown from her body, began probing at her again that she'd finally, in desperate self-preservation, picked up the gun and fired it at the man who was no longer her father, but a strange, perverse shell of the man she'd lost the day her mother had died.

"It's the last memory I have...pulling the trigger," she finished quietly, drained of emotion. "Until returning to consciousness in Ben's care."

Jack picked up the story from there. He told Emma what he thought had happened after she'd pulled the trigger. He told her how Andy must have heard the shot and come running over to her house. He came into her bedroom, found her hysterical, her father dead, and decided then and there to take the blame for her father's death. Jack had never believed Andy's version, especially after her fingerprints had been found all over the gun, but Andy had been unmoved by Jack's threats of a prison term if he didn't retract his confession. He didn't leave out Dr. Stuart's role in betraying the young teenager, and as he told of the doctor's treachery, the doctor continued to sit silently.

Emma avoided looking at her stepfather, the one man she'd thought she could trust above all others, afraid he'd see the fury in her eyes. Instead, she withheld comment about his role, reluctant to interrupt the flow of Jack's story.

Jack told of the deal he and the doctor were able to cut on Andy's behalf after they'd convinced him to revise his story a bit. He saw a light of recognition go on in Emma's eyes as he recounted Andy's stay in reform school. It seemed Andy had touched lightly on many aspects of the story Jack was re-telling, but Emma just now seemed to be putting it all together in her mind. He finished by describing how Andy had never given up hope of finding her, how Jack had got him interested in investigative work, and Andy had incorporated his search for Emma into the very fiber of his work.

As Emma listened to Jack's tale, tears began to flow freely from her eyes, tears for the man who'd given up so much for her. Tears for the loneliness Jack never came right out and admitted Andy experienced daily, but she could feel so clearly as his simply stated words flowed over her. Emma remembered how desperately Andy had wanted to follow in his father's footsteps.

And she'd shattered those dreams.

She remembered how jubilant he'd been when they'd finally come together again, consummating their love for each other after ten long years of separation.

And she'd shattered his dream once again.

With a ragged voice, she said, "But...why didn't he tell me tonight, Jack? I...I *begged* him to tell me he didn't do it, and...and he...he said he loved me too much to start lying to me."

"But don't you see, Emma? He was still trying to protect you. Did he admit he pulled the trigger?"

Thinking back, Emma realized Jack was right. Andy had never once out-and-out admitted to her he'd shot her father. Niles had said he'd done it, and Andy's own police records reflected the same—even Ben had been silent over Niles' accusations. Emma had taken Ben's silence as agreement.

But Andy hadn't said a word. He'd only said he wouldn't lie to her, that he'd never lie to her. And he hadn't.

"Oh God," she said covering her eyes. "How can he still love me after everything I've done to him? I...I *murdered my own father*!" Her anguished voice touched a deep well of tenderness in Jack, and he pulled her hands away from her face, forcing her to look at him.

"Andy never once claimed to be your knight in shining armor, Emma. He's just a man—a man who went through hell for you, gave up all his other dreams for you, because the dream of you sharing your lives meant the most to him, it always has. Everything else was a distant second for him. Don't cry for the lost dreams, revel in the one dream you *can* give back to him, the one and only dream that gave his life meaning. Some men claim they'd travel to the ends of the earth for the one they love—Andy *did* that for you." Since when had he become so profound? Jack didn't know, but he liked the sound of it. He gently took her hands in his own, holding her tearful gaze. "He must've thought it was all worth it, honey, and he's convinced me, too."

"But tonight, I sent him away..."

Jack chuckled, the tension finally draining away from him. "Hell, do you think after all he's gone through to find you, he'd let you go so easily?" He didn't feel the need to describe to her how devastated Andy had been over her rejection. What was the point?

Emma sat up in the bed, flinging aside the wet washcloth. "I've got to see him," she said, swinging her feet onto the floor.

"Wait," Ben said, moving to help her up. "It's awfully late. Why don't you wait until morning. You've gone through so much tonight, I don't think it's a good idea for you to push yourself."

Brushing off his arm, pointedly ignoring his advice, her voice firm, Emma said, "If you'll excuse me," then strode purposefully to the closet where Ben had hung her clothes up earlier. If what Jack had just said was true, she had no reservations about knocking on Andy's hotel room door at one o'clock in the morning. She had more than a sneaking suspicion he wasn't sleeping anyway.

With a grin playing at the corners of his mouth, Jack guided the unresisting Ben Stuart out of the room. A few minutes later, Emma emerged from her old bedroom, a radiant smile transforming her face from the tragic, lifeless girl of an hour ago to a woman passionately in love, going to meet the man who'd been so willing to give up his life for her.

She nearly flew down the stairs, her feet felt light as air. She knew later the impact of her role in the death of her father would hit her with a vengeance, but for now her heart was soaring. The fact that she'd been forced to pull the trigger and end the life of a man she'd adored and respected for most of her young life in an effort to preserve her own sanity did little to assuage the guilt threatening to dispel the euphoria she was feeling at the prospect of reuniting with Andy again.

With a strength she never new she was capable of, Emma closed her mind to the horrid memories, reveling in the fact that she could brush them aside, at least temporarily, without pitching back into a black void of nothingness. She rushed past the two men, intent on giving herself this one night with Andy, free of the baggage of her fearful memories.

Only later would she bravely face the reality of her past transgressions and the heavy impact they would have on her future.

Thirty-Four

He was going insane, but if this was insanity, then let it come.

Andy had been tossing and turning in his bed for what seemed like hours, unable to shake his feelings of despair, yet drifting in and out of a dream state where all was right between himself and Emma, when suddenly her visage had appeared over him, bending down to press her supple lips lightly against his. Her presence seemed so real in his groggy state of mind, and he eagerly met her searching lips with his own, only to be rewarded with the tantalizing feeling of real contact between soft, succulent lips. Liquid brown eyes, filled with passion and longing, stared deep into his soul, and Andy suddenly felt as if he knew what it felt like to die and go to heaven.

He pulled the apparition closer to him, afraid that if he let go, the dream would end, and his dismal life would be over. Murmuring words of love, he kissed her again, savoring the play of their tongues intertwining, their hands searching, caressing each other to a fevered pitch. He let go of her just long enough to remove the last vestiges of their clothing, the contact of her hot, silken flesh against his smooth, rock-hard chest felt so real he almost cried out in pain.

Insanity! Sweet, supple insanity had his mind in a vise grip so tightly he felt he could actually smell the desire welling from her, begging him to take her, long and hard.

Rolling on top of this ghostly apparition, this figure from his most desired dreams, Andy plunged deep within her; her languorous moans propelling him on and on until he was sure he would die from the pure pleasure of it all. His senses on fire, this wondrous dream mounted and mounted, her cries of pleasure mixed with his as they reached their crescendo, then slowly died as their shared climax left them totally spent, staring transfixed into one another's eyes.

Incredulous, Andy looked unbelievingly into the eyes of the only woman he'd ever loved, ever would love, amazed she hadn't disappeared, that the dream was still with him even though he felt as if he were wide awake. Slowly, ever so slowly, fearfully, he released his tight hold of her.

She didn't disappear.

Recognizing the look in his eyes, Emma said softly, "I'm not leaving, Andy." She caressed his cheek. "This time, you'll have to be the one to walk away—"

"Never!" he gasped, covering the hand softly stroking his cheek with his own, his mind finally grasping the reality of her presence. "I...I thought I was imagining you, I wanted you here with me so badly," he said, holding her close again, reassuring himself that she was, indeed, flesh and blood, not an apparition there to drive him, once and for all, over the edge of reality.

Smiling impishly, eyebrows arched, she said, "You've got one hell of an imagination." She wrapped her arms around his neck and pulled his lips down on hers again. They kissed slowly, drinking in the taste of each other. Andy still couldn't believe it wasn't all a fantasy, a trick of his own wishful mind. But there she was, her firm body pressed close to him, her eyes staring deeply into his, challenging him to deny her as real.

"Andy," she said slowly, voice wavering, her arms still wrapped tightly around his neck. "I remember. Everything. Can you ever forgive me for what I've done?" she said quietly, searching his deep blue eyes. The unwavering love she saw reflected back in answer to her hesitant question never faltered, giving her courage.

Andy smiled slowly, his white teeth flashing in the semi-darkness of the moonlit night. "There's nothing to forgive, Emma." He shifted slightly so they were lying side by side, their heads resting on the down-filled pillows, nearly touching.

"All I've worked for, all I ever wanted, is right here in this room with me. Nothing else matters, or ever will," he finished, his naturally husky voice had a tightness to it, relaying to Emma that his words came with deep, heartfelt sincerity.

A sadness suddenly came into her eyes, and she pulled slightly away from Andy. "But what about my father, Andy? I murdered him…my own father." She let the statement hang between them. She'd been determined not to talk about her role in her father's death, at least for now, but she'd lost the battle to suppress the feelings of guilt and revulsion she felt for herself over that horrible act.

Andy pulled her close again, tucking her head into his shoulder, caressing her silken hair. "He was dead long before you pulled the trigger, Emma, we both know that. Like my own mother, he wasn't the parent he was while your mom was alive, and there was nothing you could have done to save him. He was on a road to destruction, a road he chose to travel. Unfortunately, he almost destroyed you in the process. I know I'm oversimplifying this, but I think you know your will to live was his cowardly key to ultimately escape from a life he no longer felt any desire to continue with."

What Andy said made perfect sense to Emma, but it didn't erase the fact that she'd murdered someone—especially her own flesh and blood—albeit someone who wanted death to descend upon him, and she would have to confront the gruesome facts head-on. What ramifications her confession would make with her career, her friends, she didn't know. She only knew that Andy had lived ten years within the unforgiving shadow of a murder he didn't commit, closing doors and doors of opportunity for him before he'd even had a chance to grasp the handle, and she owed it to him to clear his name. It was the very least she could do.

"I want to go back to Boston with Jack, get all this straightened out," she said. Perhaps then he'd be able to fulfill some of the dreams his selfless act had taken from him.

Startled, Andy pulled her away from his shoulder, gazing at her as if she were crazy. "Emma, what's done is done. Let's leave it that way."

"But if I confess, your record will be cleared. It's not too late to follow in your dad's footsteps, Jack would help you."

"Emma, ten years is a long time, time enough for some hopes and dreams to be put to rest. But not all of them," he smiled, kissing her lightly before continuing, "I reconciled myself a long time ago to the fact that I would never do what I'd originally hoped to do."

"But I can change—"

"But don't you see, Emma? *I* don't want those things anymore. *I've* changed. The job I do now is just as important, maybe more so, than becoming a cop. It took me years to stop running from the after-shocks the events of ten years ago created, and when I stopped running, I liked what I found out about myself. And you've been running for ten years, too, you just haven't been aware of it. Your memory came back because it was time to stop running, stop running and face the truth. But don't let that truth ruin your life again. If you do, everything we've both sacrificed would all be for nothing, don't you see?"

"All I see," she said, her voice strained, "is the sacrifices you've made, not me."

Andy's eyebrows furrowed, his eyes a blue blaze as he tried to tell Emma, not with just words, but with his whole being, that the past was just that. The past should be remembered, cherished at times, able to bring deep anguish at others, but nevertheless, past.

"Emma, given a choice, I'd still do what I did all over again. It's done with, what happened so long ago. What matters between us is right here, right now, and the rest of our lives together."

"Can you really say that? I mean, not just say it, but *really* believe it?" she said, incredulous. She'd virtually ruined his life, but he claimed it was well worth it. She'd seen, not only from Jack's account, but with her own sharp perceptions, what the powers that be had forced him to give up—and she was responsible for it all. She had not been aware of what her actions had wrought, true, but they'd been hers and hers alone, and she should shoulder the blame, not him.

"Absolutely," he answered without hesitation. "I've never once regretted taking the gun from you—not once. Not back then...not now...not ever. Going back to Boston and confessing to your father's murder won't change a thing. It'll only change the honorable memories of your father to bitter, nasty ones once the papers get a hold of the true, unadulterated version of what happened that night. Aside from the fact that it *was* self-defense and you'd probably not be convicted of anything anyway, do you really want the public to know the sordid depth to which your father had plunged?" Andy could see he was making headway with this last argument, so he continued in that direction.

"There was nothing either one of us could have done for the man we'd both admired and loved before your mother's death changed him so desperately. But we can do one thing for him, deserved or not. We can keep quiet, keep quiet and let his memory with the people of Boston be unspoiled, intact."

Emma lie quietly in Andy's arms, digesting his well argued point to simply let things stand as they were. She wasn't certain she could do it though, wasn't sure her conscience would allow her to. But he had a very valid point. She could not bring her father back. She was pretty sure in her own mind that, even if she did have the power to change the events of that awful night, instead of being happy to be alive, her father would probably curse her for not leaving things be. There was no denying the look of relief that had passed through her father's eyes even as his life had ebbed away and death overtook him. No, perhaps Andy was right. Maybe it was time to truly put the past to rest. Not a forgotten past anymore, but a tragic, painful, undeniable past, finally out in the open, even if all the facts might never see the light of day.

"Besides," Andy said, reading correctly that Emma had come around to his way of thinking, "you've got a wonderful career here in Portland, I see no reason to throw a little controversy up to public scrutiny, public outcry."

Emma's eyes had a faraway look to them as she tried to pinpoint just how important her career actually was to her. She enjoyed her job immensely, yes, but how would she really feel if it were taken away from her? There would be other opportunities if the station got wind of the scandal out of her lurid past and terminated her contract.

Or would there?

She glanced up at Andy again, remembering how the specter of wrongdoing had changed the course of his life. One thing for certain, if the unforgiving public learned she'd murdered someone, her career in front of the cameras would be over.

Irreparably over.

Television stations, in an effort to conform to public opinion—their bread and butter—would never think twice about firing someone, no matter the circumstances, no matter how popular that person was, if they held the possibility of bringing an unsavory scandal down upon the station. She wouldn't try to fool herself by saying she wouldn't miss working on television terribly, but she had other talents, other options she could pursue. And with Andy at her side...well, one lost career was a small price to pay.

Sighing, she said, "I don't think I'll have a choice in the matter."

"What do you mean? They don't ever have to know, nobody does."

"But you're forgetting one element, one person," she said, regret in her voice. No matter how hard he tried to convince her that all would be as it was, she knew better, because the one person who would never give up, never stay quiet, already knew enough to get her fired, or, barring that threat, try to force her to give up Andy in deference to his keeping quiet.

"Niles," Andy said, voicing the name rolling around in Emma's morose thoughts.

"If he sees us together, he'll wonder how I can be with you knowing what he believes to be the truth of our past."

"But how can that hurt us?"

Emma smiled, but it held no warmth. She was thinking about Niles, how ruthless he could be if he felt the situation warranted it. It was an asset in many ways as an attorney, but facing him as an adversary out in the open, away from the closed doors of a courtroom, Emma knew she had to be very wary of him.

"He'll probably go to the station, fill them in on your background. If I know Niles, he'll try to paint himself as the guy in the white hat, trying to protect me from myself. The station, in turn, would put pressure on me to stop seeing you. Barring that ultimatum, they'd probably let me go if I refused." She could live with that outcome, she knew, but he wouldn't stop there, she thought grimly.

"And if I give up my position at the station for you," she added, "Niles will be doubly suspicious. I know Niles. He won't let this thing die. He'll never rest until he ferrets out the truth," she said, misery in her voice. The only real choice open to her, was to pack up and start over in another state, away from her friends, away from a job she knew she'd miss terribly.

With a gleam in his eyes, Andy said, "I wouldn't be so sure..."

Emma gazed expectantly at him, the tone of his voice telling her that, perhaps, he just might have a way out of their mess.

"The picture I've got of Niles Whitmann," Andy said, "is of a man quite concerned not only with success and money, but of his own lily-white reputation, his impeccable standing in the community, his strong ties to the high rolling corporations in this city."

"And?" she said, gaining hope from the mischievous look in his eyes.

"And I think, come tomorrow morning, after I finish with the police and we get Karen Carlson and her boys back together, I'm going to make a friendly call on Niles, point out a few little details he just might have missed in his zeal to nail me to the wall." He pulled Emma close again, already his mind turning to other, more lustful thoughts.

"But for now, I intend to make full use of this beautiful moonlight filtering through the window," he said, his eyes appreciably raking over her naked body, the desire standing out in his eyes, lighting the fire of her own burgeoning passion.

Thirty-Five

The telephone jangled on the hook, startling the intertwined lovers into groggy wakefulness. Andy was the first to recover, grabbing the unwelcome intruder off its base, answering with a gruff hello.

Seconds later, he was springing off the bed, pulling underwear out of the bedside drawer, then dashing off to the bathroom.

As he jumped under the cold, invigorating spray of the cascading shower, Emma slowly wandered into the bathroom behind him, her pace drastically different than his own harried one.

"What's going on?" she said sleepily, rubbing her eyes, trying to clear away the fog still encasing them.

"That was our friendly neighborhood detective," Andy answered as he worked up a lather on the bar of soap clutched between his two busy hands. "He's meeting me down in the lobby in about ten minutes. He's gotten a confirmation on David Carlson, and the boys, and he's ready to pick them up."

Eyes widening, Emma glanced back around at the clock on the bedside table, startled to see it was already midmorning. The half light filtering in from the windows was caused not by the early morning hours as she'd suspected, but rather an overcast, dark, dreary Portland morning. They hadn't fallen asleep until the wee hours of the morning, and now their exhausted bodies were paying them back.

With a note of panic in her voice, Emma said, "I've got to call the station, get my crew over here to interview Karen, then get the whole lot of us over to police headquarters before you get back with the boys!" She, too, began scurrying around the room.

Andy jumped out of the shower, vigorously toweling off his now rejuvenated body, his mind clear of the cobwebs. He said, "Don't worry, I called them last night." He too, glanced back at the accusing clock, the hands ticking away his precious time, spurring him along even faster. "They'll be here in about a half an hour. You've got plenty of time."

"A half an hour! Are you crazy?"

"You'll make it," he said, striding over to the closet.

"But I haven't even gone over Karen's dialogue with her..."

"She's a quick study, don't worry," he said, slipping into a pair of faded Levis. "While the film crew is setting up, you can prompt her." He grabbed a fresh shirt off the hanger in the closet, trotted back into the bathroom, swiftly buttoning his shirt along the way, then ran a quick comb through his damp hair, calling it good.

Two minutes to spare, he thought smugly. Just enough time to kiss his girl good-bye and grab a cup of coffee on the way out.

"Don't worry," he said, wrapping his arms around Emma's

now immobile form. He kissed her hard and quick, spun her around toward the bathroom and gave her a light shove. "Now go," he said. His wide grin was infectious and she smiled back as she turned and grabbed a towel. The still dripping silvery hair she loved to run her fingers through gave him such a boyish look it made her laugh despite the lateness of the hour.

"As usual, you've taken care of everything," she said lightly. He wasn't even gone yet, but already she felt the first stirrings of a longing for his presence.

"Not everything," he answered ruefully, unlocking the door. "Setting the alarm clock would definitely have been a plus."

"See you back at the station," she called out, her voice echoing behind him as he hurriedly closed the door.

A whimper instead of a bang. After months and months of searching, oftentimes frustrating, painstaking investigation, it often ended like this—so anti-climatic.

Andy and the two plain-clothed detectives first paid a visit to the babysitter, picking up the younger boy, Jacob.

Skittish at first, the boy hadn't wanted to go with them, calling for his daddy repeatedly until Andy pointed out to him that he would be riding in a real policeman's car, complete with radio and portable flashing red light.

The boy's eyes lighted up at the prospect, sweetened by the box of donuts miraculously appearing in Andy's outstretched hands. The promise of his older brother soon joining him, however, was the clincher. It was at least good to see the boy had been schooled about talking to, and accompanying, strangers.

At their next stop, Tyler's school, the principal had been appraised of the situation ahead of time and had Tyler in his office by the time Andy and the two detectives arrived. With the two detectives' permission, Andy sat the two young boys down and talked quietly about their mother.

As he'd suspected, the boys talked freely about how their mother had become very sick and hadn't been able to take care of them anymore. The younger one, Jacob, started crying, saying how he missed his mommy, but daddy said he had to be strong for her, and someday she just might get better if she had time to herself without having to look after them.

The older boy, Tyler, was a bit more suspicious, the more stalwart of the two, which was to be expected. He didn't cry, but Andy could see it took a valiant effort on his part not to do so in front of him and the two detectives. He even put his arm around his younger brother, comforting him; the small gesture tore at Andy's heart, reminding him of the many times he and Emma had consoled each other in just that very way when they were young. Two adolescent lives buffeted by forces beyond their control, just like these two brothers.

Talking quietly to the two boys, Andy explained to them that their mother was fine now, and she was waiting for them at the police station. A look of enormous joy passed over Jacob's face, but again Tyler was more skeptical. Andy could tell he wanted to believe him, but perhaps, because he was a little older, a little wiser than his brother, a little more cautious of disappointment, it took several minutes for Andy to convince him that his mother really was well and there in Portland—quite healthy—waiting to see them.

Then the questions Andy always dreaded most were voiced by Tyler. Where was his dad? Was he with mom? Why were the police there? Andy had hoped that, as young as the two boys were, they'd be so overwhelmed at the opportunity to see their mother, they'd overlook the fact that their father was nowhere in sight.

Again Andy spoke slowly, simply to the boys, trying to downplay the awful truth to them. They had to be told of their father's role in all this, but Andy was well-versed in how to soften the blow a little. He'd already arranged with the detectives not to have the boys see their father in handcuffs. The traumatic effect could be devastating on their tender, adolescent minds. Better for their mother to explain the full extent of what had happened; Andy's job was just to pave the way for the explanation. He did so by simply telling the boys that their father would be joining them all a little later at the station, but for now their mother was quite anxious to see them again. It'd been nearly five months since their last contact, and Andy could easily see the boys were overwhelmed at the thought that their mother was just minutes away from them.

Andy knew by Tyler's posture that he'd guessed there was more to Andy's simple explanation than he was saying. But he kept any additional questions to himself, perhaps afraid his little brother might start crying again.

He kept quiet, seemingly looking to Andy and the two detectives for direction. It didn't hurt that Jacob was pulling at his brother's coat, telling him they were getting to ride in a *policeman's* car. Andy could see the older boy beginning to catch his little brother's unabashed enthusiasm.

Looking solemnly up at Andy, he cautiously took his outstretched hand, putting his wary trust in him, then walked toward the waiting car.

Thirty-Six

Andy had been right when he'd said Karen was a quick study. She had no trouble following Emma's lead in the background interview, and afterwards, while the crew loaded their gear back up in the minibus, Emma took a minute or two to thank her for sharing what must have been a very painful time for her.

"To tell you the truth," Karen said, "I don't think I could have talked about it if I didn't know it was finally over, or almost anyway."

Emma glanced at her watch and said, "By now, Andy and the detectives are probably on their way back to the station, so we better head on over there. The two other detectives who went to get David are probably just now rounding him up."

Reading the worried look in her eyes, Emma said, "And don't worry, you won't even have to lay eyes on him, let alone talk to him if you don't want to. Andy'll see to it," she said confidently.

With a firm set to her jaw, Karen said, "I've spent months going over and over in my mind what I'd say to the bastard if I ever caught up with him. But now," her face relaxing, she said, "all I want is to see my boys. Andy taught me that, you know." Emma watched her closely, had seen the wave of revenge run its course through her eyes and just as quickly leave. "He kept telling me not to look back, but forward, concentrate all my energy on my sons, and he'd do the worrying about David. And he was right. I found out it was easier to keep my sanity when I concentrated harder on the love for my sons instead of the hate I fostered for David."

Emma sucked in a deep breath, the other woman's words striking a familiar chord within her. Andy had given the woman his own key to survival these many years—and now her own. She needed to focus on the good expectations instead of the bad, and maybe, just maybe, without even realizing it was gone, this new hatred for herself, her father, would melt away. The revulsion Emma felt for her father, the sickened feeling in the pit of her stomach every time she focused her thoughts on her own starring role in her father's death, Ben's despicable behavior in sacrificing Andy, even Niles' efforts to ruin her relationship with Andy—all these wretched, miserable emotions would fall away from her if only she was strong enough to break away from them and let Andy's love for her, and his hope in their future together, carry her beyond those unwholesome, debilitating feelings.

Suddenly, Emma felt light as air, knowing somehow that Andy would make good his promise to handle any threats of exposure from Niles' direction. Her mind drank in the fact that she *didn't* have to look hauntingly back over her shoulder anymore. She'd finally found the courage to face what she knew to be true, and it had made her whole again. Andy had told her there was no need to look back, and again, he'd been right. It was over, all of it, and she would never, ever look back again.

Karen, startled by the enthusiastic hug Emma suddenly bestowed upon her, had no time to reflect upon the reason for it as Emma quickly hustled her into her car. They'd have to hurry now if they were going to get to the station before Andy and his precious cargo arrived.

The reunion between Karen Carlson and her two sons, recorded discreetly by *Evening Magazine*'s crack film crew, was both uplifting and poignantly sad. The look of disbelief in the two young boys' faces as they cautiously approached their mother turned quickly to unabashed joy when they realized she truly was there, fit and fine, with open arms begging to wrap themselves around her boys, snuggle them close.

It was a struggle for Andy to maintain control, hold back the emotions that always threatened to overcome him at these moments. Emma and most of the film crew, however, felt no compunction to even try to disguise their feelings. Tears were being shed freely from most of the faces surrounding the small drama being played out before their very eyes.

But Andy knew all too well what Karen and her sons were headed for, and he felt immense sadness for the family before him. They had a rough time ahead of them, and Andy only hoped David's abduction of the boys, and it's unfortunate consequences, didn't end up tearing apart the family even more than his first illegal act had.

It was apparent that the boys loved their father, but how they reacted to his web of lies and deceit would set the tone of their relationship with him for the rest of their lives. Andy only hoped they were all strong enough to weather the stormy seas ahead of them.

But for now, he tried to take the reunion at face value, a glow of accomplishment beginning to override his bleak thoughts. With a wide grin slowly spreading across his face, he realized this investigation was finally at an end. All that remained was getting his charges onto a flight back home. Piece of cake, he thought to himself as he caught Emma's attention from across the room, flashing her the thumbs up sign.

Thirty-Seven

Life had held few surprises for Niles Whitmann, but it seemed as though he was suddenly making up for lost time. The last person he expected his secretary to buzz him and say was insisting on seeing him was Andy Brannigan.

For a few fleeting moments, Niles had been afraid; the thought that Andy Brannigan was there to seek revenge for ruining things between himself and Emma quickly ran through his mind—Andy's own police record proved he wasn't above using violence to get what he wanted.

Niles glanced around the plush office, looking for what, he wasn't sure; his eyes focused on the heavy crystal paper-weight just inches from his right hand. Not much of a weapon, especially if Andy was carrying a gun, but it was the best his office had to offer, save a dulled, hand-carved letter opener, whittled out of an elk antler, that was more decoration than anything else.

Niles warily gave the secretary his okay to let Andy through, then braced uncomfortably against his desk, senses sharp for any untoward, suspicious movement on Andy's part that might give away his motives for being there.

Andy sauntered casually into Niles' comfortable office, his unconcerned air keenly observed by the tense, unmoving man behind the desk. Niles did not stand up to greet his unwelcome guest, nor did he even try to fill the dead air with meaningless pleasantries. There was no point in trying to pretend that either of them had even the slightest liking for one another. After scrutinizing Andy closely through hooded eyes, trying to be nonchalant about it, Niles motioned him to sit down.

Niles' pointed inspection was not lost on Andy. Smirking, he said, "Would you feel better if I allowed your secretary to frisk me?"

Niles glared at Andy and said nothing. Why was he so relaxed? Last night he'd been coming apart at Emma's rejection of him. But today, he acted as though the whole episode hadn't happened. And why was he there?—to beg him to intervene on his behalf?—tell Emma it had all been a lie? Surely Andy would know he'd do no such thing. But what other reason could he possibly have for showing up at his office?

As if reading his thoughts, Andy said, "Surprised to see me? After last night, you probably thought I was holed up in my hotel room, licking my wounds."

The tight smile on Niles' face was merciless, totally lacking in warmth. He said, "The thought crossed my mind. I think Emma made it pretty clear she didn't want you around."

"She was upset," Andy agreed, then shrugged, unconcerned. He could read the confusion in Niles' eyes over his indifferent attitude.

Niles' eyes narrowed. What game was Andy playing now? He'd been devastated last night, he had witnessed it with his own eyes. And now he was acting as if the whole thing had just been a lark.

Intent on cracking through the facade of indifference, Niles said, "That's all? Pretty upset? The way I saw it, you were thrown out on your ear. Emma's finally come to her senses—"

"In more ways than one," Andy interjected, seemingly undisturbed by Niles' jibes.

"What do you mean by that?" Niles said, alert now. Something was not quite right, he could feel it. Andy was just too confident, too relaxed, and suddenly Niles knew Andy's presence in his office did not bode well for him.

"Let's just say she's had another change of heart," Andy said, watching closely the play of emotions across the other man's face.

Niles cocked his head, puzzled at Andy's innocuous statement. "What do you mean?" His mind did not want to acknowledge the obvious meaning behind Andy's oblique words.

Andy leaned forward in his chair, giving his words emphasis, "It means your inept, callous attempt to split Emma and I up didn't work." It nearly had, except for Jack's intervention.

"I don't believe you," Niles said with more conviction than he felt. Surely, with the knowledge that this man had killed her father, Emma wouldn't permit him back in her life again. It had to be a joke, and a very bad one at that, on Andy's part. Or maybe he was trying to get Niles to do something foolish, like take a swing at him or something—*anything* to give Andy an excuse to rough him up. Yes, that had to be it. Although Emma had been acting strangely the last few weeks, Niles couldn't believe she'd do something as foolhardy as to let this criminal back into her life.

"Believe it," Andy said, his voice full of steel. "I warned you last night you were sticking your nose into something you shouldn't have. But you didn't believe me. What's worse, you showed no remorse over the pain you brought Emma. All you were interested in was destroying our relationship, and it didn't work. If you really loved her, you'd never have broken the news about her father so heartlessly."

Niles was aghast. This man sitting so calmly opposite him had the nerve, the *audacity,* to question his love for Emma, when he'd *murdered* her father? The whole pathetic situation was almost laughable. Only the look in the other man's eyes kept Niles from laughing out loud at the lunacy of his remark. Years and years spent in a courtroom sizing up people from all walks of life had sharpened his senses, and the clear message he was receiving from Andy was that of pure, unadulterated truth. Somehow, some way, this convicted felon had wormed his way back in Emma's good graces, and Niles was not about to stand for it.

"You realize if you stay with her, you'll ruin her. You talk so mightily about love—is that what you want for her?"

"The way I see it, you're the only one who can ruin her."

"I'll ruin you both!" Niles hissed, trying desperately to control his growing frustration. How could she do this? He was a *murderer,* for Christ's sake!

"You mean all three of us, don't you?" Andy answered quietly, his eyes boring into the devious attorney.

Niles stared darkly at Andy. "What do you mean?" he said, willing himself to stay seated, stay calm.

"Your position in this community is pretty important to you, isn't it?" Without waiting for an answer, Andy pressed on with his attack. "How will it look to your friends and colleagues, and those big corporations you're so impressed with yourself for representing, when they find out that you, a prominent attorney, have been dumped by your girlfriend for a criminal like me? And who, actually, will be the sympathetic figure if it ever came to light that Emma's father, the Honorable Malcolm Nash, was killed because he was sexually abusing his young daughter?" After dropping that bombshell, Andy could easily see the wheels turning in Niles' eyes, realization at the predicament he'd allowed himself to become embroiled in beginning to dawn on him.

Malcolm Nash? A sexual deviant? Niles was crushed by the knowledge that not even that one aspect of Emma's tragic past could be salvaged. He didn't even question whether Andy was telling the truth or not. It was there in his eyes, his voice, and Niles wanted desperately to block out what he was saying, but he dared not.

"Of course, with Emma's talent, her television appeal, she can get a job anywhere," Andy continued, not daring to give Niles a chance to recover. "She's had offers from other stations in other cities. She could relocate without any real disruption. But you...well, you're a big fish in a little pond here in Portland, but I'm not so certain you'd ever be able to attain the status you've managed to reach here somewhere else." Shrugging his shoulders, and standing up, he added, "the choice is yours, Niles."

Andy walked to the door and opened it, trying to keep the look of triumph out of his eyes, easily reading defeat in the slackening of Nile's shoulders, his unfocused gaze. The last thing he wanted to do was goad him into ruining all their careers just for the sake of revenge.

He paused for a moment, then said, "She was mine long before you entered the picture, Niles, and I would never have given her up—ever," he finished softly, then closed the door behind him.

Niles stared, unmoving, at the closed door, trying to get in touch with what he was feeling, trying to make some sense out of the crazy things Andy had just said. This was not how it was supposed to end. Andy was supposed to be out of the picture, disgraced, vilified by the one he loved.

Instead, *he* was the one who was out in the cold, and there was nothing he could do—would do—to change the situation.

Andy had been right, of course. To make a move against either one of them would spell disaster for himself. The taste of defeat was bitter in his mouth, and Nile's stomach roiled at the unfamiliar sensation of helplessness. Twice he'd gone up against this mysterious stranger, and twice he'd lost. And now, suddenly, he didn't have the strength, or the desire, to find out if Andy's dire predictions about his career would hold true if he exposed Andy for what he was.

No, this wasn't the way Niles had pictured it ending—not by a long shot.

Andy was a murderer.

Niles' career could sustain the shock, the revelation, if it ever came to light, that an old boyfriend had killed Emma's father, but it would never survive his being dumped for that very man who'd taken her father's life, for whatever reason.

And Emma's father. Andy's words had nearly rocked Niles off his feet. He took a deep breath, spun around in his chair and looked out the window, his fingers steepled under his chin.

Emma would be a great loss, he thought, disinterestedly watching the streets fill up below with late afternoon traffic. And he would miss the status of being engaged to the most popular television personality in the city of Portland.

There would be other women—there always were.

But a career...well, one just didn't throw away a career as successful as his...

Epilogue

For the first time since the 1930's, Portland was blanketed by a light snowfall on Christmas Eve. Although the weatherman had been predicting the possibility of a white Christmas, not many had truly believed they'd actually see it happen. Oregon weather was notoriously unpredictable.

For Emma, the white Christmas was just one in a series of remarkable events that'd happened to her over the last few weeks. At first she'd been amazed that Andy had been able to convince Niles to keep his knowledge of her scandalous past to himself. But then she'd had to backtrack on her thinking a little when she remembered all the things she'd recently learned about Andy, coupled with all her past recollections now quite vivid in her own restored memory. Andy was one of those rare, complex, talented individuals who seemed to be able to accomplish virtually anything he set his mind to, at the same time inspiring others to also strive for the impossible, the unattainable.

And now, on Christmas morning, cuddled up next to Andy on the soft leather couch, a comforter thrown casually over both their legs to ward of the morning chill until the newly started fire had a chance to work its warmth throughout the room, she turned her thoughts away from Niles, away from the hours and hours spent in discussions with Jack, with Andy, and yes, even with Ben; hours spent learning how to deal with the death of her father at her own hands. Instead, she turned her attention to the two packages casually peeking out from under the gaily decorated Christmas tree.

"They won't open by themselves, you know," Andy teased, noting the direction of her pointed stare.

Sighing, Emma said, "But I thought we promised not to get each other anything this year, that we didn't have the extra time to devote to Christmas shopping, what with trying to get your story on tape, getting Karen and her boys back home, saying good-bye to Jack—"

"Shhh," Andy said, covering her lips with a long, slender finger. "If you really don't want them…"

"No," Emma quickly interjected. She had no doubt as to the contents of the small package underneath the tree. There was no way she'd give that one up. Andy had waited ten long years to make their engagement official, and she had no intention of making him wait any longer. Not that she wanted to postpone it either. But the larger package dwarfing the smaller-wrapped box sitting next to it piqued her interest more than just a little. What could it be?

"So which will it be?" Andy said. "The big one or the little one?"

Leaning forward, Emma pretended to closely study the two packages from her perch on the couch. "Ummm, they say good things come in small packages…" Making a decision, she momentarily left the warm comfort of the couch and quickly scooped up the smaller package. Once again settling into the soft spot next to Andy, she paused before opening the box. "You realize that if this isn't what I think it is, you're in big trouble," she said, no longer able to control her excitement. She ripped through the thin wrapping, exposing a black, velvet covered box.

Slowly now, savoring the moment, she opened the soft, velvety box. A dazzling, full carat, marquee-cut solitary diamond set beautifully in a gold free-form band winked back at her, begging her to slip it on her finger.

Gasping, she said, "Oh, Andy, it's gorgeous!" then threw her arms around him, holding him close.

"It's official now," Andy said between kisses, slipping the ring on her finger. "Now open your other present."

Emma sat for a few minutes, admiring the look, the feel of her beautiful new ring before she turned her attention back to the mysterious box still left under the tree.

"Any hints?"

"Nope. You've got to open it."

"Can I shake it?"

"If you can lift it, you can shake it."

"Really? It's that heavy? What is it, a chain saw or something?"

"Just open it." Actually, Andy wasn't exactly sure how Emma was going to react to what was inside the heavy box. He only hoped the contents would make her happy, not depressed.

Again she left the comfort of the soft, warm couch, but this time Andy followed her to the waiting package. Kneeling down next to it, Emma tried to pull it toward her.

"You weren't kidding, were you?" she said, wrestling the package closer to her lap. Cautious now, she tore the outer wrapping off, a little dubious of what lay inside.

"Just rip it," Andy encouraged. "It won't bite, I promise."

Throwing caution to the wind, Emma ripped off the last remaining pieces of wrapping paper only to reveal a plain brown corrugated box underneath. Free of any markings on the sides, the contents still remained a mystery.

Emma sat back on her heels and studied the box. At a nod of encouragement from Andy, she unfolded the top of the box, the contents now fully exposed.

Emma stared down into the depths of the box, her eyes wide in amazement. She felt as if the wind had been knocked out of her.

Spilling out in front of her were the hundreds of momentos of her younger years; her family albums, report cards, year books, love letters from Andy—all the precious collections of her youth she'd thought were long gone, forgotten or destroyed many years ago, restored to her possession.

"Jack and I have been sitting on those for you. He got them out of your house before they closed the place up. I had him send it to me after he went back home."

Emma turned to Andy, her eyes brimming over with delight. This man who'd given up so much for her, had given her—besides his undying love—the greatest present of all: he'd given her back her past.